I0573006

ELIZA NEVIUS

The Key to Wonderland

First published by Phantom Publishing LLC 2025

Copyright © 2025 by Eliza Nevius

All rights reserved. No part of this publication may be reproduced, stored or transmitted in any form or by any means, electronic, mechanical, photocopying, recording, scanning, or otherwise without written permission from the publisher. It is illegal to copy this book, post it to a website, or distribute it by any other means without permission.

This novel is entirely a work of fiction. The names, characters and incidents portrayed in it are the work of the author's imagination. Any resemblance to actual persons, living or dead, events or localities is entirely coincidental.

Eliza Nevius asserts the moral right to be identified as the author of this work.

Eliza Nevius has no responsibility for the persistence or accuracy of URLs for external or third-party Internet Websites referred to in this publication and does not guarantee that any content on such Websites is, or will remain, accurate or appropriate.

Designations used by companies to distinguish their products are often claimed as trademarks. All brand names and product names used in this book and on its cover are trade names, service marks, trademarks and registered trademarks of their respective owners. The publishers and the book are not associated with any product or vendor mentioned in this book. None of the companies referenced within the book have endorsed the book.

First edition

ISBN: 979-8-9988569-8-3

Cover art by Tatiana Villa

This book was professionally typeset on Reedsy.
Find out more at reedsy.com

For those who have ever felt like they didn't fit in the story they were given—
this is your key. Unlock the door, and see where it leads.

Contents

Acknowledgments

Writing *The Key to Wonderland* has been a mad tea party of its own, and I wouldn't have survived it without the incredible people who joined me at the table.

First, to my family— Nick, Tristan, Kedzie, and Harrison: you are my anchor in every storm, my laughter in the chaos, and my proof that unconditional love exists even in the darkest timelines. Thank you for tolerating my late nights, my caffeine consumption that bordered on war crimes, and my endless rambling about Wonderland politics.

To my friends and early readers, who devoured drafts, gave feedback, and cheered me on when I questioned if this book would ever see daylight—you are the true heroes of this story.

To my readers: you are the magic. Your support breathes life into every page, and you give me the courage to keep weaving worlds that are as strange, beautiful, and unpredictable as this one.

And finally, to Wonderland itself—thank you for reminding me that the best stories are the ones that change us along the way.

Now, grab your keys. There's always another door waiting.

1

Open Books and Closed Minds

Alicia

The key turns in the lock with a whisper, like the universe is trying not to wake me up too fast. The bell above the door gives its usual chiming yawn, and just like that, another thrilling day at *Thistle & Thorn Books* begins.

Cue the imaginary applause.

The familiar scent of old paper, wood polish, and probably some deeply embedded cat dander wraps around me like a well-worn sweater. I inhale deeply, because if I'm going to spiral into existential monotony, at least let it smell like vintage novels and forgotten dreams.

I flick the lights on and do my usual slow stroll through the aisles—my sacred little kingdom of ink and spines. I touch covers like I'm blessing them, straightening crooked books and silently judging whoever shelved romance in with political thrillers. Probably Chad. Or maybe it was me yesterday. No one needs to know.

"Morning," I mumble to no one in particular, then correct myself. "Well, morning to *you*, weird haunted Jane Austen cut-out." I nod at her cardboard form near the classics section. She doesn't reply, but I'm pretty sure she's judging my outfit.

After a few minutes of robotic shelf-straightening, my hands drift to the fantasy section—my safe space, my escape hatch, my coping mechanism. I linger there, eyes flicking across dragons, dystopias, vampire love triangles. All fictional. All preferable to real life.

And then—because I hate myself—I glance at the bottom shelf where *Alice's Adventures in Wonderland* mocks me with its frilly title and pastel cover.

"I still don't get the appeal," I mutter. "A fever dream with tea and trauma."

The book twitches.

I freeze.

…Nope. Just my imagination. Definitely not the book. It definitely is not back-lit by an otherworldly glow. I am definitely not unraveling this early in the morning.

I shake off the weird and march to the front door, flipping the sign to OPEN with the flair of someone pretending they aren't actively dissociating.

Ten minutes later, Mrs. Thompson enters like a suburban hurricane in a cardigan. The bell chimes politely, but her perfume punches me in the face.

"Good morning, Alicia!" she chirps, clutching her purse like it's full of secrets and Werther's Originals.

"Mrs. Thompson," I smile, feeling dead inside. "Back for more murder and midlife crisis lit?"

She giggles. "Of course! I finished *Death by Darjeeling* last night. It was… okay."

"So just a decaffeinated disappointment."

She winks. "Hit me with something spicier."

I guide her to the mystery section with the practiced ease of someone who should probably charge more for therapy sessions disguised as book recs.

As she leaves with her latest paperback fling, I return to the front, only mildly questioning my existence. Through the window, Main Street bustles with purpose. Everyone rushing somewhere. Doing things. Living lives that, at the very least, amount to aimlessly wandering.

I glance at my reflection in the glass. Same tired green eyes. Same messy ponytail. Same bookstore shirt I swore I'd burn two years ago. Behind me, rows of stories wait for someone—anyone—to give a damn.

The next customer is an elderly man who wanders in with a limp and a thousand-yard stare. I help him find a book on Viking raids and human sacrifice.

"Something light, right?" I offer.

He grunts, which I assume means yes.

Then come the teenagers. Loud. Energy-drink-buzzed. One's wearing a hoodie that says "No Thoughts, Just Vibes." Honestly? Respect.

"Got anything… epic?" one asks, eyeing me like I might be hiding a secret stash of forbidden knowledge.

"Vampires or werewolves?"

"Both?"

I hand them a romance with fangs on the cover and abs on the spine. They squeal. I pretend I'm not silently judging their taste while also remembering I read that exact book three months ago.

* * *

As the day wore on, the shop became quiet. It was the kind of quiet only bookstores and graveyards seem to master—soft, slightly dusty, and filled with the low hum of secrets.

I was half-asleep behind the register, mentally debating the ethics of organizing the self-help books by author name or by level of delusion, when the door creaked open.

Not chimed. Not jingled. *Creaked.* Like the sound from an old horror movie.

That was new.

The man who stepped in didn't belong in Main Street, Illinois. Or possibly this century. His suit looked older than my great-aunt's floral wallpaper—pinstripes, pocket watch, and all. He walked like someone who had nowhere to be but everywhere to remember.

"Can I help you find something?" I asked, because I am a professional—or at least someone who pretends really well on weekdays.

He glanced at me with pale, stormy eyes that made me feel like a poorly filed receipt under fluorescent lighting.

"I'm looking for a specific title," he said, voice soft but precise-a faint English accent barely discernable. "I believe you carry it."

I blinked. "Uh, maybe. What's the title?"

He smiled slightly. *"Through the Veil: Lost Histories of the Unwritten Realms."*

"That… doesn't sound familiar," I said, already rising from my stool. "But I'll check the system."

Spoiler: I didn't have a "system." I had a rickety outdated

iPad running a spreadsheet with passive-aggressive tabs. Still, I searched it. Nothing.

"I'm sorry," I said, glancing up. "We've never had—"

But he was already walking.

Past the counter. Past the fantasy section. Straight to the back corner—where we kept the rare books and misprints. The "Weird Section," lovingly curated by yours truly and aggressively ignored by the general public.

He stopped. Tilted his head. And pulled a book from the shelf I *swear* wasn't there five minutes ago.

A black leather cover. Silver embossing. A strange rune etched into the spine.

"That's not—" I started, stepping toward him.

He held up a hand. Not threatening. Just… absolute. "It's always here, Alicia."

My blood chilled. "How do you know my name?"

He opened the book. Not like a customer. Like a priest at an altar, flipping pages that hummed under his fingertips.

I was torn between calling the cops and asking if he had a LinkedIn profile for cult recruitment. But I just stood there, rubbernecking the reality-warp like a hungover mall Santa with no escape from a food court stampede.

He smiled down at the page. "You're wondering about the book. You're wondering about me. Both are reasonable instincts."

I tried to laugh. Instead something between a cough and a whimper slithered out. "People don't usually quote my inner monologue at me, sir."

He touched the page, tracing a sentence that shimmered— actually shimmered—like heat above asphalt. When he spoke next, his words vibrated in the dusty stillness. "What do you do, Alicia, when a story needs fixing?"

For a heartbeat I actually considered all the times I'd jokingly talked to the books here. I felt the red creep up my cheeks, silly and spooked.

"Uh, mostly I make coffee and ring up the occasional true crime junkie, sir. I'm no writer."

"No, you are the key." He replies simply, placing the book gently in front of me.

Not sure how to respond to that odd little tidbit, I chose avoidance, pretending I didn't hear . "No price tag," I murmured, stalling. "And it's not in the system…"

"It's not for the system," he said. "Just for me."

He handed me a coin. Not a bill. A **coin**. Heavy, strange, etched with a heart split down the middle.

The moment it touched my palm, the air buzzed—like the silence before a thunderclap.

I blinked.

He was gone.

Door didn't open. Bell didn't ring.

Gone.

The book, too.

Only the coin remained.

And the faintest smell of roses and smoke.

I held the coin up, inspecting the split heart. It looked handmade, maybe even antique, the line between halves uneven like a wound that hadn't healed right. I tried to remember if I'd ever read about currency like this—something occult or ceremonial in my years of mainlining fantasy. Nothing came to mind except a sense of deja vu, faded and sticky and not quite comfortable.

When I closed my hand, the coin stayed warm. The warmth

ran up my wrist. I pressed my thumb over the split heart, waiting for a hidden mechanism or message or maybe just some clue about what happened.

Nothing. Just a weight, a charge, like the air before a tornado, or the moment before you say something you can't take back.

I hid the coin in the pocket of my jeans. It felt safer out of sight. On the off chance this was a prank—or worse, a memory slip—I'd deal with it after closing.

The day limped on. A package delivery. A toddler dropping crackers in the coloring books. A grad student arguing with someone on FaceTime about post-structuralism right by the register. I fielded it all, but my brain kept snagging on the morning. On the book. On the man's voice.

How did he know my name?

Once the shop was finally empty, I locked the door and leaned against it, soaking in the dusty silence. The dim lights cast sharp shadows around me. It felt like the perfect night for a breakdown or a ghost story— possibly both. I reached into my pocket to retrieve the coin, my curiosity overtaking me once more. It wasn't there.

2

In The Still of The Night

Below the quiet apartment, the bookstore breathed with a life of its own, as if it were a sleeping giant dreaming in the depths of night. The lights were off, casting the room into a deep, restful slumber, where shadows whispered across the floor like a gentle lullaby. The door was locked tight, yet someone—or perhaps something—was already nestled within its embrace, cradled by the store's silent promise of secrets untold. Moonlight spilled through the tall, grand windows, sliding like quicksilver across the polished wood floors and painting long, haunting shadows between the towering shelves that stood like sentinels guarding ancient knowledge. The air shimmered faintly above the "Wonderland Collection," an ethereal mirage like heat rising off a forbidden secret, untouched by mortal hands, as if daring someone to discover what lay beneath its shimmering veil.

Three figures glided silently between the stacks, their movements fluid and purposeful, like phantoms weaving through a tapestry of shadows. The first—a tall man draped in flowing robes of black and crimson—had his face obscured behind an intricate mask, shaped like a heart shattered into jagged pieces, each fragment catching the light with a glint of mystery. He moved with an intimate familiarity, as if he knew every creaking floorboard and hidden passage carved into the very grain of the wood, his presence as much a part of the bookstore as the shelves themselves. His gloved fingers hovered just above the spines of the books, never making contact, for he had no need to touch. He already knew their secrets, the stories that whispered in the silence.

"She's beginning to hear it," he spoke, his voice low and resonant with an eerie, melodic quality that seemed to echo through the room, curling around the shelves like smoke. "The whispers are waking her."

Behind him, a woman stepped into the slanted cascade of moonlight. Her gown flowed behind her like a river of spilled blood, pooling around her feet with a rich, crimson sheen. Her mask—crafted of enameled ivory, its edges as sharp as rose thorns—concealed a visage carved from ice and fury, a face that promised both beauty and danger. She stood, a regal figure in the moonlit gloom, commanding the space with her presence.

The Queen.

She did not speak immediately. Instead, her gaze drifted upward toward the ceiling, toward the girl resting just beyond it.

"Too early," she murmured, her voice a soft, thoughtful whisper. "But not unexpected."

"She touched the book," the Knave continued, his eyes fixed ahead.

"It's speaking to her."

The Queen glided toward the register, her fingers trailing

lightly over the counter where Alicia had stood just hours before. She picked up a receipt—a mere ghost of its former self, its ink faded to nothingness.

"She doesn't know who she is," the Knave remarked.

The Queen's voice sharpened, slicing through the silence. "Good."

A pause. Then, her voice descended into a sinister whisper: "Let her wander. Let her doubt. The deeper she falls, the simpler it will be to shatter her."

The Knave tilted his head, his eyes flickering toward the door, shadows dancing across his mask. "And when she arrives in Wonderland?"

The Queen turned to him, her movements slow and deliberate as if savoring the moment. "Then," she hissed with chilling finality,

"the true torment begins. The Key must reach Wonderland. The contract makes no promises about her success. Or her survival."

She dropped the ghostly receipt back to the counter, where it settled without a sound.

At a nearby shelf, the Keeper—the third figure—watched with eyes ringed in memory. The old man's hand closed around a silver coin similar to the one he had pressed into the girl's palm the day before, setting this perilous chain of fate in motion. "This will be your greatest challenge yet, Majesty," he murmured, recalling the stubbornness that had burned in the girl's gaze.

The Queen's gloved hand flexed, pale fingertips weaving invisible threads through the stagnant air. "She will not escape us, Rabbit," she vowed, porcelain mask unmoving. The tension hummed, threads snapping taut across unseen planes.

"You will make it challenging for her; I have no doubt." He agreed. "This one is different. She is resilient, stubborn, and likely to change minds in the people of Wonderland. She will inspire change unlike the Keys who came before her."

The Queen's posture stiffened, as though affronted by the very suggestion that a mere Key—the girl from above—could influence the sprawling madness of the world below. Her mask betrayed nothing, but the slow clenching of her hands betrayed a fury banked, not extinguished.

"She will break like all the rest," she spat, though her voice lacked the certainty it once carried. "The people of Wonderland are loyal to me because they know what happens if they step out of line."

The Knave glanced at her sidelong, the intricate mosaics of his mask catching the moonlight in new, unsettling ways. "She will not be alone, Majesty. Your adversaries will move to greet her."

The Queen drummed her fingers on the hallowed wood of the counter, the rhythm sharp enough to startle dust motes from their slumber. "They are no threat," she dismissed, but her voice sounded as though she were speaking more to herself than the others. She swept her gaze through the darkness, as if she could see through timber, bone, and dreaming flesh. "All wonder bends, in the end."

The Keeper watched the Queen, silent, seeing in her the age-old tremor of rulers who know the hourglass is bleeding its last grains. He had seen many Keys before, but this one glinted different, as if she were cut from the stubbornest diamond. He wondered, not for the first time, if Wonderland itself was ready for the changes she would bring.

In the center of the room, a table stood piled with leather-bound tomes, titles faded, pages warped by centuries of handling. The Knave reached out, gloved hand hovering over the slick surface of a book titled *Historia Obscura: The Dreams That Became Us*. He hesitated, then tapped the cover once—hollow, expectant. The book shuddered, then opened itself as if guided by an invisible hand, pages riffling to a half-torn chapter near the center.

His gaze lingered on the passage, though the text itself shifted like ink on water—names slipping sideways, fates rearranging themselves with every blink. And yet… one line remained constant.

The Key will bring change. Will you help her, or let her fall?

The Knave stared at the words, unmoving. Something in the page tugged at him—a flicker of déjà vu wrapped in grief. He closed the book softly, almost reverently.

"You seem invested," the Queen said behind him, her tone too smooth, too sharp. "Only in the outcome," the Knave replied, but his voice was a shade quieter than before. The Queen's footsteps echoed as she approached. "She's just another lost girl with a pretty face. Like the others. We break her early, we spare her the agony of hope."

The Knave's jaw flexed beneath his shattered-heart mask. "Hope is resilient. More dangerous than any blade." "And yet it always bleeds."

Silence stretched between them. Then, as if catching himself in the mirror of her words, the Knave drew back his hand from the book like it had burned him. Whatever softness had ghosted through him—uncertainty, memory, something older—vanished in a blink.

He straightened.

"She won't survive long enough to hope," he said, coldly

now. "Not if I'm the one who greets her."

The Queen's smile was slow and cruel. "Good. Let that be the last thing she learns."

Above them, in the silent loft, Alicia trembled in her dream filled sleep. A quiver ran through her limbs; stray tendrils of hair clung to her forehead, lips parting as if on the verge of a cry.

The Knave remained motionless beneath the ceiling's cracked beams, as though bracing for the room itself to collapse. He waited with the cold patience of a lurking predator—every heartbeat a soft scratch against the shroud of night.

Around them, the Queen prowled the cramped shop, each step bending the stale air. Shelves quivered in her wake, and dust fled before her silent, furious power.

The keeper lingered by the ancient oak desk, his fingers absently tracing the contours of a weathered set of books. These books, steeped in the coloration of age, had unlocked secrets and gateways never intended for the light of day. Each breath he took caused the coins in his pocket to chime softly, an eerie melody that foretold a journey steeped in horrors yet to unfold.

The Queen and her shadow cast their eyes upward, their gaze fixed on the ceiling as they listened to the shallow, rhythmic cadence of Alicia's breath. Her presence felt precarious, like a porcelain figure teetering on the edge of a shelf. "Such a fragile vessel," the Queen mused aloud, her voice a blend of curiosity and disdain. "Are you afraid she'll break?"

"No," the Knave responded, his tone laced with a dark anticipation. "I hope she does."

The Queen turned her attention to the Keeper, her command slicing through the silence like a blade, leaving the air filled with anxious, jagged fragments. "Send her in, then," she ordered. "The edges of the dream are thinning. Prepare the way."

Above them, Alicia's body spasmed, her chest rising sharply as if she had inhaled the oppressive, stagnant heat. Even from a distance, the Queen could sense the erratic, thready pulse of the girl, an invisible thread connecting them. It was a pulse driven by dreams she would never recall and fears that roamed the shadowed corners of her mind, yet to be given form or language.

3

Night Reading

Alicia

That night I dreamt of a man in a mask. His eyes an ever changing of colors. We were in a meadow, but not like any I'd ever seen before. The colors were vivid and impossible all at once. Plants seemed to be alive, judgment evident in their movements. The man stops just before me, bowing as though he was snatched out of a different time.

"Alicia," he said, in a voice made for late-night radio. "Time is running thinner than you think."

I wanted to say something sarcastic, to divert from the intensity of the moment. The mask's eye holes flickered—teal, then gold, then the sickly blue of a dying TV screen. I lost my words somewhere between my molars.

He extended a hand, palm up. On it, the coin—the very same as earlier, split-heart, jagged as a confession. "A story needs finishing."

"What story?"

He smiled, all teeth and intent. "Yours, ours, theirs," he said, and pressed the coin into my hand. The warmth of it spread up my arm a second time, thick and insistent. I felt my heart stutter like a misfiring carburetor.

"You're not the author," he murmured, voice lowering, "but you are the Key to righting what has been wronged."

Then—his expression shifted. Not fear, exactly. Something heavier. Sadder.

"If the Key fails to turn," he said, eyes flicking skyward where clouds swirled unnaturally, "the story fractures. Wonderland collapses in on itself. What's real becomes unremembered. And she…"

"She who?" I asked, suddenly breathless.

"The Queen remembers what the world forgot. And she will rewrite the ending in her own image." He stepped back, gaze hardening. "That's why she fears you. Why she's already hunting you." I swallowed. "Why me? Why now?"

"Because you're the version that might survive it."

I opened my mouth to respond—but he wasn't finished.

"You are wondering what the Key is," he said, stepping forward again. "It's not a weapon. Not a crown. It's not even power in the way most people understand it."

His voice softened, as if reciting something sacred. "The Key is the influence. The story-shaper. The one who can tilt hearts toward change and restore the balance of Wonderland—not through force, but by guiding others to remember who they truly are."

I stared at him. "So… I'm supposed to give everyone magical therapy?"

That earned a faint smile. "You're job is to *unwrite the ending* the Queen has forced into place. To awaken what's been buried. Wonderland isn't ruled by swords or thrones—it bends the story. And the story has rotted."

"But why me? Why now?"

He glanced toward the violet sky. "Because the Key is chosen every hundred years. A safeguard created by the Keeper himself, long before Wonderland turned cruel. Each Key is sent to guide the realm back from the edge. To balance chaos with conscience. To remind Wonderland of what it was before it broke."

"Let me guess," I said slowly. "It hasn't gone well."

His jaw tightened. "The First Key chose power over promise."

My stomach dropped.

"Since then," he continued, voice like thunder wrapped in silk, "The Queen has destroyed every Key who followed. Quickly. Quietly. Before they could disrupt her version of the tale. And now?" He looked back at me, and for the first time, I saw fear in those ever-changing eyes.

"Now, Wonderland is bleeding. Time collapses. Memory unravels. The land rots beneath its flowers. If the Key fails again—there won't be another century. There won't be another chance."

I felt the weight of it settle over me like wet stone. My breath caught in my throat.

"So... no pressure."

"You're not expected to fight her, Alicia. You're expected to change the story." The man smiled, sad and strange. "The keeper has chosen you for your love of stories and your yearning for adventure."

Dream logic dictated I accept this at face value. I nodded, numbed by a thrum that was part adrenaline, part nostalgia, part terror. Around us, the wildflowers craned closer, greedy onlookers at the gallows. One of them bared tiny, perfect teeth.

"The rules are simple," he said, voice dropping as though for privacy. "Save them. Fill the silences with honesty. Change the story. And—" here, he leaned forward, voice sweet and brutal, "—help him write the last page."

"Who is him?"

He didn't respond to this directly, instead, he went back to my role in all of this. "You will be tested, terrorized, and betrayed. Wonderland will not make it easy, but you are strong enough to believe in change and rather, you are inspiring enough to make the people of Wonderland believe."

"Okay, but why does Wonderland need me? Why not just find some local, functional Alice and hand-off the apocalypse?"

He laughed, actually laughed, like I'd told him the world's oldest joke, and he was tired of pretending it wasn't funny. "Because you already know how to unstick a broken narrative. You do it every day—reshelving, reframing, refusing to let even a failed story go to waste." His tone grew gentle. "It's not a story if no one remembers how it ends. And Wonderland has forgotten everything except how to hurt."

"What makes it so broken?" I ask softly, afraid of the answer.

"The first Key I spoke of earlier; she was picked by the Keeper of Wonderland to restore balance to the world that was overrun by a king who ruled with an iron fist. Taxes were high, residents were starving, and despair was at an all-time high." The handsome masked stranger explained. "The first Key was given trials, faced certain death, but prevailed in the end at overthrowing the king. Unfortunately, this gave way to a new kind of tyrant; one more monstrous and diabolical than any ruler before."

"The Queen of Hearts," I whisper.

"The very one," he confirms.

His mask seemed to flicker—something sad and human behind its shimmer. "They say she was once gentle. She loved riddles. She wrote her own dreams and willed her nightmares to be silent. But in the vacuum left by the old king, she rewrote the world so that pain and panic were the only truths. She erased whole families with a decree; she delighted in watching hope collapse. Wonderland became her diary, and her ink was blood."

A long, slow shudder rolled through the grass. In the distance, sky fractured into jigsaw pieces, all different colors and seasons. Rain fell upward; trees bloomed in the shape of hearts, then bled their petals out like cauterized wounds.

The man in the mask stood, turning to me with a gentleness I didn't know how to absorb. "The Keeper's rules for Key's are simple but resolute. The Queen has no choice but to let you into Wonderland, it is part of a contract he created which is written in blood. If she refuses to allow you in, she dies. But that doesn't mean she can't kill you once you arrive. Trust me, she will try."

"And if I don't play the part?" I asked, mostly to see if I still had a choice.

He shrugged. "Wonderland will decay into memory. The balance is too far off. You are the last Key; there's not enough time for another. Then it's only a matter of time before your world follows."

I frowned. "That seems a little dramatic."

He smiled, closer now, the shimmer in his eyes darkening

to a stormy gray. "It's Wonderland," he said quietly. "Drama is the only currency." I chewed the inside of my cheek, feeling the pressure of a choice that wasn't mine to begin with. "I run a bookstore. I have zero sense of direction. I'm not a Key. I'm not even a spare library card." He shrugged, as if I'd said something inevitable. "You're all of those things, and also more. The Key is always ordinary, until the moment she can't be." Suddenly, I felt it—a deep, dragging pain, as if some invisible claw had pierced my sternum and was threading me to the air itself. My hands went numb. The world started to dissolve: the meadow flickered, the wildflowers trembled, the mask's eyes brightened until everything was only color and heat and the tang of blood and ozone. I groaned, clutching for the masked man's arm, but my fingers slipped through him, through the grass, through the pulsing sky. "You'll see me again," his voice echoed from somewhere, "but not as you expect. Remember—the Queen lies with every breath, but Wonderland lies with its silence. Speak truth. Listen deeper." He pressed the coin into my palm, his hand suddenly so very real and heavy. "Try to hold onto it this time." He says with a wink. The world folded in on itself like the end of a bad dream, and my last glimpse of him was a flicker of teeth, of heat, of desperate hope.

I jolted awake, ensnared in the sheets, sweat clinging to my collarbones. My room was bathed in the strange light and shadow of post-dream haze, with whites too bright and shadows eerily standing. Though the clock showed midnight, it felt much later. I attempted to recall the dream, but it was already vanishing into the depths of my mind, never to resurface.

* * *

It was precisely 2:37 A.M, and I'd long since abandoned any pretense of sleep. Outside my window, the city lay muted under a low, oil-slick sky—broken only by the hiss of tires carving wet asphalt and the distant, restless hum of headlights weaving through midnight streets. Inside, the air tasted faintly of chamomile tea gone cold in its mug, while the curtains still wore the ghost of lavender detergent. It was oddly comforting, in that "haunted but make it aesthetic" sort of way.

I sat cross-legged on the sagging couch, wrapped in a knitted blanket burrito that smelled faintly of cedarwood. To my side rested the book: *Alice's Adventures in Wonderland*. The very same used copy that was in my store downstairs— the one that had inexplicably twitched on the shelf during my afternoon of hallucination. Totally normal.

With a careful exhale, I cracked it open. The pages were supple, their edges feathered from gentle overuse, and someone— a former owner perhaps—had underlined certain lines in perfect, spidery pencil:

"Curiouser and curiouser..."

"We're all mad here."

"It's no use going back to yesterday, because I was a different person then."

My eyes snagged on that last line, circled twice in the same precise scrawl. Something about that line struck a chord with me.

I trailed a fingertip over the warm page—warm not with fresh ink, but with a slow, almost organic heat, like the paper was breathing beneath my touch. My spine stiffened. A floorboard creaked somewhere behind me.

I whipped around. The living room yawned empty, shadows pooling in their usual corners. No cultists. No writhing tentacles. Not yet.

I sank back against the cushions. Then—so faint I nearly missed it—a soft whisper curled through the air.

I could've blamed it on a draft, except the windows were shut tight.

Heart thudding, I leaned forward, blanket slipping from my shoulders.

"...*Alicia*..."

The voice was a breath of silk—masculine, intimate, alarmingly familiar. I sat bolt upright, yanking the book shut. The whisper died.

My pulse hammered. I held the tome out before me as if it might snap its cover and bite.

A beat. Then another.

"...*Open the door*..."

It came again, low and insistent, emanating from the very binding.

With trembling fingers, I cracked the cover once more. The next page was blank—except for one line I'd never seen before:

"*It is time, Key. Wonderland awaits.*"

I blinked. That couldn't be Carroll. I flipped to the front: identical edition, same worn barcode, same sticker reading "$2 or best offer."

"What the hell..." I murmured.

The words on the page began to shift, letters melting like

dripping candle wax before refolding themselves into chilling new text:

"She's coming for you. Soon."

I slammed the book shut, the sound echoing through the silent room.

Nope. Nope, nope, nope.

I flung it across the floor and bolted for the kitchen, flicking on every light switch—each bulb flaring to life, even the oven's. Suddenly the apartment felt glaringly bright, clinical.

The book lay where it fell: silent. Innocent.

Sleep became impossible.

Instead, I scrolled through my phone, aimlessly ping-ponging between news feeds and memes, desperate for banality. But everything—the ads, the notifications, even the wallpaper—seemed laced with allusion, as if the world itself was in on some enormous joke at my expense.

At 3:20 A.M, I surrendered. I threw on an oversized hoodie, pulled up my socks, and pointedly did not glance at the book on the carpet as I left it for dead. Halfway to the stairwell, I heard a soft, shivery giggle echo up the shaft, then nothing. My heart stuttered, but the snark came back automatically: probably just the ghost of a bad decision.

Outside, a fine mist feathered the air. I walked two blocks to the 24-hour donut place, past rows of sleeping storefronts and the singular flicker of a neon barber pole. The shop was staffed by the world's least judgmental cashier and one elderly man in a fedora, nursing a bear claw and the crossword section. I ordered a black coffee and a glazed twist, then sat in the plastic corner booth, and waited for the caffeine to banish whatever defective neurotransmitters were in revolt.

Instead, I found myself replaying the hallucination—

because there was no other word for it—in vivid, slow-motion recall. The feel of that not-right heat on the page; the cadence of the ghostly voice; the coin, still inexplicably gone. I searched everywhere, but it was nowhere to be found.

Maybe I'd freaked myself out so badly I'd dropped it. Maybe it was wedged between the couch cushions or fallen through a wormhole in the universe.

I got home with a sugary film on my teeth and the ambient unease of a person who's read too much urban fantasy and now suspects the shadows are lobbying for a union. The sun was rising—a half-hearted, milky dilution of light. The city looked more like a sepia-tinted TV special than anything real. Back in my apartment, the book was gone.

Confession: I'd expected this.

As inevitable as spoiled milk in the back of the fridge or that ex texting "u up?" the very second you're emotionally stable.

Just an empty spot on the carpet, like someone scooped out the nightmare and left me with a carpet stain.

I checked the apartment anyway. Hall closet, behind the shoe pile. Under the bathroom sink with the half-used bottles of hair detangler. Even the freezer—because who doesn't play hide and seek with possibly cursed objects? But no Alice. No Wonderland. No sign of the split-heart coin, either.

I poured myself another coffee and stared at my reflection in the stainless steel of the electric kettle. My face looked like someone had tried to model anxiety in the shape of a balloon animal. Not even the Instagram filter of kitchen sunrise could save it.

I continued my search, checking under the couch, between the couch and the wall, behind the TV stand, inside the fridge (just in case, okay), and even behind the toilet. I scoured bookshelves, coat pockets, and the mysterious void at the back of my pantry that ate Tupperware lids and hope. No book. No coin. Nothing but dust bunnies and the grim reality that I had, in fact, definitely not hallucinated a magical book and a sinister coin.

The rest of Sunday passed in a haze. I did chores I'd been putting off for months, alphabetized my tea collection, and executed the sort of deep clean that normally signals a nervous breakdown or a breakup. Still, I couldn't shake the sense of being watched, stalked by the memory of that voice. By the insatiable itch in my palm where the coin had pressed itself into my fate.

I didn't sleep. Instead, I watched the sunrise sweep across the windowpane and waited for something—anything—to return.

4

Google Didn't Prepare Me For This

Alicia

The next afternoon drug on like a raccoon wearing yesterday's mascara. At some point, I make coffee. At another, I try to reorganize the Staff Picks shelf (it's just my picks). The sun slants through the windows, golden and too cheerful for the inside of my skull.

As the day wears on my mind goes back to last night's dream. The man in the mask, his features eluding me. The prismatic meadow. The threat, the warning, the story that wanted fixing. It lingered with the tacky weight of déjà vu and the tickle of horror movie aftertaste. What gnawed most was that the dream felt more real than the burnt tongue I'd earned from my morning coffee, or the pinprick cuts on my finger from the damn recalcitrant tape gun. I think of what it would be like if the dream were real. Adventure, danger, it would be much different than my monotonous life.

My father passed when I was a teenager, my mother following him a few years later. I found solace in books and, when that wasn't enough, in the act of cataloguing and curating. The world outside rarely provided a plot worth following; inside these walls, stories could at least pretend to tie up their loose ends. Maybe that's why the morning's dream bothered me so much—it was a mystery I couldn't shelve, a riddle that refused to play by the rules.

At 25, I have finally given up on adventure, excitement, or even companionship. Occasionally I would feel a spark of adventure. Every few months I'd feel the inertia shift, the universe's cruel trick where it made you believe something could change, but then there'd be a mortgage to pay, or a leak under the bathroom sink, or a dry spell at the register, and the momentum snuffed out. The city didn't care, and it certainly didn't notice. But here I was, living what should have been another day in the dusty slow bleed of the workweek, with the muscle memory of last night's fever dream curling tighter around my limbs.

I ran a fingertip over the counter, trying to focus on the texture of peeling laminate, anything but the dream. It was pointless though as I kept seeing the mask's eyes, flickering, relentless. It was almost enough to make me laugh. Okay, so maybe I was unraveling a little. Maybe I was overdue for a vacation. Or a Valium. Maybe both.

At closing, I secured the heavy wooden door of *Thistle & Thorn Books*, effectively putting an end to the madness of the day. The street outside lay in a serene stillness as twilight began to wrap the town in its gentle embrace. Flicking off the lights, shadows pirouetted across the book-lined walls, transforming my little sanctuary into a haven of soft silhouettes and whispered secrets, as if the books themselves were sharing tales of ancient lore.

I lingered by the door, my hand resting on the cool, aged metal of the lock. The past few day's events swirled in my mind like leaves caught in a brisk autumn breeze, their colors vivid and wild.

"Get a grip, Alicia," I muttered to myself, shaking my head with a smile that was half amusement, half disbelief. "You're letting your imagination run wild again."

But as I turned to head upstairs to my apartment, a flicker of movement outside of the window caught my eye—a rabbit, sitting boldly on the sidewalk next to a rickety signpost outside my shop. Its snow-white fur shimmered with an almost metallic sheen in the fading light, and its eyes… Were they glowing with an ethereal luminescence? I blinked hard, convinced my mind was playing tricks on me.

The rabbit cocked its head, regarding me with an intelligence that sent shivers cascading down my spine. For a fleeting moment, I could have sworn it winked, a gesture filled with mischief and mystery.

"Okay, that's it. No more late-night fantasy marathons for you," I scolded myself, tearing my gaze away from the enigmatic bunny. I turned, hurrying up the narrow stairs to my apartment, my hands trembling slightly with a mix of excitement and unease. Once inside, I slammed the door shut, craving the security of a barrier between myself and the mysterious happenings below. I leaned against the door, releasing a long breath I hadn't realized I'd been holding.

"You're losing it, Alicia," I said aloud, my voice echoing in the familiar clutter of my living room. "Mysterious strangers, stalking rabbits… What's next? A neon striped cat with ethical issues?"

But even as I tried to laugh it off, a part of me thrilled at the tantalizing possibility. What if it was all real? What if, just beyond the thin veil of my ordinary life, there truly was a world of magic and wonder waiting to be discovered?

I moved to the window, peering out at the darkening street below. For a moment, I thought I saw a flash of crimson-colored robes disappearing around a corner. My heart leaped into my throat.

"Tomorrow," I whispered, my breath fogging the glass. "Tomorrow, I'll get to the bottom of this."

As I turned away from the window, my gaze falls on my bookshelf. There, nestled between well-worn paperbacks and dog-eared classics, was the copy of *Alice's Adventures in Wonderland*. Next to it, sat the coin. How does it keep getting here and more importantly, why is it glowing faintly? A weird feeling of intense pressure starts to take hold.

I glance around.

Books. Still.

Shelves. Still.

Clock. Ticking.

Except... not.

The second hand on the wall clock has stopped. Mid-tick. Frozen.

So. That's not ominous.

I reach slowly for the coin and the Alice in Wonderland book with stalker tendencies on the shelf. It's warm now. Buzzing. Like it's alive—or at least better caffeinated than I am.

"Okay," I say, my voice suddenly dry. "Fun prank. Very immersive. I give it five stars. But I really need to—"

The moment I touch the book, the room shifts.

The smell of ink and paper vanishes. The fluorescent lights flicker like they're gasping. And then—

Boom.

Colors burst behind my eyes in a dazzling explosion. A kaleidoscope of swirling ink, vibrant light, and resonant sound engulfs the bedroom, transforming it into a surreal canvas. I attempt to scream, but my voice is swallowed by an inexplicable indoor gale. The ground beneath me vanishes—or perhaps I dissolve into nothingness. My body is tossed and twirled as though flushed down the world's most opulent, disorienting toilet.

This is it, I think, acknowledging my descent into madness. They'll discover me babbling to a cardboard cutout of Jane Austen, a book fused to my hand, and a mountain of unpaid bills languishing on the counter.

Suddenly, everything halts. It's as if someone has pressed pause on a wildly expensive, illicit light show.

When I finally regain consciousness, the world spins like a top. I sluggishly pry open my eyes, straining to sharpen my vision through a fog of disorientation. My cozy apartment with its comforting clutter and the lingering scent of cheap wine has vanished. In its place is a lush forest glade, enclosed by towering trees painted in psychedelic hues of purple and blue. My limbs are ensnared in the soft, dewy grass. The air is rich with the fragrance of flowers and the bewildering scent of freshly-baked absurdity. Above me stretches a lavender sky—true lavender, not the artificial tint of a "sunset filter"—adorned with clouds whimsically shaped like punctuation marks.

"Oh," I croak, rolling onto my side. "This isn't Illinois."

I'm ensconced within a hedge maze. Because, naturally,

that's where I find myself. Nearby, a sign marks the entrance:
"This Way to Certain Doom →
← That Way to Slightly Less Certain Doom
Or Just Wait Here and Be Found"
I choose the most logical option: full-blown internal panic grips me like a vise. "Okay, Alicia," I mutter to myself, brushing the clingy blades of grass off my jeans with jittery fingers. "Let's recap. You touched a book with boundary issues and a coin that plays hide and seek. Got sucked into a Lisa Frank nightmare. And now you're in a foreboding hedge maze." The absurdity of my situation hangs heavily in the air.

Somewhere nearby, a flower emits a high-pitched giggle, its sound as delicate as the tinkling of tiny bells.

I whip around, my heart pounding like a wild drum. "Don't like that," I declare, my voice echoing through the uncanny silence of the maze. The hedge labyrinth seems to mock me with its twisting, shifting paths and the dead ends that appear from thin air only to vanish just as suddenly. "Sure," I grumble under my breath, as I navigate yet another corner, the foliage whispering secrets I can't understand. "Let's add 'manipulative greenery' to the list of things that want me six feet under."

Just when the thought of leaving a trail of breadcrumbs behind me seems like my only hope, the maze abruptly gives way to an unexpected clearing. In front of me unfolds a scene plucked straight from the most whimsical corner of my imagination: a towering rabbit—no, man-sized—sits serenely at a long, elegantly set table that stretches across the path. He's adorned in a perfectly perched top hat and a monocle that glints in the dappled sunlight, and—because why not—he's checking a gleaming pocket watch with a sense of urgency.

"Late, late, late," he mutters in a voice that carries the weight of perpetual tardiness. "For everything, really. But mostly destiny."

I stand there, eyes wide, locked in a staring contest with the fantastical creature before me.

He meets my gaze, his eyes as inscrutable as the depths of the ocean.

I continue to stare back, my mind racing to catch up with reality.

Then he sighs, the sound full of a world-weary disappointment. "You're late," he declares in a soft British accent that reeks of boarding school trauma and herbal infusions. It also sounds exactly like the old man from my shop a few days before.

"You!" I reply, my words tinged with bewilderment. "Why are you a rabbit?"

The Rabbit straightens his cravat, sets the watch down with a click and gives me an expression I can only describe as withering patience. "I am always a rabbit. You simply could not see me clearly in your world." His whiskers flare with the arrogance of someone who's both right and has had centuries to practice being so.

I look down at my hands for signs of hallucinogens or, failing that, possession. Still human, unless anxiety counts as a mutation.

This time, when he gestures at the empty chair beside him, I do not hesitate. I sit, half expecting the furniture to bite. "Why am I here?"

With the air of someone accustomed to strange occurrences, he gestures lazily with an ornate sugar spoon. "You've been summoned. Obviously."

"Obviously," I echo, my voice hollow, as I grasp for words that don't come.

"Welcome to Wonderland," he announces, taking a dainty sip of his tea as though it's the most ordinary of affairs.

I remain rooted to the spot, stunned into silence, until a bird—its feathers a patchwork of playing cards—flutters overhead and releases a tiny envelope onto the table beside him.

He deftly snatches it from the air, his movements fluid and precise, breaks the seal, and hands it to me without so much as a glance.

Alicia Hightower,

Welcome to Wonderland. We are delighted you have arrived. Try not to die.

—The Knave of Hearts

"Oh. Good," I say, sarcasm dripping from my voice. "A threatening welcome letter." The Rabbit, with his coat of snowy fur and eyes like polished onyx, raises one inquisitive brow.

"You'll want to be moving along now. The maze doesn't like loitering." As if responding to his words, the hedges around us shudder, leaves rustling ominously.

"Wait," I protest, clutching the note tightly. "Why me? I'm just a bookshop girl who talks to cardboard cutouts and has very questionable opinions on Lewis Carroll." His smirk widens, a mischievous glint in his eye. "That's exactly why you were chosen."

I stand there, dumbfounded, watching him hop away before my survival instincts jolt me into action. If the White Rabbit knows who I am and where I come from, surely, he knows the way back home. With a resigned sigh, I brush the dust off my skirt and trail after him, muttering under my breath, "Well, this'll teach me to stop touching random glowing items." Although you would think that I would already know that.

The path through the hedge maze, which previously twisted and turned against me with every step, now guides me unerringly as though an invisible hand charts the course. Wonderland, it seems, flows on a whim, unfettered by logic or clocks.

Every twist and turn reveals something more absurd than the last: towering topiary dragons that sneeze bursts of glitter into the air, fountains that spurt fragrant tea instead of water, and one particularly aggressive tulip that swipes at me with its broad leaf, as if affronted by my presence.

I ignore it all, keeping my head down and my focus sharp. Mission: Get. Out. But before I can take another step, a hand clamps onto my wrist with an iron grip.

I whirl around, fists clenched and poised to fight off whatever fresh terror this world throws my way. Instead, I find myself staring into the startled eyes of... myself?

5

Doppelgängers & Other Mildly Inconvenient Revelations

Alicia

No, not quite – this version of me had the same strikingly vivid green eyes, flecked with golden sparks where the light caught them, and the same wild mop of golden hair cascading in loose, luxurious curls around her face. But while my cheekbones curved gently, hers were sharply etched, as if an artisan had meticulously carved them with a fine-tipped pencil. Her lips curved into an amused smirk, one corner lifting upward, as if she harbored some delicious secret—probably an accurate assumption, given the entire scenario.

Her makeup was impeccable: smokey bronze eye shadow that made her eyes smolder with intensity, a touch of highlighter that shimmered along her brow bone, and lips painted in a polished rose hue that completed the look. Her outfit was extravagant, tailored fabric that draped perfectly over her lean hips, gleaming accessories that whispered of wealth and unshakable confidence. She was me, reborn with luxury, power, and a dangerously high level of self-esteem.

She crossed her arms, the leather of her jacket creasing softly with the movement, and tilted her head so that one light curl swept dramatically across her forehead. "Finally caught up, huh?" she purred, her voice smooth and silky as the finest satin.

"…Okay," I managed to say, my voice hoarse and strained. My heart pounded so loudly that I felt it reverberate in my throat. "Is this, like, a magic-mirror thing? Or am I hallucinating from trauma?"

She grinned broadly, her sharp teeth flashing under the light. "You always were slow on the uptake."

I rubbed my temples in exasperation. "Cool. A sarcastic hallucination. Love that for me."

"I'm not a hallucination," she declared, stepping forward with a confidence that made the air around her crackle with energy. "And I'm not your evil twin, either, before you get too excited."

"Define 'evil,'" I muttered under my breath, my skepticism barely concealed.

She ignored my comment entirely. "I'm you. Sort of. A version of you—the one who said yes when the universe knocked, the one who didn't bury her head in the sand."

"Oh good," I replied flatly, feeling as though I'd stumbled into a multiverse of bad decisions.

She rolled her eyes and snapped her fingers—a sharp, crisp sound that made the air shimmer like heated glass. The world around us blurred and then snapped back into focus. We were standing in a bookstore.

Except it wasn't my dusty little corner shop. This place

gleamed with a polished brilliance. Shelves of books glowed faintly, as if each spine held its own heartbeat. The pale walls pulsed rhythmically, like the building itself was alive, breathing and watching us with a silent, mysterious gaze. Above the doorway flickered a sign in luminous script:

Chapter One: Begin Again

I swallowed, pulse thrumming like a drum. "Okay," I said, voice as steady as I could manage. "What. The hell."

Not-Me hovered before me, lips curved in that sly grin, her voice reverberating like distant thunder. "This," she whispered, "is where your real story begins." She drifted down the plush, burgundy carpet, her every step lit by holographic constellations spiraling overhead and archaic runes glowing around her outstretched fingertips.

"You are The Key," she intoned, eyes alight with starfire. "Capital K. You possess the power to change. To inspire a world to fight for itself."

My stomach knotted. "Why me?" I blurted, flinging my hands up as if warding off invisible blades. "Why not some sword-wielding elf girl with a tragic backstory and a dangerously handsome assassin boyfriend?"

She arched a single brow, a playful smirk tugging at her lips. "Because they're busy on Kindle Unlimited."

My laugh echoed between the towering shelves—sharp, brittle. "Fair point."

She leaned in, close enough that I could see the runes flickering on her collarbone, like ghostly tattoos. "You've been chosen as the Key, Alicia. The magic, the power needs you to believe in it."

I wrapped my arms around myself, heat creeping up my neck. "That feels like a hell of a burden for someone who once locked herself out of her own apartment—twice—in one week."

Her voice dropped to a velvet murmur, weighty with destiny. "Then perhaps it's time to stop being the girl who can't open a door—and become the one who unlocks happily ever after's."

Just what I needed: a motivational speech from my deluxe doppelgänger.

She was already moving, trailing her fingers along the luminous spines as if reading their secrets by touch. "It's all here, you know. Stories of every possible you. Every choice you never made, every heartbreak you never nursed, every monster under your childhood bed. All documented." I trailed behind her, and the shelves seemed to warp and curve away from my peripheral vision, creating an endless carousel of options. The ambient light felt both natural and utterly alien; there was sun through the transom, but also a phosphorescent glow coming from between the books themselves, illuminating the dust motes in slow, lazy orbits. She continued, plucking a particularly battered volume and thumbing the edges with reverence. "You always liked to believe in hidden worlds. But most people, Alicia, they never look past the surface. They see a book on a shelf, or a girl in a shop, and that's the whole of it." She snapped the book shut and slid it back home. "You, though. You squint at the cracks. You notice the odd seams." There was a question implied in the statement, but I didn't know how to answer. Instead, I watched—not-Me select a new book from a high shelf, its gilt edging haloed by faint blue light. "You're the Key," she says holding up the book. "You determine how this story ends."

Before I could ask, "How?" the bookstore walls dissolved into flurries of dusty paper and ink. A gale-force wind whipped through my clothes, and a dizzying lurch sent me tumbling onto cool, damp grass.

I found myself in Wonderland's twisted reflection beneath a bruised purple sky. Magnolia blossoms and damp earth mingled with a faint metallic tang. I was alone—that is until a single ebony feather drifted past my cheek, jagged and singed. I looked up and saw a raven perched on a manicured hedge, its glossy eyes unnervingly knowing.

A whisper, slick and cold as satin, curled around my throat: *"Find the Knave."*

My heart pounded against my ribs. "Yeah. Sure," I muttered, voice as dry as parchment. "That sounds perfectly harmless."

The raven's wings beat once, soundless, then it vanished in a swirl of inky smoke.

I stood, brushing dew and loose shreds of plot off my jeans. The path before me was cut with shadows, hedged in by topiary that now seemed to leer with the faces of forgotten teachers and exes. Every angle bristled with implied danger, on-the-record weirdness. Maybe that's how it worked here in Wonderland. I walked on, keeping to the flagstone at the labyrinth's edge, half-expecting the flora to reach out and trip me up. Instead, the world seemed to hold its breath. My head throbbed with the echo of my other self's lecture—a motivational TED Talk, except the PowerPoint was my own insecurities dressed up as ominous threats. What was it she'd said? Every possible you. Every story you never lived. I shuddered. "A Choose-Your-Own-Adventure with optional suffering," I whispered.

Ahead, the path split in two—one paved in what looked like licorice, the other blanketed in velvet moss. From somewhere distant, music wafted: strings and cacophony and the distinct rhythm of a tap-dancing typewriter. A crooked wooden sign with more directions sprouted from the hedge, its letters carved deep and charred:

← This way to Answers.

This way to Certain Doom. →

I stared at the twin arrows, wood grain twisting like veins. "Same thing, really," I murmured.

Bracing myself, I exhaled and stepped beneath the arching hedges, letting the maze swallow me whole. After all, it seemed I hadn't tumbled down enough rabbit holes just yet.

6

The Puzzle Path

Alicia

The hedge maze loomed around me like a living predator, each towering wall of leaf and branch poised to strike. After my fifth dead end—each time the hedges seemed to shuffle themselves into a new configuration with the smug precision of a GPS possessed by a god complex—I had come to one inescapable conclusion: this maze was definitely trying to kill me.

My breath came in jagged bursts as I leaned forward with trembling hands on my knees, chest heaving. "Okay," I managed, voice tight with sarcasm. "That's fine. I didn't need to get anywhere. I adore being trapped in sentient shrubbery. It's just like a spa day—if your spa therapist specialized in dread and psychological torment."

The hedge to my left rustled, leaves quivering as if chuckling at my misery. Somewhere behind me, a lone flower on a tall stalk quivered—and then sneezed, a delicate "achoo" scattering pollen like golden dust into the humid air.

Swallowing hard, I turned the next corner—and froze. A wall of thorns spiked across the path, every black, obsidian-like barb glinting menacingly even in the dappled light. At its center stood a gate wrought from tangled gold branches, curling into the shape of a gigantic question mark whose dot hovered just above the ground. Beyond it, the trimmed hedges glinted, hinting at a clear corridor leading deeper into the labyrinth.

Suddenly a plaque shimmered into existence on the golden gate, its surface rippling as letters unfurled like living vines curling in mid-air:

"Answer true or walk in circles. The door opens to wisdom, not wit."

Then, from everywhere and nowhere all at once, a voice boomed—resonant, echoing through my chest like distant thunder. "Speak, Key. Solve the riddle, and the path shall open."

At that moment, a single card drifted down from the canopy overhead, spiraling until it landed at my feet. I picked it up gingerly—the parchment was cool and grainy, its edges curling as though alive. In looping, eerie script, the riddle read:

"I turn once, what is out will not get in. I turn again, what is in will not get out. What am I?"

I blinked once, twice. "Okay," I muttered under my breath. "Escape-room puzzles now. That's exactly what I wanted on top of everything else."

I studied the riddle anew, heart thudding so loud I was sure it echoed through the hedges. And then it clicked. My pulse surged.

"Not a lock," I whispered, stepping closer to the gate. "A

key."

Instantly, the golden branches trembled, recoiling as though scalded. They uncoiled in slow motion—serpentine vines shedding tension—until, with a deep, creaking groan, the gate swung inward and the thorn wall dissolved into motes of shadow.

A soft, musical voice drifted from the thinning thicket, gentle as a breeze through chimes: *"Find him."*

I crossed the threshold cautiously, as if the ground might vanish beneath me. The air shifted the moment I passed inside—cooler, older, tinged with anticipation. The hedges ahead rose taller and darker, their leaves dense and unreadable, but the path at least lay open, bathed in a pale green light.

Behind me, the golden gate snapped shut with a final, echoing click. Silent. Absolute.

I didn't bother to say thank you. But as I moved forward, something in the wind sighed back, carrying a single, exasperated whispered reply: *"You're welcome."*

The twisting path narrowed until I was practically squeezing through vine-curtained hedges, emerald leaves brushing my arms as the air turned damp and heavy—thick with the sharp, citrusy perfume of bergamot… and something darker, like impending doom. My heart thudded as I rounded one last mossy corner and stepped directly into madness.

In the center of a moonlit clearing stood a single table, draped in lace-trimmed linens that shimmered ghost-white in the muted light. Bone-white china teacups and saucers were arranged with mathematical precision, while porcelain teapots—glazed to a perfect sheen—hovered midair like smug, slow-moving airships, drifting and rotating as though caught in an invisible breeze. Four chairs encircled this surreal tea party, each more bizarre than the last.

One chair had rococo curves and gilded carvings fit for Marie Antoinette's ghost, its pale upholstery embroidered with roses. The second was a jagged throne of polished swords, their hilts crossing like a metallic bouquet. The third resembled a dentist's chair—cold, clinical leather and gleaming steel foot pedals. The final seat was a colossal, plush flamingo, its downy pink feathers soft and warm where a cushion should be, its long neck arched protectively.

"Absolutely not," I muttered, eyes locked on that feathered oddity as if it might honk at any moment.

Dangling from the center of the table by a silken ribbon was a small chalkboard sign, neat white letters scrawled in an elegant hand:

"One chair saves. One chair traps. One spills. One snaps. Choose wisely. Tea is mandatory."

Beside it, a slender silver hourglass flipped itself over—black sand beginning its steady descent, ten seconds displayed in bold numerals along the glass. A tinny voice—possibly the flamingo's—squeaked with menacing cheer: "SEAT YOUR-SELF OR BE SEATED."

My pulse hammered. "Okay, okay!" I gasped, pivoting wildly among the four cursed choices. The swords flashed in the dim light. The dentist's chair let out a mechanical whirr. The flamingo's glassy eye seemed to blink.

The hourglass grain hissed as ten dwindled to three. I let out a strangled sound halfway between a scream and a whimper and collapsed onto the Marie Antoinette–style chair. Immediately, the world exploded into motion.

The hovering teapots swooped down with graceful arcs, porcelain lids clinking like distant bells, and poured steaming amber liquid into fragile cups. Tiny sugar cubes were flung from a lace doily in perfect parabolic arcs, landing neatly in teaspoons. A butter dish at the table's edge popped open, sending pats of golden butter dancing across the linen.

And then… nothing. Silence, except for my own ragged breathing.

"Did I—did I pick right?" I stammered, staring at the table as if it would answer me.

With a sudden SNAP, the flamingo chair's plush body snapped shut like a gaping maw, feathers rustling. The dentist's chair spun wildly on its axis before ejecting itself backward into the hedge with a tortured squeal. The sword throne ignited in a flash of sparks, swords clattering as the whole contraption combusted into sizzling embers.

I blinked at the scorched earth and drifting ashes, clutching my teacup so tightly my knuckles whitened. Then one of the floating teapots purred, its voice smooth as cream: "Good choice." A second teapot, its handle looped like a curving swan's neck, added in reverent tones, "You get Earl Grey."

"…What happens if I didn't?" I whispered, voice small.

A third teapot, its spout tilted in sorrow, offered in a hushed lament, "English Breakfast," as if pitying my fate.

I lifted the delicate cup to my lips and took a cautious sip. The tea was perfect—velvety, fragrant, with that bright citrus note of bergamot dancing on my tongue.

"Was this… a test?" I ventured, trying to calm the frantic pounding of my heart.

The remaining items didn't answer. They were far too occupied smoldering or gnawing at the surrounding hedges.

Beyond the clearing, the path reopened—this time with only a polite rustle of leaves, no sinister fanfare. I rose, brushing imaginary crumpet crumbs from my shirt, and muttered into the still night, "I swear, if this maze makes me fight a macaroon next, I'm filing a formal complaint."

The hedge snickered, its leaves trembling in amused agreement. Of course it did.

7

The Queen's Games

Far beyond the hedge maze, in a tower that was a phantom on any map yet loomed ominously over all of Wonderland, the Queen watched with unyielding eyes. The air surrounding her shimmered like molten glass, swirling to conjure an image in midair: Alicia, treading carefully over the charred remnants of a chair, steam curling lazily from the tea in her cup.

"She adapts quickly," the Queen mused, her voice a soft, dangerous whisper that could chill the warmest heart.

"She survives," the Knave replied, in a bored tone. "That's different."

He stood just behind her, his presence a shadow, one hand resting lightly on the hilt of a blade that had materialized as if summoned by thought. His mask, crafted from obsidian and cleaved down the center, mirrored the flickering image of Alicia's uncertain path.

"She is amusing," the Queen noted, taking a delicate sip from a goblet brimming with a liquid too crimson to pass for wine. "A wild card. I will enjoy breaking her piece by piece."

47

The Knave let his gaze drop to the scrying pool at their feet—water black as mourning silk, disturbed only by the faintest ripple each time Alicia stuttered or stammered or, in her own stubborn way, refused to collapse. "She's different from the last Key." He didn't say it as a compliment, and the word hung in the air with the same weight as the dozens of predecessors whose puddled stories now inked the Queen's transcript.

The Queen turned, an imperceptible shift of her head akin to a guillotine poised to drop.

"Different, yes. She is strong willed and naive," she declared. "Every step forward disentangles the threads. Every riddle she unravels tightens the snare. It will be a pleasure to watch her shatter."

"The Beast?" he inquired.

"She'll face it next," the Queen purred, setting her goblet down on a surface that materialized only when required. "It will pursue her. Compel her to flee. We shall see what she does when cleverness deserts her."

The Knave's jaw clenched beneath his mask. "You've rigged the game."

"I am the game," she replied, her smile as sharp and thin as a blade. "And she is the piece neither of us can predict."

He remained silent.

Alicia reappeared in the shimmering image, halted at a fork in the road, her brow furrowed in thought.

"What do you think of the girl?" the Queen inquired, her voice a blend of silk and smoke.

The Knave did not answer.

The image flickered. A new shape emerged just beyond Alicia's sightline.

The Queen's gaze skated over him, as if she could see beyond the black glass of his mask, into the very cut and grain of his intentions. "I remember when you were that unpredictable," she said. There was a fondness in her tone, but also a warning. He inclined his head just enough, the strands of his ebony hair falling forward. "Not every game is played with cards," he replied. "True," she said, eyes already returning to the image of Alicia. "Sometimes the heart is wagered." A fresh flicker in the glass—Alicia moved, setting her jaw, marching down the moss path, umbrella brandished at her side. The picture warped and refocused, tracking her as she sped up, as the wind in Wonderland changed and the hush grew tighter, more expectant. The Queen watched, eyes narrowed to razors. "Call up the Beast." "Majesty—" "Now, Knave." He bowed. At his gesture, the shadows along the tower wall thickened, bulged, condensed into gears. Talons. Eyes glinting with malice and teeth wreathed in smoke.

The Clockwork Beast.

The Queen's smile broadened.

"Let the games begin."

8

The Clockwork Beast

Alicia

The tea had barely cooled in my stomach when the hedge path narrowed once more, then suddenly widened with dramatic flair—as if the maze itself was throwing its arms wide open and screaming, "Surprise! It's trauma time!"

I stepped cautiously into a clearing where the silence was abrupt and absolute, like a vacuum pulling at the edges of reality.

Too abrupt.

There was no wind rustling through leaves, no birds chirping their usual melodies. Not even a single flower, passive-aggressive or otherwise, dared to show its face. The air was thick with a mechanical tension—a tautness like a music box wound too tight, ready to snap at any moment.

Something clicked. Not in my head—well, maybe also in my head—but somewhere above. I craned my neck squinting through the dense topiary ceiling. But still, I saw nothing but a random umbrella casually floating in the air as though the laws of both gravity and decency had entirely checked out.

I took a tentative step forward.

Another menacing click sliced sharply through the air.

Then came a whirr, a cacophony like a thousand mechanical bees swarming with relentless purpose.

Then a growl followed—a deep, guttural reverberation that seemed to shake the very marrow of my bones.

At the far end of the clearing, the hedge tore open with a dreadful screech, reminiscent of steel claws scraping against bone. From that gaping, sinister maw, it emerged:

Towering at an intimidating eight feet, it was a monstrous chimera of churning gears and glistening bronze plating. Its head was an enormous clock face, split jaggedly down the middle, with the hands spinning frantically, chaotically out of sync. When its jaws parted, it revealed rows upon rows of vicious metal teeth, each one a reflecting silver needle poised to shred anything in its path. Its eyes were blazing hourglasses, tipped sideways and aflame with malevolence.

I barely managed to breathe the words, "Why me?" before it unleashed a deafening roar, a sound so powerful it shattered the stillness of the clearing.

Chaos erupted around me. I reacted on pure adrenaline, flinging myself sideways behind a particularly dense tangle of hedge, the scent of torn earth and panic flooding my nose as jagged metal claws gouged a trench in the grass where I'd just stood. A shower of splinters and metal filings rained down; I spat something gritty from my mouth, praying it wasn't a crucial part of my own dental work.

I then sprinted, adrenaline surging through my veins as the beast thundered after me, each monstrous step a seismic shockwave, like a ticking bomb destined to explode. Trees recoiled in terror, and the hedges peeled away like eager spectators at a gladiatorial spectacle, eager to witness my impending doom.

I veered left, narrowly avoiding a twisted root that curled up from the earth like a mocking question mark. My legs screamed in agony, muscles burning with exertion. My lungs felt like they were aflame, each breath a desperate gasp for survival.

It lunged again, impossibly fast for anything built of metal and hate. I ducked, rolled, and somehow snagged the floating umbrella I'd glimpsed earlier at the edge of the clearing. It was heavy, cold. The handle thrummed with a pulse, like a miniature generator set to "overachiever."

I thrust the umbrella instinctively, channeling every bad martial arts movie I'd ever watched alone at 2AM. To my absolute horror-slash-delight, the tip ignited with a ribbon of blue-green flame, yet the beast was relentless, gaining ground with every passing second.

"WHY," I gasped hoarsely, mid-sprint, "IS THIS PLACE OBSESSED WITH MURDEROUS HOUSEWARE?!"

I careened around a corner, heart pounding like a war drum in my chest, only to face another dead end—no escape, no salvation in sight.

The beast loomed behind me, steam curling ominously from its nostrils like the breath of an impending storm, ready to consume everything in its path.

It hesitated for half a breath, mechanical jaw beginning to split in what almost resembled anticipation. I sucked in a ragged gasp—lungs owned by terror, arms rigid—and thumbed an indent on the umbrella's handle that screamed

"I'm going to die." The flame at the tip erupted, not outward, but upward, a torrent of turquoise lightning that painted every leaf and blade of grass in mad, sidereal light. Too bad it had no effect on the beast.

"Thinkthinkthinkthink," I hissed, retreating until my spine pressed against the rough texture of a vine-laden tree. The clock-face on the creature ticked faster, a relentless countdown marking impending doom. Its chest clicked open, exposing a mesmerizing display of intricate gears, whirring furiously around a glowing blue core that pulsed like a miniature furnace. A low, ominous hum began to emanate from it.

It was about to explode.

My eyes darted frantically around the clearing. Twisting vines snaked over the ground, jagged rocks jutted up like teeth, and a lone, cracked teacup rested in the hedge, oddly placed like a forgotten trophy. But then, there was also a mirror.

A tall, cracked standing mirror, half-swallowed by the encroaching ivy, placed there like a relic from another time.

Screw it.

I don't know what made me do it, but in a desperate move, I snatched the teacup and hurled it at the mirror with all my might. I don't know why I did it, it just seemed like the right thing to do in that moment, like an instinct. As the teacup collided, the mirror's glass fractured into a thousand shimmering shards.

A brilliant pulse of light exploded outward from the mirror, engulfing the beast mid-charge in a radiant, blinding wave.

Time stopped.

Literally.

The relentless ticking ceased. Wisps of steam hung suspended in the air, frozen in their ascent. Even my own breath caught, stalled halfway up my throat as if caught in amber.

The beast stood immobilized, caught in a mid-lunge, like a corrupted gif frozen between one frame and the next.

I slowly exhaled, the sound echoing in the unnatural stillness.

"Holy hell," I whispered, my voice barely audible against the silence. "I broke physics with a teacup."

Gradually, the brilliant light faded, and the mirror seamlessly re-formed as if it had never shattered.

And the beast… it began to rewind, its movements reversing in a surreal dance as time started to flow backward. Piece by piece, it folded itself backward, retreating into the hedge from which it came.

When it was gone, the clearing went still again.

My knees gave out. I dropped onto the ground and stared up at the lavender sky, laughing like someone who had officially *had enough*.

"Wonderland," I panted, "is not for me."

Except a voice inside me—my own or maybe the version of me with better hair and worse impulse control—snipped, *not yet*. I dragged myself upright, dusted imaginary debris off my clothes, and clutched the umbrella like it was the only thing keeping me tethered to reality. The world was still locked in that hushed, post-detonation calm; even the colors seemed saturated with shock. I didn't want to move. I wanted to collapse in the moss and let Wonderland chew me up and spit me out. But the path forward had miraculously—and ominously—cleared once more as if I was in a video game and I needed to defeat the level to progress.

The vines shifted beside me. I stumbled up, legs weak,

expecting at any moment for the universe to reassert itself and throw another obstacle at my head. Instead, the maze path gently invited me on, the scent of citrus and old books pressing forward like a memory I wasn't sure belonged to me.

The hedges leaned in conspiratorial, whispering leaf-to-leaf as I passed, and somewhere above, the sky began to shift from lavender to a bruised mulberry. Each step sloughed exhaustion off me, though it kept trying to crawl back up my ankles, hungry as guilt. By the time I reached the next opening, my breathing was almost normal. Almost.

I emerged into a sunken garden—a perfect circle with a gnarled tree at its center, draped in Spanish moss and silver ribbons knotted around every limb. I didn't so much walk as drift into the garden, feet moving because they hadn't yet received the quit memo from my brain. The hedges fell away behind me, like they knew this place wasn't theirs to interfere with.

The silence here wasn't threatening.

It was *reverent.*

The air held still. Watching. Waiting.

I dropped to the ground under the tree, the mossy base cool and soft like the world's weirdest memory foam mattress. The silver ribbons tied to the branches fluttered despite the absence of wind, each one etched with delicate script I couldn't quite read.

I closed my eyes.

Just for a second.

The ground beneath me hummed. Like a heartbeat.

Or maybe it was mine.

I placed a hand on the tree's bark, rough and cool beneath my palm.

And that's when it happened.

A *pull.*

Not physical. Not even magical, exactly.

I stood slowly, pressing my palm to the bark once more. It pulsed under my touch. "Okay," I told the tree with all the false confidence of someone who's definitely not unraveling. "You're probably enchanted. Or high. Maybe I am. Either way, I'm going to ask nicely—can you point me toward civilization?" The tree blinked. *IT BLINKED*. I blinked back. We stared at each other like two raccoons caught in a philosophical debate.

The tree never did answer. By this point the tree had gone still again, but the air around it still thrummed with energy, like I'd only scratched the surface of something massive and buried. My fingers brushed the mossy ground. And stopped. A patch of soil didn't feel right. Too smooth. Too symmetrical. I pulled at the moss. Beneath it, a square of dark stone emerged—etched with lines I couldn't quite place. I cleared more away. It wasn't just a stone. It was a door.

Circular markings spiraled out from a central symbol— something that looked almost like a keyhole, but shaped like a stylized **heart split down the middle**, just like the coin from the collector. The moment I saw it, my palm burned.

"I really don't like this," I muttered. "Which probably means I have to do it." I pressed my hand to the heart. The stone glowed blue, then gold, then burst into white light. The door cracked open with a low, resonant groan like something had just *woken up*. A staircase descended into darkness, carved of polished stone that pulsed with faint veins of light.

Before I could take a step inside, a raven appeared once more, tossing a letter at me before disappearing again. Unraveling the parchment my breath shuttered as I took in the threatening letter from the Knave written in blood red.

My Dearest Alicia,

By now, surely you realize that Wonderland is not fiction, and your life—your insipid, charming, tragic little life—was the daydream. Consider also that, as of this moment, every step you take is watched by the Queen. Every word, weighed by the tower's obsidian heart. You have made it farther than any Key in the past three centuries. Congratulations. The question is, will you survive what's next? It is your curse, and your gift, to choose. Tick tock, darling. She is expecting you.

You always wanted to know how the story ends, Alicia. Down you go.

— The Knave

P.S. The Beast is not dead. Only hungry. Don't keep it waiting.

"Definitely going to die," I said to no one, as I stepped down.

Nothing about this underworld of Wonderland was what I expected. The air was neither cold nor hot, but crisp—tinged with the ozone of a distant thunderstorm and the sweetness of old paper. The walls, barely more than rough-hewn rock, twitched with odd veins of fluorescent gold that pulsed in rhythm with my own pulse. There were no torches, but there was light enough, as though the rock skin itself had decided to glow just for me.

The air inside was cooler, stiller—heavy with the scent of

parchment, candle wax, and time.

The staircase wound downward far longer than any illusionist's basement had a right to. I felt the physics of my old world peeling away with every echoing step.

At the bottom, the staircase opened into a chamber lined in bookshelves carved from the roots of the tree above. Shelves curved like spirals, wrapping around a central pedestal made of crystal and thorns.

And resting on it—was a map.

Old. Unfurling slowly on its own. Its surface shimmered, showing a maze, a forest, a castle that flickered between shadow and light, and a sea of ink where no paths yet existed.

As I stepped closer, new details appeared—*my* path through the hedge maze, still glowing faintly. And at the far edge, flickering in red, two names I didn't like:

Knave. Queen.

Below that, words bloomed across the page in a language I shouldn't be able to read. But I could read them. I knew what they meant, even before I realized it:

Only the Key may choose the next chapter.

I reached out, fingers trembling, and the map rolled itself shut, sealing with a gold ribbon and a single silver wax seal in the shape of a spade.

"Excellent," I whispered. "A creepy door, a map that watches me, and now I'm the protagonist in a magically binding Choose-Your-Own-Adrenaline-Nightmare."

9

The Masked Stranger

Alicia

There was a door at the far end, ominously waiting to be opened. I should not have opened it. I staggered through the ragged door, every limb vibrating with leftover adrenaline and residual emotional stress. The umbrella-turned-flamethrower still dangled in my grip, humming faintly like it had opinions. The trees ahead pressed inward, shadows stretching too long for the time of day, like Wonderland's lighting crew had gotten artsy and unhinged.

I should have turned back.

Instead, I pressed on, stepping into an open field. It wasn't much—just a low bowl of velvet grass hemmed in by twisted trees that whispered to each other without wind. But it felt wrong. Not bad wrong. *Off.* Like the silence was listening. Like I'd wandered onto a stage right before the final act and forgotten my lines.

That's when I saw him.

Tall. Still. Centered like a statue in the eye of a storm. He wore black and crimson, cloak rippling slightly as if the air around him refused to settle. A mask obscured his face—cracked down the center like a broken heart, the pieces stitched together in jagged red. His eyes—if they were eyes—were dark as night, and just as dangerous. They narrowed as I stepped closer, my stomach twisting like a wrung-out rag.

He didn't move. Didn't speak. Just watched.

My fingers tightened on the umbrella.

"Okay," I croaked. "Are you here to kill me, too? Because honestly, I am *not* emotionally equipped for round two with a sentient blender."

A pause. Then, slowly, he took a single step forward.

"No," he said. His voice was low and precise, the kind that didn't need to raise volume to command attention. "If I meant to hurt you, Alicia, you'd already be broken."

I blinked. "Cool. Love that confidence. Who are you?"

He tilted his head, as if I'd asked the wrong question.

"Names are masks," he said. "And I'm not the only one wearing one."

That was… not an answer.

"I've had a long day," I said, pointing the umbrella at him like a polite threat. "I've been screamed at by an exploding clock-beast, gaslit by sentient furniture, and I may or may not have broken time with a teacup. So, unless you're here to explain what the hell is happening or hand me a Xanax, I suggest you—"

He raised a gloved hand, and my voice stopped. Not magically. Just… instinctively.

"There's a war beneath the whimsy," he said. "And you're in its center, whether you choose to be or not." I narrowed my eyes. "You sound like the world's least helpful narrator."

He didn't react. Instead, he reached into his coat and withdrew a card. A single playing card, aged and yellowed, with a heart on it—not the sweet, Valentine's kind, but one cracked down the middle and bleeding at the seam. He held it out between two fingers.

I hesitated.

Then I took it.

It burned cold.

"When the time comes," he said, "will you have what it takes to change Wonderland, or will you fail in spectacular fashion? Personally, I am hoping for option two."

He lingered in the clearing, gaze fixed unblinking on me, as if he'd always been my audience and I was just now noticing the spotlight. Somewhere behind us, the distant chime of a clock stuttered and died.

I tried to hand the card back, but he shook his head. "It's yours. You've always had a part to play, Alicia Hightower. You just never wanted to read the script." His thumb caressed the edge of his mask, tracing the ragged split; I wondered, for one unhinged moment, if that mask would fit me just as well. I'm a sucker for fashion statements.

"Look," I said, card slick with sweat between my fingers, "I don't even know the rules." I sounded shrill. "Are there rules? Or do you just set things on fire and hope for the best?"

He laughed—a real sound, surprisingly human, threaded with something like pain. "Rules are for those who fear consequence." He stepped closer and, though every cell in my body screamed run, I stood rooted. "Wonderland has always bent to the will of those who dared rewrite it."

"This has got to be a dream." I mutter. "Or a nightmare."

He lifted my chin with a gloved knuckle, holding my gaze. "You're not dreaming, Alicia. *You* are the dream. Wonderland doesn't live in maps—it lives in you. Wakes up every time you lose your place or forget your way." His voice was gentler now, quieter. "You broke the Beast. You mended the heart. The Queen can't have that, which is why I'm here."

My blood ran cold at his words. This wasn't just any masked stranger, this was the Queen's right hand man, her assassin, The Knave. He saw the recognition click behind my eyes and smiled—an ugly, knowing twist beneath his mask. "Looks like someone read ahead," he said in a smug tone that made me want to cry. Or slap him. "Relax," he soothed with fake reassurance, as though we were sharing a cigarette outside a bar and not standing in the crossroads of a metaphysical coup. "If I were here to collect, you'd already be carted off in pieces."

"Reassuring." My voice went small and cynical in self-defense. "Why don't you just kill me, then? You already know the Queen's watching. What difference does it make?"

He took another measured step forward. Light licked the sheen off his boots. "Where would be the fun in that?" He asked, false innocence coloring his tone. "I much prefer the game little, Alicia."

The trees pressed closer around the clearing, as if bracing for an incoming storm. In the distance, a bell tolled—a resonant sound that vibrated the pit of my stomach. He didn't turn to look; for one grotesque moment, I wondered if I could run, if I could vanish into the brush before he bared his teeth. But, as it turns out, there was no need.

When I looked back at where he was standing, he was gone. No sound. No gust of wind. Just vanished. Like a trick of light—or memory.

The clearing around me had already begun to fade, the shadows pulling back like curtains after a show. I turned in a slow circle, but the grass was just grass again. The trees, normal. No sign of him.

No proof he was real at all.

Somewhere behind me, I thought I heard laughter.

Soft.

And heartbreakingly familiar.

10

An Alice, A Cat, and a Complete Mental Breakdown

Alicia

The path winds like a drunk spaghetti noodle with a vendetta against straight lines. Every time I think I'm making progress, it doubles back, throws up a talking rock with a questionable accent, or dead ends into a wall of whispering ivy that seems to be gossiping about my outfit choices. I'm starting to suspect the map is just a suggestion. Meanwhile, I'm as lost as a super model at a goat farm. At this point, the trail is gaslighting me with the dedication of a method actor.

After what could be minutes or decades (Wonderland runs on its own battery), I trip a root, nearly perform dental surgery on a mossy stone, and am greeted by the sound of gentle sobbing. At first, I assume it's me, but the wail is too melodic, too determined. Following the noise, I burst through a curtain of suspiciously soft brambles and nearly run straight over a girl curled at the base of a gnarled willow, nose buried in her knees.

She looks familiar. Not in the "we took chem together" way, but in the "I saw you in an oil painting and you blinked back" way. She's clad in layers of blue and white, her apron muddy and torn, and her hair—much blonder than mine—falls in a tumble down her back. It's not possible, and yet the proof is right in front of me.

"Alice?" I say, with measured disbelief.

She peeks up. Her eyes are bloodshot and glistening, her nose practically luminescent with misery. But then she refocuses and gives me the kind of up-down appraisal reserved for loan officers or especially judgmental baristas.

"Oh good," she sniffs. "The new Key has arrived. It has been a century since the last one came. You're the last hope to save the story."

The last hope. Not a new chapter. The final page.

Then she scowls and wipes her nose with a sleeve. "You're late," she adds, though I have a strong suspicion time is more of a party trick here than a functional concept.

I swallow and glance around, looking for cameras, witnesses, or an exit sign. No such luck. Just me, Alice (?), and an audience of silent, judgmental willow leaves.

"I didn't get a user manual," I tell her. "In fact, I was hoping the position of 'Key' would go to someone with better spatial awareness." I gesture back at the maze. "I've spent the last hour being berated by shrubbery and possibly emotionally manipulated by a masked stranger with epic villain energy."

Her head jerks up slightly at that, eyes narrowing—not with surprise, but recognition. "The Knave," she mutters, like the word tastes foul. "He always finds the Key first. He likes to watch them falter."

Alice stands. At first she seems fragile, but once upright she radiates a certain feral competence, like a cat who's been through three lives and learned how to weaponize each one. She regards me with a frown so profound it is almost regal.

We lock eyes, and for the briefest moment I see something ancient flicker behind her glare—an undercurrent of exhaustion so deep it probably predates the concept of sleep.

"So, uh," I offer, dusting bramble-bits off my sweater, "what exactly was wrong with the previous Key? Did they, I don't know, reset the universe and forget to leave instructions?"

She mops her nose with the corner of her skirt, unashamed. "The last Key lost. That's what Keys do. They lose themselves. The world decays. Story lines tangle. Wonderland becomes…this." She gestures around, indicating the aggressively mismanaged topiary, the perpetual overcast, the subtle but pervasive sense that even the birds would unionize if they could.

"But you—" she adds, voice softening a fraction, "you might be different. You've already changed something. The whispers are louder. Wonderland is paying attention."

I pick my way closer, half-expecting the ground to collapse into a sinkhole of symbolism. "Well," I say, "if it's any consolation, my sense of direction is so bad I usually get lost in IKEA. Maybe it's fate."

Alice shrugs, eyes gone glassy over some distant trauma. "The maze is adaptive. The more you doubt yourself, the more it doubts you. Eventually, you forget you were ever real."

"That's bleak," I reply, oddly comforted.

She stands, knees cracking, and for the first time I realize she's older than I expected. Not old-old, but there's crow's feet around her eyes.

"One Key comes every century," she says finally. "You are not here to fight. You are here to inspire. To make the people remember. The Keeper created the Key to help Wonderland choose another path."

Her voice drops. "The first Key chose power instead of balance. The others never made it far enough to change anything."

She looks at me like she's waiting for me to break. When I don't, she adds, "But some say this Key—the one who hears the story whisper and makes it sing—might be the one who turns the tide."

With that, she turns on her heel, takes two steps, and disappears.

I stare at the spot where she vanished, wondering if this is how one inherits a collapse of narrative structure, and also whether the ground is safe to sit on, or if it's the kind that will try to unionize and usurp your pants.

The wind shifts, and for a brief, brilliant moment I hear a different sound: laughter, somewhere ahead, deep and bright and so unlike the wilting sadness of Alice that I get up, dust myself off, and follow it.

The maze, perhaps sensing I'm less afraid now—if only because I'm too tired to properly panic—reluctantly parts before me. The walls are less menacing, more draped in curious blossoms and soft, downy fuzz. I get the feeling the maze is reconsidering its life choices. Good for it, honestly. So am I.

* * *

After another indeterminate interval of twisty-time, I step into a new area—and immediately regret it.

The air here is *too* still. Not peaceful-still. Trapped-in-a-snow-globe not yet shaken kind of still. The sky overhead is bruised lavender, and the grass beneath my boots makes a soft crunch like it's been listening to secrets it shouldn't.

Which is when I meet the elusive meddler.

He must be roughly six feet five inches tall, dressed in purple and pink with clothes like a Victorian thief who moonlights as a magician, and wears an expression that screams, *"I know what you're thinking and I'm going to use it against you."*

He appears—literally—from nowhere. One second, I'm alone. The next, he's lounging upside-down on a branch directly above me like gravity owes him money.

"Well, if it isn't our reluctant heroine," he purrs, his voice as honey-smooth and razor-sharp as a bee that's taken up fencing.

I jump, heart doing its best impression of a startled squirrel. "Seriously?"

"Seriously," he replies, flipping to the ground without a sound, like air was designed just to carry him. "You've got the scent of destiny on you. Or maybe just bookstore dust. Hard to tell without a monocle."

He circles me like a predator. Or a fashion consultant on a caffeine high. His movements are fluid, unnaturally graceful—like every muscle is choreographed to music I can't hear.

"You're Cheshire," I say, mostly to feel like I still have control over anything more complicated than a toaster.

He gives a dramatic bow—one hand to his chest, the other sweeping off a top hat I *swear* wasn't there a second ago, as if auditioning for the role of Most Extravagant Figment of My

Imagination.

"At your service, Alicia Hightower. Chosen One. Key. Slightly disheveled interdimensional tourist."

"You know my name," I say flatly, like I'm reading a menu with too many truffle options.

"I know many things," he replies, flashing a grin that looks like it should come with a warning label and a nondisclosure agreement.

"Know how to get out of here?"

"Define *here*," he says, tilting his head like an owl who's just discovered sarcasm.

I rub my temples. "Do you always answer questions with riddles and smugness?"

"It's either that or therapy," he sighs. "And I haven't been licensed in centuries. Plus, paperwork's a nightmare."

I sigh back, louder. "Fine. Let's say I *am* this 'Key' person. What am I supposed to unlock, exactly?"

"That," he says, eyes gleaming like a cat who's just spotted the world's slowest mouse, "is the question." He steps closer, and for the first time, his grin fades. His voice lowers. Gravity leans in. "But if I were you," he says slowly, "I'd worry less about what you unlock—and more on how the story ends."

My mouth opens to ask what that means, but he's already gone. Not walking away—vanishing. Just *gone*. A curl of shimmering purple mist hangs in the air where he stood. The scent of cardamom and static. The weight of a presence that shouldn't have fit in something as simple as a body.

And completely unhelpful.

And somehow, more terrifying than the Knave.

11

Caterpillar and Confusion

Alicia

I set off down the path once more, the scenery changing on a whim—like the forest couldn't decide whether it wanted to be haunted or whimsical, so it chose both and added mood lighting. I don't wander far before I stumble on the mushroom.

Calling it a "mushroom" feels wrong. It's massive—easily the size of a minivan—and glows with an otherworldly blue that practically hisses, *do not touch.* It radiates the sort of energy that says licking it would either unlock the secrets of the cosmos or kill you instantly. Possibly both. And, of course, there's a spiral staircase carved right into its stalk. Lacking self-preservation and decent judgment, I climb.

The stairs creak with every step, releasing little clouds of bioluminescent spores that cling to my clothes and shimmer like static electricity. The air gets colder the higher I go, thick with something like ozone and forgotten words.

At the summit, a velvet cushion hovers just above the

mushroom's cap like a levitating throne. Seated cross-legged on it—no seatbelt, no gravity, just vibes—is Caterpillar.

If you squint, he's human-shaped. But only just. He's cocooned in robes that shift colors faster than a malfunctioning smart bulb—indigo, emerald, copper, back again—never the same hue twice. His face is a picture of disinterest draped in ancient patience. One hand holds the stem of a hookah that seems to breathe on its own. The other taps lazily on a small hourglass filled with what looks mysteriously like falling starlight.

Smoke curls from his lips, unfurling into the shape of a key. It spins, flickers, then dissolves into the ether.

"Alicia Hightower," he says, voice slow and smoky, like a haunted grandfather clock refusing to chime.

I'm winded and sore and increasingly suspicious of reality. "Let me guess," I mutter. "You've been expecting me."

He sighs, long and theatrical. "No. I've been avoiding you. But the future is pushy, and time has teeth. So here you are."

I blink at him. "You all talk like fortune cookies having existential crises."

He gestures to the cushion beside him. I sit because standing on a swaying mushroom cap feels like tempting fate and/or death. The cushion squeaks as I sink into it, sending up a puff of shimmering dust.

"You seek answers," he says.

"I seek an exit," I correct. "Answers would be a bonus."

He exhales another smoky shape—a crown this time, cracked down the middle—and watches as it evaporates. "Wonderland is unraveling. The Queen rewrote the rules, erased the heroes, and chained the story to her will. The Key"—his gaze flicks toward me—"was meant to inspire change. Not fight. Not conquer. Influence."

"Cool," I say. "So I'm magical peer pressure?"

"You're the reminder," he counters. "That madness doesn't mean cruelty. That power can be rewritten. That Wonderland is still listening—even if it's forgotten how to speak."

I shiver, the air thinner here than before. "And the Knave?" I ask, trying to sound casual. "What is he to her?"

Caterpillar's eyes narrow, their color shifting to something sharp and metallic. "He is what happens when loyalty forgets why it began."

That hits harder than I expect. "So he's a weapon."

He nods once. "And a consequence."

I swallow hard.

"The Queen commands the suits. The Knave eliminates threats. But it is the Key who stirs hearts. That is your power. That is why she fears you."

"Fears me?" I scoff. "I nearly died tripping over a toadstool."

"Not yet," he says, and it's not quite comforting.

Another long silence.

"You will be offered choices. Illusions wrapped in prophecy. The Queen will test you. So will the Knave." He leans closer, hookah forgotten. "But remember, Alicia: stories only end when you stop telling them. And your story—this story—has been waiting for you to change it."

The wind rises. He exhales one last plume, this time in the shape of a shattered mask.

When it fades, he's gone.

So is the cushion.

So is the warmth.

I sit on the cold cap of the mushroom, the weight of his words heavier than gravity. Below, the spiral stairs look steeper than before—darker, less welcoming. The forest hums with anticipation.

And somewhere—just out of reach—I think I hear the Knave's laughter again.

This time, it sounds like a warning.

I turn—and discover a path that wasn't there before, winding off into the glowing fungal forest, like an open invitation to a road trip on acid.

I follow, because in Wonderland, as I am quickly learning, the only thing more dangerous than moving forward is standing still. The path pulses under my sneakers—breathing, almost, like some nervous organism—and each footstep leaves a print that lingers in the luminous moss before fading into memory. In the darkness between the trees, things scuttle and watch; sometimes they laugh, sometimes they just stare, and sometimes they offer helpful home décor tips in faint, piping voices. (Wonderland is terrifying, but at least the ambiance is on point.)

I wonder if I'm supposed to be afraid. Technically, yes. But mostly I'm running on empty, maybe even below empty. That's how you get through a day in retail. That's how you get through Wonderland, apparently.

The path deposits me at a crossroads. An actual, honest-to-God, fairy-tale crossroads. There's yet another signpost in the middle, its wood darkened by years and something less savory. The signs spiral and loop around each other:

UP: To the Queen
  LEFT: To the Knave
  RIGHT: To Yourself

DOWN: To Regret

The last is just a hole in the ground with a pair of cartoon eyes blinking up at me. I step carefully around it.

I consider my options. The Queen's probably not my first stop, given that she wants me dead or rewritten or both. The Knave? No, thank you. I am not interviewing the local villain without preparation. Which, of course, leaves: To yourself.

To the right I go.

I find myself growing increasingly weary as the day drags on, prompting me to seek solace by the babbling creek bank. The gentle murmur of water lulls me into a tranquil state, and before I can resist, sleep descends upon me like a thick, enveloping fog—soft, all-consuming, and eerily silent.

I can't recall the moment my eyes closed. One instant, I was gazing up at the intricate weave of silver-knotted branches above me, their leaves whispering secrets in the breeze. The next, I found myself transported to an entirely different realm.

A seemingly endless hallway stretched out in both directions, shrouded in dim, shadowy light. Mirrors lined the walls, yet they failed to reflect anything but distorted versions of myself I couldn't recognize. Each reflection was slightly askew—some older, others younger, some adorned in elegant gowns, others clad in formidable armor or cloaks stained with crimson blood. None of these reflections blinked, their eyes fixed and unyielding.

I began to walk slowly, the mirrors emitting a faint, melodious hum as I passed them by. Then, one mirror shivered with a subtle, ethereal shimmer.

I halted in my tracks.

This mirror displayed a memory.

A girl who bore a striking resemblance to me stood barefoot in a candlelit chamber. Her eyes glistened with tears, though her expression remained calm, almost regal. In her delicate hands, she clutched a key crafted from blackened silver.

She was not alone.

A tall man stood before her, his dark hair curling at his collar like ink-stained waves. A teacup dangled from his fingers, its design a fractured heart, split down the middle. His eyes burned fiercely, illuminated by a stormy inner light—filled with anger and an overwhelming sense of grief.

I couldn't hear their words, but the raw emotion hit me like a visceral blow.

The girl stepped toward him, her movements deliberate and graceful. She reached out, placing the key in his hand with a solemn gesture.

He remained motionless.

He stared at her as if she had handed him a dagger and commanded him to finish a perilous task.

Suddenly, the room around them fractured like fragile glass.

The mirror cracked down the center with a sound akin to a piercing scream, and I recoiled just in time before it shattered completely—leaving nothing but swirling smoke in its wake.

"Too soon," a whispering voice murmured behind me.

I spun around swiftly.

But there was no one there.

Just another mirror, its surface coated in a delicate layer of frost.

Etched upon it, in fine frostbite handwriting, were the

chilling words:

"You gave me the key." He whispers, either horrified or touched I couldn't tell. "Now find me in the waking hours."

I awoke with a gasp, my heart pounding furiously in my chest.

The garden remained still, the tree above me silent.

Yet the air was charged with an electric tension.

As if something was approaching.

Or watching.

Or both.

12

Wandering Through Whimsical Wonderland

Alicia

Once I get my bearing's, or some semblance of them at least, I follow the path I was on yesterday; mainly because I didn't have any other choice. As I venture deeper into Wonderland, the scenery around me transforms like a swirling, chaotic masterpiece painted by a drunken artist. The colors bleed and blend into one another, creating an ever-shifting tapestry of wonder. I tread cautiously on the unsteady ground, every step a delicate dance as my senses remain on high alert. Though the Cheshire Cat and Caterpillar have imparted their cryptic *wisdom*, uncertainty clings to me like a shadow in this whimsical realm. Yet, the anticipation swirling in my clenched belly is a tantalizing mix of exhilaration and dread.

Ahead, a rabbit hole yawns invitingly in the ground, its entrance adorned with a crudely-painted sign that reads: *"Fall in here for adventure!"* The familiarity of it all tugs insistently at my memory, but its source eludes me, leaving me in a fog of confusion. Summoning my newfound courage, I inch closer and peer into the dark tunnel. The space within pulses with an iridescent glow, a kaleidoscope of colors beckoning me forward like a siren's call, promising secrets and discoveries unknown.

"Well," I say aloud, addressing the hole as if it were a sentient being, "here goes nothing—or everything, I suppose." With a deep, steadying breath, I plunge feet-first into the unknown, mirroring the fateful dive a certain Alice took so many years ago.

The fall is both brief and eternal; time stretches and contracts, losing all meaning as I plummet through the rabbit hole. Disoriented, I land in a heap on a lush meadow painted in vibrant shades of emerald and gold, the hues so vivid they seem to pulse with life. Dazed but unhurt, I push myself upright and take in my surroundings with wide eyes.

Wonderland has shifted again.

Instead of the psychedelic plants and animals I had grown accustomed to, this new realm unfolds before me like a storybook illustration come to life. Enchanting gardens stretch out in every direction, reminiscent of an old English estate—if such an estate were managed by fairies on a sugar high. Tall trellises, intricately woven with rose vines that change colors in a mesmerizing display, line perfectly manicured paths. A grand fountain shoots out sparkling water that glitters like a cascade of diamonds, sending rainbows dancing through the canopy of trees.

From around the back of the estate, the raucous sounds of a party float through the air, a symphony of laughter and music that beckons irresistibly. Naturally, my curiosity gets the best of me. In hindsight, I probably should have just kept walking, but really, who can resist the allure of a good party?

As I turned the corner into the backyard, I was greeted with a scene that left me speechless. A long table sat in the middle of a wild, trippy dream of a party. People dressed in fancy clothes while other strange creatures wandered around, singing about unbirthdays, arguing over tea, and generally acting like total lunatics.

To my surprise and confusion, both Caterpillar and Cheshire were among the madness. At the head of the table sat a man wearing an outrageous top hat. He had dark hair escaping in every direction from underneath the hat. Despite his crazy outfit, even from here I could tell that there was no denying he was incredibly attractive. Looking at him sent a jolt of recognition through me, though I had no idea why. Shaking off the odd feeling, I refocused on the festivities in front of me.

This must be the famous Mad Hatter's tea party. I try to take in the party goers, but my eyes only want to appreciate the Mad Hatter's exquisite looks. The man is a work of chaotic art. He is tall with an athletic build. His features are sharp in the way of a tragic romantic hero—jawline you could scythe wheat with, cheekbones carved from heartbreak, and eyes the green-gold of an absinthe hallucination. Boy did the movies get this one wrong.

The guests at this zany gathering are like something straight out of a fever dream, possibly concocted by someone who'd had one too many late-night experiences with acid. Over to my left, a flamboyant trio of flamingos, decked out in sequined waistcoats that would make any disco ball envious, are fluttering their eyelashes at a sentient bundle of balloons that appears to be trying to maintain its composure while floating just a little too high. Meanwhile, a pair of twin girls, who could easily be mistaken for mirror images if it weren't for the fact that one is defying gravity by sitting upside-down on her chair, are engaged in a heated debate on the critical question of whether cake falls under the category of soup. What?

At the far end of this carnival of curiosities, a woman draped in a gown made entirely of rose petals—who probably leaves a trail of potpourri wherever she goes—is locked in an intense staring contest with a hedgehog. The hedgehog, for its part, appears to be winning, possibly due to its natural advantage of not understanding that it's a challenge.

As I absorb the bewildering tableau before me, I'm downright amazed that my brain hasn't thrown in the towel and decided to take an extended vacation.

Just as I'm about to dive headfirst into yet another whirlwind of wild theories about how I ended up in this theatrical spectacle, the Caterpillar, who's been munching on a leaf at the end of the table, finally notices my presence. He swivels his head in my direction and, with a tone that suggests he's been expecting me all along, says, "Alicia, you made it."

13

Tea, Trauma, and Theo in a Top Hat

Alicia

Abruptly, the music cuts off, plunging the party into a profound silence as every head swiveled towards me. It was as if I had been thrust into a glaring spotlight, a minuscule insect pinned under the merciless scrutiny of a microscope. The air crackled with tension as the Mad Hatter's eyes met mine with a fiery intensity that threatened to sear my very soul.

For a beat, no one moved. As the party goers remained focused on me and only me. They stared at me like I was the weirdest thing at this party. Maybe I was.

Naturally, I did what any rational human would do and gave a tiny, awkward wave. "Uh. Hi?" A few partygoers erupted into applause, more shocked than admiring.

I tried to act cool and pretend like I meant to crash this crazy party, so I straightened my skirt, flipped my long hair over my shoulder, and sauntered over to the table as if I belonged there.

As I drew nearer, the allure of the Mad Hatter intensified, revealing details that were even more captivating up close. His jawline was impeccably chiseled, sharp enough to slice through the finest crystal, and those eyes… Oh boy, those eyes! They were a marvel on their own, shifting in a mesmerizing dance of colors. One moment, they gleamed with the vibrant green of the lush gardens surrounding us, brimming with life and vitality; the next, they deepened into a profound blue, akin to the depths of a moonless, star-studded night sky. Finally, they settled into a piercing gray, a hue so striking it sparked a fleeting memory within me, like a whisper from a dream almost remembered. Yet, just as I reached out to grasp that elusive recollection, it slipped away, vanishing like mist in the dawn light. A shiver coursed down my spine—not from any sudden chill in the air, which remained warm and still, but from the sheer intensity and depth of his penetrating gaze that seemed to see into my very soul.

"Caterpillar," I said nonchalantly, as I finally reached him, trying to ignore the intense, silent stares from everyone around me. "I didn't expect to find you here… or— all of this." I waved my hand toward the eclectic assembly encircling me, each member more peculiar than the last.

The Mad Hatter cocked an eyebrow at me, his expression wavering between curiosity and amusement, causing my heart to skip a beat in response to the sudden attention. The Cheshire, with his wide, mischievous grin, seemed to be reveling in the spectacle, his eyes gleaming with delight. Just what I needed – a captivated audience savoring every moment of my awkwardness.

The moment stretched on as no one seemed to want to

speak.

In the silence, I became acutely aware of my every fail point: the way my hands fidgeted with the hem of my jacket, the tremble in my breath, the catch of my teeth against my lip. The party's colors seemed to pulse, synchronized to my escalating heartbeat, and I realized in that instant that Wonderland didn't just warp space and time—it broadcasted your anxiety to surround-sound.

Standing from his chair, the Mad Hatter bowed gracefully to me, a mischievous grin on his handsome face. "Alicia," his voice was nothing like I'd imagined. It was warm, but with an undertow: a gentle river laced with undertones of something much darker. "It is a pleasure to finally meet you."

He tipped his fancy top hat, the motion so smooth it belonged in an infomercial for "how to flourish dramatically." In one motion, he swept an arm to the seat beside him. "Care to join our little soiree?"

I hesitated, every neuron screaming "stranger danger," but all eyes remained locked on me, waiting. I nodded and stepped closer.

"Alice – sorry, Alicia," The hatter spoke in a voice smooth and rich like velvet, "allow me to introduce you to some… ahem… friends of mine." His words dripped with sarcasm, a thick layer that hung heavier than the dark, aromatic tea he casually sipped from a delicate porcelain cup.

"Everyone, meet Alicia –"

"The Key!" screeched a high-pitched voice, sharp and sudden like the squeal of a rusty hinge. My eyes darted to the source – a tiny mouse perched precariously on the ornate handle of the teapot, its whiskers twitching with excitement. "She's the one who can unlock the story."

"Dormouse!" The March Hare, I presumed from his long ears and frenzied demeanor, yelped through a mouthful of crumbly cake. "I forgot you were there!" He smacked his forehead with a silver spoon, its handle adorned with intricate designs, before shoveling another piece into his eager mouth.

The table erupted into chaos once more, a cacophony of voices clashing like discordant music, each one trying to outdo the other with wild and fantastical tales about me and my supposed "powers." The air buzzed with the energy of their frantic chatter, like a hive of bees disturbed from their work.

"That's enough!" The Mad Hatter declared, slamming his teacup down with a decisive clatter that echoed through the clearing, effectively silencing the group. His eyes, those mesmerizing orbs of swirling color, locked onto mine with an intensity that could pin you in place. "You'll pardon my… guests," he said, his voice laced with disdain, "they tend to get carried away at times."

I could only nod in response, my mind too occupied with the overwhelming effort to hold myself together and not dissolve into a puddle under his penetrating gaze. Get it together, Alicia! I chided myself. You can drool over the eye candy later.

Mutters and grumbles followed as the motley crew dispersed, leaving me alone at the table with Caterpillar, Cheshire, Hatter, and a host of judging teacups.

Hatter sat back in his ornate chair, his eyes twinkling mischievously as he extended a strong hand towards me. "Please, Alicia, have a seat," he said, his voice smooth and inviting. "Let me make it up to you for my… guests' behavior." His smile was warm and disarming, like a beam of sunlight breaking through a stormy sky, and it made my heart skip a beat, fluttering like a captive bird. I swallowed hard, trying to dissolve the knot of apprehension lodged in my throat, and hesitantly placed my hand in his. A surprising jolt, like a tiny electric current, tingled through my fingers at the contact. He gently guided me down into an empty seat beside him, our closeness enveloping me in an aura of unexpected familiarity and intrigue.

"So," I began awkwardly, my voice tinged with disbelief, "you're really the Mad Hatter? And these are—"

"I prefer Theo," he interrupted smoothly, his words sliding into the air like silk. "And these fine… folks are merely… associates of mine. You know how it is." His eyes twinkled with mischief as he winked at me, his voice a dangerous blend of velvet and knives. "Care for a cup?"

"Is it cursed?" I asked, half in jest, half in genuine concern.

"That depends. Do you like surprises?" he inquired, a playful challenge in his tone.

"No. I run a bookstore. My idea of danger is ordering the wrong edition," I replied, my voice dry with irony.

He grinned, a subtle curve of his lips that spoke of impending chaos—like a storm cloud brooding on the horizon, ready to unleash its thunder.

"Then I'll pour carefully," he promised, a dare gleaming in his eyes like hidden jewels.

I glanced around the table, my gaze full of wonderment, taking in the motley crew gathered nearby. Curiosity buzzed within me, accompanied by a weariness that clung to my bones. And a small flicker of irritation at how impossibly dashing he looked in his impeccably tailored attire.

With a magician-like flourish, he slid a delicate teacup

toward me, the porcelain gleaming in the soft light.

I eyed it with suspicion. "What's in it?"

"Truth," he replied, his voice smooth and enigmatic.

"So, poison," I retorted flatly.

His laughter erupted—a single, low, genuine sound that resonated like a secret shared. It unsettled me more than anything else so far.

I took a cautious sip. The tea was a curious blend, honeyed and complex, offering both comfort and an unsettling mystery in its depths.

He watched me intently over the rim of his cup, his gaze unyielding, as if he were waiting for me to crack first.

I held steady.

"So," I said, setting the cup down with a deliberate clink, "what's your deal? Are you Wonderland's emotional support representative, or do you just have a flair for the dramatic?"

"Wouldn't you like to know," he smirked, a challenge dancing in his eyes. "But I suppose that's fair. You've been pulled from your world, declared the Key, nearly vaporized by literature, and now you're sipping tea with a man in a cravat." After a pause, he begins again. "Tell me, Alicia, what excites you most about Wonderland."

My heart skipped a beat, a stowaway aboard the vessel of my chest that longed to dock at the shores of intrigue and mystery. The dimly lit room, with its flickering candlelight casting whimsical shadows against the walls, seemed to pulse with the energy of secrets waiting to be uncovered. I needed to know about my journey, my purpose. I also needed to know the Queen's weaknesses—vital knowledge for what lay ahead—but oh, how easily my resolve wavered under the weight of his piercing, inquisitive gaze that seemed to see right through to my very soul!

"The curiosity, Mr. Hatter," I answered, reaching for my own cup, its rim chipped and worn like a secret shared between old friends, the porcelain cool against my fingertips. "Pure, unadulterated curiosity."

"Ah," he replied, his voice rich and smooth, layered with notes of secrets yet to be spilled, like a well-aged wine waiting to be tasted. "The most potent of brews."

Suddenly, a commotion erupted behind me, a flurry of activity that drew Theo from the table, his movements fluid and swift. "I'll be right back," he muttered, shooting me a glance that made my heart skip another beat (still not helping, heart! I admonished myself), his eyes dancing with a mix of apology and promise. "I'll just… deal with this."

The instant he departed, Caterpillar leaned in close, his eyes narrowing to thin, menacing slits. "Be cautious around him, Alicia," he murmured, his voice low and deliberate, each syllable dripping with enough venom to bring down lesser beings. "The Mad Hatter… he's not who he appears to be."

A chill ran down my spine, causing it to stiffen like a board. "What do you mean?" I inquired, my voice steady and resolute, despite the swarm of butterflies performing acrobatics in my stomach. Caterpillar shook his head slowly, as though weighing the decision to reveal more. "You'll find out soon enough," he uttered enigmatically before sauntering off in pursuit of Theo. Fantastic, just what I needed—more mystery and intrigue to untangle.

Left alone with my swirling thoughts and the increasingly judgmental gaze of the Dormouse, I seized the moment to regain my composure. So, Theo—or rather, The Mad Hatter—

was concealing something? How utterly predictable in a place as bizarre as Wonderland. Yet, I couldn't shake off a pang of betrayal. He appeared so… ordinary for someone reputedly insane. Of course, 'ordinary' was a relative concept here.

As I mulled over Caterpillar's ominous warning, Cheshire slinked up to me, his perpetual smirk doing little to assuage my mounting anxiety. "Pay no heed to the Caterpillar, my dear," he purred smoothly, "he's been indulging in his hookah a tad excessively of late."

I regarded him with suspicion. "You mean I should place my trust in you, instead?"

"Why, Alicia," he feigned a wounded demeanor, "I'm deeply hurt by your lack of appreciation and trust!" His grin reappeared as swiftly as it had vanished. "In all seriousness, though, Theo may have his… eccentricities, but his intentions are… mostly pure."

I arched an eyebrow at that less-than-reassuring endorsement. "Mostly?"

"Oh, come now," Cheshire said with a casual flick of his hand, "who among us isn't a touch mad? Besides, don't you find it invigorating to be around someone with a dash of… spice?"

I couldn't deny that. It was true—Theo was unlike anyone I'd ever encountered, in the most exhilarating way possible. There was a sense of danger and unpredictability about him that was simultaneously thrilling and terrifying. And those eyes! They held more secrets than the pages of a dusty tome hidden in the library's forbidden section. He also sparked recognition, like I had met him before. I just don't know where.

The ball of noise and chaotic color rippled and shifted as a hush spread through the crowd. The party seemed to merge into the background, the edges of the garden blurring into shadowed, oily brushstrokes. It was just me, Cheshire, and the last dregs of lukewarm tea. He leaned against the table, his gaze flicking between the people and the sky.

"You know," Cheshire said, voice dropping into a conspiratorial purr, "you are not the first Key to pass through Wonderland. The archives say you are the… fourth? Fifth, perhaps. But you are the first to make it so far since the very first Key. Most lose themselves on contact." He watched me with an unsettling intensity, his pupils narrowing until they were mere slits of black in rings of melting gold.

"Oh," I replied. "So, my superpower is stubbornness and sarcasm?" He laughed, the sound curling around me like fog. "That is exactly why you will succeed, Alicia."

Before I could respond further, Theo reappeared at my side, a deep furrow of concern etched into his handsome features. His eyes, dark and penetrating, seemed to search for reassurance. "Apologies for the interruption," he said smoothly, as he reclaimed his seat. "Where were we?"

"Ah yes," I said, trying to regain my train of thought amidst the whirlwind of emotions and secrets swirling around me like so many tea leaves in a delicate fine china cup. The room felt alive with whispers of unspoken truths, "curiosity and its many… side effects." Theo chuckled low in his throat, a sound that rumbled warmly and sent shivers dancing down my spine, igniting a fire beneath my skin. "One must always take caution when dabbling with such potent concoctions."

He leaned in closer, a subtle shift that brought him into my space, lowering his voice to a hushed whisper that sent goosebumps prickling along my skin. His breath was warm against my ear, and his words hung heavy in the air between us, like a thread of spun sugar, delicate and ephemeral, yet strong enough to bind two souls in the whirlwind of Wonderland's secrets. "Allow me to share a bit of advice, my lovely companion. Some curiosities are better left unanswered." His gaze was intense, more potent than any tea leaf's foretelling, as if trying to unravel my very soul with its depth.

In that moment, I knew I had to know more—about him, about this enigmatic world, and about my own role in the twisted tapestry of madness that was my newfound reality. The air crackled with possibility. "I've never been one to shy away from a challenge," I said with a grin that belied the quiver in my voice. The room seemed to close in around us, charged with an electric intrigue. "Besides, where's the fun in unraveling a mystery if it comes without a little… intrigue?"

The corner of his mouth quirked upward, revealing a playful dimple that sent a warm flutter through my stomach. Sunlight danced in his breathtaking eyes as he regarded me. "I admire your spirit, Alicia." Each syllable of my name dripped from his lips like melted chocolate, velvet-soft and heady. "But even the bravest of hearts can be broken by Wonderland's secrets."

I swallowed, my pulse thrumming in my ears. "Then I'm glad I have you to guide me," I blurted, too eager to filter my words. He held my gaze a heartbeat too long—an electric moment in which I could almost taste the charged air between us. Finally, he tipped his head and winked. "I'll do my best not to steer you wrong."

Shortly thereafter, Theo was cornered by Cheshire over near the rose-laden archway. Seeing this as an opportunity, I seized my chance for reconnaissance. I needed to learn everything I could about the Red Queen. What better hunting ground than this madcap soirée?

"Alright, Alicia, time to play detective," I murmured, brushing aside the warmth of Theo's lingering look. Though every fiber of me yearned to overanalyze his every inflection, duty called. I rose from my velvet-upholstered chair, smoothing an imagined wrinkle from my crisp white sweater. Drawing in a steadying breath, I summoned my inner confidence.

Time to mingle with Wonderland's crème de la crème, I told myself, exhaling. Here goes nothing.

The party swirled with laughter and clinking crystal. Creatures of all kinds. Sleek feline humanoids, rabbits the size of a grown man, dressed in their afternoon finery sipping tea, some tipsily weaving through the crowd like boats on a moonlit sea. Top hats bobbed over voluminous petticoats, and the air smelled of rosewater and candied ginger.

As I edged past a gilded buffet of teacakes, a flamingo-pink lady in a rushed gown declared to her lanky companion, "She's simply dreadful, that Red Queen—and that Knave of Hearts!" Her voice was a sharp hiss, like a porcelain teacup cracking on stone. "He's just as bad." My heart stuttered. The Knave of Hearts. His name alone enough to send shivers racing up and down my spine.

"Pardon me, ladies," I interjected, sliding into their circle with what I hoped passed for nonchalance. "I couldn't help overhearing. You're familiar with the Knave of Hearts?"

They turned, eyes glinting like polished jet. The flamingo lady—Priscilla, if the name embroidered on her fan was any clue—purred, "Well, well, a new face in our midst. Yes, to your question." She leaned in. "The Knave is quite the enigma.

He appears out of nowhere, settles the queen's affairs, then vanishes before anyone can pin him down."

Her companion, clad in a frothy mint-green dress, fanned herself with delicate, butterfly-adorned feathers. "And so… dashing," she sighed, each word fluttering like a wingbeat. That gave me pause. Mainly because I had a similar reaction. "He sets our hearts aflutter." I pressed my lips together to stifle a groan. Fangirls of my arch-nemesis may not be a reliable intelligence source. But the curiosity gnawed at me, so I leaned closer, my voice barely a whisper.

"But what does he do for the Red Queen? Is he her general, her assassin…?"

Priscilla's eyes sparkled. "My dear, you must understand— he serves the Queen in ways whispered only in shadows." She leaned in conspiratorially. "He does her dirty work. But don't worry—no one's quite sure what that entails." She gave a knowing wink. I nodded, tucking that nugget of information into the pocket of my mind. The game was afoot—as was the Red Queen's menacing shadow.

Their faces twisted in distaste at the mere mention of her name, and they leaned in closer once more, speaking in hushed tones as if hiding secrets. "He's her right-hand… man," Priscilla whispered with a sense of intrigue, her voice barely above a murmur. "Or so the rumors say. No one truly knows the mysteries that unfold behind the ornate doors of the Red Court. What we do know is that he is perilously dangerous— and undeniably handsome." Right-hand man? As in her second-in-command? Did my doppelganger not suggest I attend the Knave's dinner party? Is that where the climactic confrontation of this tale occurs?

Before I could probe further, a shadow stretched over us,

casting a brief reprieve from the sun. "Ladies," Theo greeted, tipping his top hat with a polite flourish. "I trust you aren't monopolizing our newest guest excessively." His eyes zeroed in on me, lingering just a heartbeat longer than what felt appropriate. I could feel a warm flush creeping across my cheeks under his analyzing gaze. Ah, nothing like a dash of awkwardness to accompany my looming sense of doom. "Oh no," Priscilla purred, fanning herself with a fervor that bordered on theatrical. "We were just about to take our leave." She clasped her friend's arm with a deliberate motion and whisked her away, leaving me standing with Theo once more. Or as alone as one could feel amidst a swirling sea of chaos.

"So," he began in a casual tone, as though he hadn't just sent shivers cascading down my spine with his glance. "Are you enjoying yourself?"

"Oh, you know," I replied with an air of breezy nonchalance, striving to mask any trace of nervousness. "Just mingling with the perpetrators of madness." I gestured toward the vibrant, chaotic scene enveloping us. "Quite the eclectic crowd you've assembled here."

He laughed, a sound that both unsettled and amused me, causing my composure to waver in the most delightful way. "You know how it goes in Wonderland: we're all mad here." I couldn't suppress a laugh, feeling the tension in my shoulders ease slightly in the face of his infectious humor. "Well, at least I'm in good company then," I quipped with a sly grin. "So, this Knave of Hearts everyone whispers about... I gather he's quite the character?"

Theo's expression darkened briefly, a shadow flitting across his features so swiftly I questioned if it had been real. "He is... unpredictable," he replied with measured caution. "A master of disguises, skilled at slipping through the fingers of pursuit. Why do you ask?"

I couldn't tell him I was fishing for scraps of intelligence on my enemies. My heart drummed beneath my ribs, but I forced a light laugh and waved my hand as though swatting away a fly. "Oh, no reason in particular," I said, keeping my voice easy. "I just overheard people whispering about him. I was curious—what's so important about the Knave of Hearts?"

Theo's eyes, sharp and silver in the dappled sunlight, bored into mine. I felt exposed, as if every thought was a butterfly pinned beneath his gaze. "Well, Alicia," he said at last, his tone deceptively casual, "if you truly wish to meet the Knave, I imagine we could arrange it."

A hot wedge slid into my stomach. "No, we've met before!" I blurted, voice rushing out too high. "It didn't go well—I'm sure he's a… perfectly nice… murderer?" My words scattered like a poor shuffle of cards.

He chuckled then, low and amused, a sound that seemed to echo against the ever arching trees around us. He laid a hand on my arm—light as moth wings—and an electric prickle raced up my skin. "Fear not, Alicia. I was only teasing." His fingers lingered for a heartbeat, and I shivered. "Best not concern yourself with the Knave," he whispered. "He's not someone you want to cross your path."

"But why?" My voice shook as I edged away, though my pulse hammered with a mix of fear and something like longing.

"Trust me," he said, his tone folding into a rare gravity. "Let him stay in the shadows where he belongs. It's safer that way." Reluctantly, I offered a nod, though the rain of unspoken questions dripped down my spine.

He leaned forward, elbow resting against the intricate patterns of the wall. "The Queen wants you dead," he said quietly. "You need to be more careful."

I lifted my cup—porcelain so thin it trembled in my fingers—and managed a wry smile. "Is this part of your charming small-talk routine?"

"I just think you should know where we stand." His voice was calm as a grave. "This isn't a fairy tale. No one here is safe. Especially not you."

I swallowed hard. "You know, this is really putting a damper on your party."

He shrugged, but the gesture was stark, like a blade. "And yet you're still here."

I stared down at the tea swirling in my cup—dark amber flecked with steam. "I haven't decided if that's bravery or stupidity."

"Don't worry," he murmured, leaning close enough that I smelled mint and iron, "Wonderland will decide for you."

A hush fell over the clearing. Even the teacups seemed to pause mid-tilt. I couldn't help the question that spilled out: "Who are you?"

Theo tilted his head, sunlight flickering off the sharp angle of his jaw. "Theo."

"No—you know what I mean. You know things you shouldn't. You seem cunning..." My words trailed off. "Like Cheshire."

He grew still, the air around him suddenly colder. "I'm not like Cheshire," he said, voice firm but not defensive.

"Then who are you?"

He tapped a finger in a rhythmic beat, as if marking each truth. "Bound."

"To the Queen?"

"To the rules," he corrected, gaze drifting to the twisting boughs overhead.

I watched him—the tension in his shoulders, the way he forced every line of his body into crisp control. There was something cracked inside him, a fracture hidden beneath charm and steel. Something achingly familiar.

"You don't like being here," I said softly.

He met my eyes again. "I never said that."

"You didn't have to."

He offered no reply.

Instead, he turned and padded the length of the table to where a silver teapot—its spout shaped like a snarling dragon—glinted in the half-light. He lifted the lid, peered in, frowned, then turned back to me.

"She'll come for you soon," he said, voice low. "The Queen. Or worse—the Knave."

I frowned. "Let me guess. I have to unlock something before they do?"

He inclined his head once. "Only you can decide what happens next."

"And you're here to help me?"

He paused so long that the world seemed to stop. Finally: "No," he said softly. "I'm here to watch."

"Spy on me."

He shrugged—half amused, half mournful. "Call it what you like. Wonderland watches back."

"And what if I refuse to play along?"

He closed the distance between us, and for an instant the forest light glinted off his eyes with something like pity. "Then we all lose."

We stood there beneath the hush of ancient trees, the wind teasing the teacups on the table, carrying secrets we dared not speak. In his gaze I saw a flicker of something human—recognition, perhaps. A crack in his mask. And I realized, trembling: maybe he was asking the same thing I was.

If it was possible to drown in someone else, I was halfway under already.

"We all lose," I repeated, the words pulling at a memory I couldn't quite reach. "What happens if we win?"

He stilled, looking off toward the woods, where the branches tangled into chaotic, beautiful knots. "No one knows. No one's ever done it."

14

The Queens Pet Murderer (And Other Fun Rumors)

Alicia

By late that evening, the tea party was still going strong. No idea how. I decided I had gotten all the information I was going to get from this lot, so it was time move along. I needed to focus on getting home. By all signs, it seems that is only going to happen after a run in with the Queen of Hearts and her Knave sidekick. I silently stepped away from the madness, hoping to blend into the shadows as I made my escape.

I couldn't help but cast one final glance over my shoulder at Theo. He was still surrounded by a swarm of Wonderlandians, his maddening grin and captivating eyes on full display. It took every ounce of willpower I possessed not to dive back into the fray and take my chances with the Mad Hatter. But no, I reminded myself sternly, I had a mission to complete and a world to save.

"I need to find the Queen of Hearts and her Knave, and

98

quick." I say to myself.

The problem was, I had no idea where to start. Wonderland was a big place, and logic wasn't exactly its strong suit. Sighing, I slumped against a tree (or at least, what I thought was a tree) and tried to think. "Okay, Alicia," I muttered to myself, "you can do this. You've read enough books and watched enough movies to know how this works."

Just as I righted myself and started onto the path, a voice from behind broke the eerily silence of the night. "Leaving so soon, Alicia?"

I froze in my tracks, my heart leaping into my throat. Slowly, I turned around, trying to keep my expression neutral. "Theo! I-I, um, thought the party was over," I said lamely, cursing my traitorous voice as it quavered.

The Hatter was leaning against a twisted tree; his top hat tipped at a jaunty angle. He wore a knowing smirk as he watched me squirm under his intense gaze. "Forgive me for eavesdropping," he drawled, "but I could have sworn you were headed in a specific direction."

"Y-you were eavesdropping?" I sputtered, heat creeping into my cheeks.

Theo's grin widened. "In my defense, your 'silent' escape wasn't quite as silent as you'd hoped." He chuckled and straightened up, sauntering over to me with a predatory grace that made my knees feel like Jell-O. "But I digress," he continued, his voice low and thrumming with an undercurrent of… something. "You're looking for the Queen?"

I swallowed hard and forced myself to meet his gaze, trying to project an air of confidence I didn't feel. "Yes, and her Knave. Who or whatever he is." I say, my voice getting stronger with conviction. "It's my only hope of going home, of getting out of this crazy place."

Theo's eyes narrowed, but he didn't deny the accusation about his land. "Fair enough," he said after a tense moment of silence. "I can understand wanting to return home." His voice held a hint of anger that was at odds with his usual jovial demeanor. "At least stay for the evening and get some rest. I have a room prepared in the East wing, come let me show you." His invitation was polite, but his tone made it clear it wasn't a request.

I hesitated, weighing the risks of following a man who'd openly admitted to spying on me versus wandering Wonderland alone at night. Honestly, I didn't trust either option, but my record of solo adventure in this place was… spotty.

"Lead the way," I said, angling my chin up so I wouldn't look as tired as I felt.

Theo's eyes sparkled, and for the briefest second he looked less like a caricature and more like a person—someone with secrets, sure, but maybe not every secret was out to kill me.

We walked in companionable silence through the winding gardens, past rows of night-blooming lilies that sang to themselves and by the hedge were animals sculpted mid-pounce. Occasional fireworks erupted overhead, throwing violent neon over Theo's sharp features and giving the whole scene a low-budget Burton vibe.

"The Queen won't make it easy," Theo said, not looking at me. "Especially now that she knows you're here."

I shivered. "I got the impression people don't keep secrets well in Wonderland."

"We don't," he agreed. "But sometimes the truth is even more dangerous."

We reached the mansion (castle? They never clarified)

and entered through a side door. The hallways were empty, echoey, and painted in stripes of moonlight and shadow. I cast a glance at the mirrors as we passed. They winked at me, but it seemed less threatening and more… encouraging.

Theo stopped outside a door trimmed in emerald velvet. "Your room," he announced, with a bow so ornate it bordered on theatrical insult. "You'll find the wardrobe pre-stocked with essentials: pajamas, a dagger, and a couple volumes of bedtime reading. If you need anything else, don't call me."

I can't tell if he's joking or serious.

He grinned as he caught my confusion, producing a skeleton key from thin air, weighing it on his palm before flicking it in a lazy arc. "Unless, of course, you're locked out." The key vanished before it landed.

"Charming," I said, arms folded.

"If you value your life," he began, the teasing tone dimming, "you'll stay inside tonight. There are worse things than nightmares that haunt these halls at dusk." He hesitated on the threshold, his silhouette all angles and afterthoughts, his shadow somehow sharper than the man himself. "Lock the door, Alicia."

He left before I could utter a word.

I stared at the door a moment before turning the knob, half-expecting it to bite me.

Inside, the room was—unexpected. A soft gold glow. Huge window with a view of the moon smudged over the gardens. The moon itself was huge, swollen and blue, like a bruise in the sky. Thick blankets, a pile of pillows, and—yeah—on the bedside table, a proper dagger and two books: *Sun Tzu* and *Sense and Sensibility*. Someone was either a comedian or genuinely concerned about my odds of survival.

I flopped onto the bed. The mattress courted me down into its depths. For a second, I considered not moving ever again. *Falter*, a little voice in my head warned. *They'll eat you alive.* But if anyone had earned a night of literal beauty sleep, it was me.

15

The Invitation

Alicia

My one night at Theo's estate turned into two. Then three. Then a week. I was aimless, unsure of my purpose, or where to go. I was overwhelmed, confused, and possibly going mad.

The room I'd been assigned—if "gifted" is the appropriate term for a space with wallpaper that seemed to breathe and a vanity that mischievously rearranged my freckles— had finally settled into an eerie silence for the night. I was curled up on the bed, attempting to delve into a book that stubbornly blocked me at Chapter Two unless I solved a cryptic riddle, when the window began to rattle ominously. It then creaked open with an unsettling slowness, as if moved by some invisible hand.

I sat up cautiously, ready to hurl either the book or the entire lamp beside me, when something drifted inside the room. Not with the briskness of flight, but with the languid grace of a leaf on the breeze—a black envelope, sealed with a striking violet wax. Naturally. This peculiar place couldn't even manage to deliver mail in a conventional manner. I snatched it out of the air, its seal emblazoned with a familiar emblem—a heart, neatly bisected, with one side eerily hollow.

Inside was a single card, the words elegantly penned in flowing ink.

"You are cordially summoned to the Midnight Masquerade. Dress accordingly. Speak sparingly. Nothing is ever quite as it seems.—T."

There was no return address, no RSVP, and certainly no clause to safeguard my sanity. I stared at the signature, composed of merely a single letter: T. My heart betrayed me, executing a flutter that was both unexpected and unwelcome.

"Okay," I declared to the room, breaking the silence, "That's officially the creepiest invite I've ever gotten, and I once got a Save the Date for a dog's Quinceanera." The vanity reorganized my hairbrushes in what I interpreted as applause.

I lay back on the bed, envelope in hand, and stared up at the writhing paisley on the ceiling. The air tingled with possibilities—the kind that made my skin fizz and my brain spiral into a thousand what-ifs. I pressed the card to my lips, just to see if it would unlock some hidden message, but it tasted only of paper, wax, and desperation.

You are cordially summoned.
  Dress accordingly.
  Speak sparingly.
  Nothing is ever quite as it seems.

I couldn't decide whether it sounded more like a death threat or the invitation it claims to be. A flicker in the corner of the room caught my eye. The wardrobe door, which I'd sworn was closed and locked with one of those Victorian mechanisms only professional burglars or housecats could defeat, had drifted open by a hair. I padded across the plush rug and peered inside.It now glowed with a soft, ethereal gold, draped in luxurious silks and bathed in the gentle flicker of candlelight. Around me, dresses spun slowly in the air, swirling like ethereal dancers auditioning for a role in a fairy tale.

"I'm not Cinderella," I warned the room, my voice a whisper against the enchantment.

It was a riot of masquerade finery. Silk. Satin. Velvet the color of dried wine stains. Every dress, pantsuit, and, unsettlingly, cloak seemed tailored to my most secret aesthetic wishlist, which I was certain I had not discussed with anyone. I rifled past a sharp-shouldered, bottle-green suit, a corset dress with more buckles than technically advisable, and finally settled on a gown of midnight blue silk. It was embroidered with silver thread that shimmered like a tapestry of constellations against the night sky. The bodice was daringly cut, exuding confidence, while the voluminous skirt promised drama with every swish. It hovered expectantly, as if waiting for my approval.

"Oh fine," I conceded with a resigned sigh. "Let's go bother some nobles."

The moment my fingers brushed the fabric, it wrapped around me with a life of its own, fitting perfectly to my form. It wasn't tight, nor was it stiff—just… right, as if crafted by some magical tailor who knew my soul.

A mask floated into view next—an exquisite piece of black velvet adorned with intricate silver lace and a glint of something ancient that hinted at forgotten secrets. It concealed most of my face, leaving just enough mystery to qualify me for a poetry slam or embroil me in a political scandal.

I stared at my reflection in the mirror, not recognizing the woman who gazed back.

This woman wore shadows like armor, her eyes gleaming with concealed secrets. She appeared powerful, dangerous, like someone who belonged in this world of enchantment and intrigue.

I swallowed hard, my throat tight with anticipation. "Just a dance," I whispered to myself. "A little music. A little mystery. A little betrayal probably. No big deal."

The mirror offered no argument.

A moment later, a soft, deliberate knock echoed on the door—three gentle taps that resonated with anticipation.

When I opened it,

I was greeted by a rabbit. Not the White Rabbit—no, this one wore a wine-red waistcoat and sported a goatee that made him look like he moonlighted as an indie record store manager. He bowed, offered his velvet-pawed arm, and said, "Allow me to escort you, Miss Hightower."

I considered slamming the door again, preferring to hide out in my room, but he was already herding me down the hall. We whisked past florid tapestries that seemed to wink and gossip behind our back—*Which one is she? Is she the one? Oh do hurry*—and soon descended a staircase that should not have fit inside the building's geometry. At the bottom was a chandeliered foyer thick with anticipation and the scent of burning vanilla. The entire mansion pulsed with the expectant hush of an orchestra seconds before the downbeat.

The doors to the ballroom loomed ahead—massive, filigreed with silver and gold, and guarded by twin men in masks so perfect they resembled faces carved from ice. As I approached, the hush sharpened, then shattered into applause as the doors swung wide and the crowd took me in.

I stand corrected. If I hadn't already died from embarrassment, I might have fainted on the spot. There were hundreds of them. Not people, not exactly; Wonderland's finest and worst, all distilled into glamour, lace, and the palpable tension of a high-stakes hostage negotiation. Some were beautiful in a way that hurt; others were beautiful in a way that hurt other people. But every eye in the place was on me now, and for one horrifying moment, I became the prop in someone else's theater—a marionette whose strings were pulled by a hand drunk on chaos.

I did what I always did when backed into a corner: I faked confidence and looked for exits. The dance floor stretched before me like a chessboard, its patterns shifting subtly with the movement of masked guests. Overhead, a thousand candles snickered among the chandeliers, their light reflecting off faces transformed by velvet, paint, and artful deception. The air was heavy with the scent of rosewater and something metallic, like nostalgia with a nosebleed.

The rabbit with the goatee bowed again and receded into the crowd, leaving me standing at the top of a grand double staircase that curved down into the sea of revelers. I caught a glimpse of Cheshire, in the midst of the masses wrapped in a haze of violet smoke, his grin stretching uncomfortably wide as he raised a glass in my direction. I respond with my best side eye, which only made his smile sharpen.

I caught sight of the Mad Hatter—Theo—almost at once.

He was impossible to miss, standing dead center beneath the chandeliers, his suit a patchwork of midnight hues and iridescent threads that caught the light and scattered it, prismatic, across the room. His mask was simple—just a thin black band that left his jaw and mouth exposed, which was a power move and he knew it. His eyes, mercurial as always, found mine through the crowd. He didn't move. He just watched me, daring me to flinch.

A hush hung between us, a gossamer line drawn through the crowd, taut and electric. I walked toward him, letting the motion carry me past a swirling stratocumulus of perfume, the glint of predatory teeth behind painted lips, and the sidelong stares of creatures so beautiful and strange I didn't know which were human and which were not. I felt the shifting ground beneath my shoes tilt, like the whole world sliding inexorably toward Theo.

A string quartet somewhere above and to the left began a tremulous, anticipatory air. The music was delicate, intricate—it was a Bach fugue, if Bach had written it while on a three-day bender and then thrown the pages down a spiral staircase. The dancers began to fall into pairs, the colored whirl of skirts and sharp black forms moving in clockwork that made me dizzy.

Theo waited, his hands clasped behind his back, body rigid as a sword in a scabbard. The crowd folded away from him as I approached, and time dilated: I could see individual beads of sweat on a gryphon's feathered brow, the momentary glimmer of recognition in the eyes of a girl in a thistle-purple gown, and the way Theo's jaw flickered with some secret tension as I stopped within arm's reach.

"My compliments, Miss Hightower," he said. "You look

every inch the legend they expect."

"You're a flatterer," I murmured, uncertain if I was meant to flirt my way into or out of danger.

His posture lazy, confident, like he owned the very air between us.

His eyes locked with mine—gray, unreadable, electric.

"You're late by the way," he said, voice low and amused.

My pulse stuttered.

"Is this the part where you try to sweep me into a dance and then betray me three minutes later?"

"Would it ruin the mystery if I said yes?"

"Only a little."

He offered his hand. Gloved. Elegant. Dangerous.

I stared at it for a beat too long.

Then took it.

The moment our fingers touched, the music swelled—and the room blurred at the edges, like the universe was giving us privacy. Or warning everyone else to stand back.

He led me to the center of the ballroom, and we began to move.

I hadn't danced in years, and never like this. Somehow, our steps matched perfectly—like muscle memory that belonged to someone else.

We didn't speak.

We didn't need to.

His hand slid to my waist, the other guiding mine to his shoulder. My heart was beating like it was trying to break curfew.

"You're acting weird," I said, finally.

"No," he replied. "But you are."

"I'm not."

"You will be."

I narrowed my eyes. "Do you always talk in riddles?"

"No. Only when the truth is too dangerous."

That pulled a breath from me. "For you or for me?"

"Does it matter?"

We spun. The chandeliers flickered. I wasn't sure if we were still being watched or if we were the only ones left.

His mask was more intricate up close under the light—small runes and symbols barely visible in the blackened setting.

Something about it tugged at me.

"You feel… different," I whispered, before I could stop myself.

He didn't answer.

Just stared at me like he could see the version of me I hadn't become yet. The music slowed. The last note hung in the air like a breath that didn't want to exhale.

And still, we didn't let go. "You should leave," he said finally, voice softer now. "Before she comes for you."

I blinked. He stepped back. And vanished into the crowd.

I stood in the reflux of his absence, hand out like a dope, cooled by the sudden lack of his touch. Around me, the masquerade surged back with doubled force, the noise and color clashing so loudly that it all became too much.

I stumbled out into the night air like someone had yanked the record off the turntable mid-song.

The ballroom was gone.

Just… gone.

Where glass and music had shimmered a heartbeat ago, there was now only an open glade under a bruised purple sky. Crickets chirped like nothing had happened. Like I hadn't just slow-danced with a man who may or may not be unraveling the entire universe with his cheekbones and cryptic riddles.

I yanked the mask off and threw it to the grass, then immediately regretted it.

It looked so elegant lying there. Like something from a life that didn't belong to me.

"What the hell was that?" I asked no one in particular.

The wind, apparently fluent in sarcasm, offered no response.

I turned in a slow circle. No sign of Theo. No sign of anyone. Just me, my racing pulse, and the faint scent of his cologne still clinging to my dress like a bad idea I couldn't quite shake.

He'd been different.

More composed. More dangerous. More... *watchful.*

But he'd still looked at me the same way—like I was the riddle he couldn't solve, and maybe didn't want to.

You should leave, he had said. *Before she comes for you.*

I didn't need a name to guess who *she* was. I could feel her watching again, just past the edges of the trees. A presence like cold breath on the back of my neck.

I crossed my arms, glaring at the empty space where the ballroom had been.

"So, to recap," I muttered, "I got magically summoned to a ball, slow danced with the one person who makes Wonderland or maybe me feel real, and am now about to have my soul eaten by the Queen of Hearts. Great. Sensible. Perfectly on brand for this entire fever dream."

A branch cracked nearby.

I froze.

But it was only the wind.

Probably.

I scooped up the mask, brushed it off, and tucked it under my arm.

Because even if I didn't know what was going on, I knew one thing:

I needed to find Theo.

Not the charmingly chaotic Hatter version.

The *real* one.

Whoever that was.

16

Confessions in the Garden

Alicia

The garden felt like a dream half-remembered. Instead of clear walkways, there were only hushed suggestions: a dew-slick stone here, a broad leaf there, each gesture pointing me deeper into the tangle. I couldn't say how I'd ended up here—perhaps the forest had coaxed me through knotted roots, or perhaps I'd simply followed a desperate need to breathe air untainted by illusions and old regret.

Moonflowers unfurled their milky petals in the darkness, each bloom glowing like a ghostly lantern wound around wrought-iron trellises that seemed to sprout naturally from the earth. Crickets wove a three-part harmony, their song as gentle as a lullaby—if lullabies had fangs. The air was thick and warm, a velvet caress that whispered promises I wasn't sure I wanted to keep.

I sank onto a crumbling stone bench, its surface cracked and rimmed with foliage. My gaze fell to my hands, where the

113

mask still dangled from one finger. Its silver filigree mirrored slivers of moonlight, intricate swirls and arabesques shimmering against my palm as if pleading for me to remember something I'd never learned.

Soft, deliberate footsteps approached behind me. I didn't flinch. Somehow, I already knew who it was.

"Theo," I murmured without turning.

He settled beside me—close enough to offer warmth, distant enough to remain a choice rather than a threat. No masquerade finery now: just a shirt collar undone, sleeves rolled to his elbows, every detail of his look carefully untidy. Moonlight caught stray strands of his hair, and in his eyes, I saw a quiet wariness I couldn't name.

"What brings you out here?" I ask.

He shrugged, that infuriating half-smile tracing his lips. "You."

A long pause stretched between us, filled only by insects and rustling leaves. Then he asked, voice low and oddly gentle, "Did you enjoy the dance?" I turned to face him. "Which part? When reality bent in on itself, or when you disappeared without a word—again?"

His lips twitched. "You sure are inquisitive."

"I'd like to think most people would be in my situation."

"The ball disappeared because you left. You are in charge of the story, Wonderland is bending itself like a mold and you are the artist." He glanced away after that, quiet. Stoic. His fingertips drumming a silent beat on his knee. When he spoke again, his voice was hushed. "I wasn't supposed to see you here. Not yet."

I studied his profile, the moonlight tracing the sharp line of his jaw. "Why?"

He closed his eyes, as if my question cut too close. When he spoke, his words were softer still: "Because the truth… has teeth."

I swallowed, voice barely a whisper. "You mean things aren't already completely insane?"

A ghost of laughter drifted from him. "Not insane, maybe. But everything comes with a price." He turned, and for the first time, I saw the exhaustion etched all the way through him. Not just the kind that comes from too little sleep, but the sort that seeps in past the marrow—an account of sleepless nights and ancient debts, rung up long before I'd stumbled into this thicket. He reached out, slow so I could see every intention, and took the mask from my hand. He held it between us, balanced on his fingertips, examining it like some beloved artifact unearthed in a dig. "These things are supposed to conceal us," he said. "But they only reveal us in the end." The crickets fell momentarily silent, as if the universe, too, was listening. I looked down at my dress, mosquitoes orbiting my knees. "Who am I hiding from?" I asked him. Theo hesitated. "From the person you were before you came here. And from the person you'll be if you leave." A blunt truth, delivered without ceremony. I admired him for that. Honest cowardice was more comforting than brave deceit. He set the silver mask on the bench between us and folded his hands atop it. "Did you notice the moonflowers?" he asked. "I think they're beautiful." "They only open in darkness." His eyes stayed on the blooms, his voice growing soft. "That's why I come here. Everyone thinks the day brings clarity, but sometimes you see better when the world's asleep." He paused to let the words settle, then brushed his thumb along the edge of the mask as if it might feel pain.

"I suppose I'm not as fond of darkness as you are," I said. My voice came out steadier than I felt. "Some of us lose ourselves out here. I'm not brave enough for that."

"You're still here, aren't you?" Theo asked, not unkindly, echoing words he'd said before. I wanted to snap something clever, but the cicadas had resumed their symphony, and the silence between us felt too honest for deflection. Instead, I let my head tip back—just enough to catch the corona of mist lighting up the moon. For a few heartbeats, I let the weight of it press against me: the humming garden, the soupy air, the sense that even the stars were old conspirators to whatever was happening now. I didn't notice his hand until it landed, gentle as a sigh, on my wrist. I looked down and saw the faintest tremor in his fingers, a fraying of resolve at the edges. He was afraid, too, which by some convoluted calculus made it easier to stay still.

"I didn't want you to come tonight," Theo said eventually. I braced for the sting, but there was no cruelty in his voice, only a sort of desperate sincerity. "If you knew what I know, you'd understand." "And what is it you know?" I asked. He looked at me then, really looked, as though cataloguing every feature for evidence he could trust. "That you're braver than you think. That you'll keep asking questions no matter how much it hurts. That you deserve something better than all this... theater." He flicked the silver mask; it made a thin, metallic chime. "And that even if I try to warn you off, you'll follow the trail of breadcrumbs anyway." I didn't know whether to be flattered or insulted, so I settled for curiosity.

"What's at the end of the trail?" For a moment, in the pause between syllables and the next breath, I thought he might tell me the truth. The real truth, not the half-shadows that made up our conversations. He just pressed his lips into a line. "Maybe it's better you lose the scent."

He bent down and plucked a petal from a nearby moonflower, rolling it between his thumb and finger. I could see the veins in it, tiny capillaries all branching from a single point, just like the nerves that spiderwebbed beneath the skin of my own hand. He seemed to weigh something invisible before offering the petal to me. I took it, because not taking it would have felt like breaking a spell.

The silence between us threatened to fill with all the unasked questions: about the masked figures gliding through the mansion's corridors. About the way the clocks ticked backwards at midnight and the servants never seemed to blink quite often enough. Instead, Theo broke it with a laugh—quiet, almost apologetic. "I forget how much you see." Another pause.

"I never wanted you involved," Theo said quietly. "You keep saying that, but I'm here." I picked up the mask, feeling the chill of the metal bite my palm. "What happens next? Do you vanish again, or—" "Or you do." He said it like an apology, eyes on the moonflowers, chin tilted as if awaiting the verdict of the stars. I wanted to ask what he was so afraid of, wanted to reach out and touch the place behind his ribs where the truth must be rotting. Instead, I pressed the mask to my face, aligning its impossible perfection with the scars and ordinariness beneath. The world shrank further, tunneled through the cutwork of the filigree, and on the other side was Theo: battered, beautiful, and bound to me by some uneasy truce. "Would it be easier if you hated me?" I asked. He shook his head, a trace of real pain in the gesture. "No. And you don't make it easy anyway."

I allowed myself a bittersweet smile. "I was never good at games. Not the kind where you can't tell the rules."

"Then let's stop playing," Theo murmured. There was an edge to it, as if he was hurling the words at a precipice inside himself.

All around, the garden listened: an audience of shifting leaves and velvet petals and the quiet wet heartbeat of deep summer.

He stood in one smooth movement, palms flattening on either side of the mask as he did. For a moment I thought he'd leave, the way he always did, but instead he stooped and offered me his hand.

I looked up at him, getting lost for a moment in his gaze. In his aura. I took his hand as though offered a life line. His grip was dry, strong, worlds away from the measured uncertainty I'd seen before. He drew me to my feet, causing the night to spin a little, the scent of earth and cut grass sharper now, the hot hush replaced by the possibility of wind.

He didn't let go. "Do you trust me?"

"No." I tried to smile. "But I trust myself."

His answering smile was lopsided, but more real than any I'd seen via candlelight or crystal glass. "You're my favorite kind of dangerous." He slipped his hand into his coat and withdrew something small, turning it between his fingers as though it contained all his regrets. He pressed a coin into my palm—silver, cool, etched with a heart split down the middle. Just like the one from my store that disappeared on me. "What is this?" I traced the fragile fissure.

"A good luck charm." Our hands lingered, warmth mingling in the dim light for a heartbeat too long. Then he stepped back into the moonlit shadows. He paused, one shoulder turned toward me.

"If I told you who I really am," he said quietly, "you wouldn't believe me." I stood as well, feeling the coin burn against my skin. "Try me." He tilted his head, and the moon revealed the sharp curve of his smile. Then he was gone—vanished like a fragment of a dream at dawn.

For a while I stood there, listening to the world reknit itself after his departure. When the hush grew too heavy, I pressed the coin to my lips and tasted iron and old secrets. "Try me," I whispered, though the only witnesses were the crickets and the fevered hush of green things reaching for light.

I could've turned back to the manor. Its windows flickered with party-lights—warm, insistent, the way a home you don't quite trust tries to lure you back to itself. I could've gone to my room, locked the door, and willed myself to believe none of it happened. Instead, I let my feet decide, and they led me deeper.

Past the moonflowers, the air changed. Branches arched overhead, laced so densely with vines that the night bled into a single, impossible shadow. Someone had trimmed the topiary into menageries: wolves with mouths frozen in mute howls, a peacock tail fanned in greenish splendor, twin foxes curled nose to tail around each other. All of it rendered in leaves and absence. I pressed on until the path vanished and my only light was the glimmer in my hand.

The coin grew heavier the longer I held it. By the time I found the crumbling archway, my fingers ached from its insistence. There was a door beyond the arch, wood so old it had forgotten its own grain. I expected resistance, but the door swung open at my push, exhaling the scent of damp earth and something old enough to feel sacred.

I found myself inside a planter's paradise. The door whispered shut behind me like it didn't want to wake the past. I stood in the heart of the greenhouse—though *greenhouse* felt like too small a word for it. This was a cathedral of glass and ivy, long abandoned but still alive in ways that defied logic. Moonlight filtered through warped panes above, painting fractured constellations on the mossy floor.

Everything was blooming—and decaying.

Roses with obsidian petals curled around skeletal vines. Trees bore fruit shaped like clocks. A lily the size of a wagon wheel opened and exhaled something that smelled like winter and thunder.

At the center of the room was a pedestal.

On it: a locked box. Tarnished silver, edges etched with the same heart-split symbol from the coin.

I approached slowly, fingers twitching at my sides.

The box didn't look threatening.

But it *felt*… sentient.

It pulsed once, softly, like it knew I was there.

I reached for it, causing the plants around me to move. Not violently. At least not yet. But the vines reared back like snakes tasting the air. A tree creaked, its bark forming the ghost of a face—sad and watching. The air turned syrupy with magic.

I froze. Then pulled the coin from my pocket. It glowed faintly in my palm. I stepped forward and laid it against the box. It clicked.

The vines tensed—but did not strike. The box opened. Inside: a map.

Or something like it. Not ink on parchment, but light. A projection of Wonderland itself—ever-shifting, alive, the paths rearranging like a living riddle. In the center of the glowing web pulsed a single symbol: a **key**, surrounded by the same split-heart crest.

As I stared, the map shifted. And for a moment, I saw **myself**. Not just now, but layered—different versions of me, fractured through different scenarios. One wore armor. One carried a blade. One held a crown she clearly didn't want.

I stumbled back, breath shallow.

The light vanished.

And the plants fell still.

The box sealed itself once more.

I tucked the coin away, heart thundering.

Whatever this was—it was tied to me. To the Key. To the truth no one wanted to say aloud.

And I had the sinking feeling that something had just begun.

17

The Dreaming Path

Alicia

Back in my room, the image of the map was seared into my mind. Even with the box securely sealed and the coin nestled snugly beneath my pillow, those haunting images lingered—undulating paths, mirrored versions of myself, and that pulsating key etched at the center like a heartbeat seeking to sync with mine. Sleep overtook me abruptly. Too abruptly. As if something with icy fingers had dragged me under, heedless of my consent. When I opened my eyes, I found myself standing barefoot on an expansive stretch of marble tile that shimmered like moonlight dancing on water. Above me loomed not a sky but a ceiling composed of fragmented mirrors. My reflection stared down in disjointed pieces, each segment capturing a different incarnation of me. Some were familiar. Others… were not.

Ahead lay an arched door, seemingly suspended in midair, rotating gently, yet firmly locked. Beside it, a riddle was inscribed into the floor in shifting, liquid gold.

"To pass through the door, you must name what you lost, what you fear, and what you will never be."

A phantom wind whispered through me, though there was no actual breeze, just the ghostly memory of one. I turned, but behind me lay only impenetrable darkness. No way to retreat. I knelt to trace the riddle with my fingertips, the words sparking like static electricity. What had I lost? Too many things. My bookstore, my reality, my dignity—What did I fear? That was simpler. Losing myself. What would I never be? A hero, a chosen one, a legend. I was just a woman equipped with sarcasm and a half-dead houseplant, not a myth yearning to be unveiled.

I stood, the answers poised on the edge of my lips—and the instant I voiced them, the mirrors overhead shattered. Not with violence, but with a sense of liberation. The shards cascaded around me like a glittering rainfall. And the door swung open. Beyond it lay a winding path crafted entirely from typewriter keys and torn-out pages. Trees grew at odd angles, and lanterns dangled from invisible hooks. Far in the distance, a flicker of movement—a figure walking. Someone who looked just like—me.

I followed the flickering figure down a winding corridor of torn pages that carpeted the earth like brittle autumn leaves and bent, crooked keys that jutted from the ground like ancient tombstones. With each step, the air rippled and warped; the sky folded in on itself. Underfoot, the paper murmured stories I couldn't place, yet every fragment bore my name in curling calligraphy.

A sudden gust rattled the pages. Was it wind or an exhalation from some unseen beast? Above me, the skeletal branches leaned in, whispering like a congregation of elderly crones.

The figure halted before a doorframe built of stacked tomes, their leather spines stitched with gleaming gold thread. She didn't look back—she simply stepped through. My chest tightened. I hesitated, then followed.

The world shifted again. One blink later, I stood inside *Thistle & Thorn*, my bookstore. The air was thick with lemon-cleaner tang and the musty comfort of aged paper. Overhead, brass lamps glowed softly. A beeswax candle flickered on the counter. On the romance shelf, Mrs. Thompson's silver-rimmed glasses perched atop a paper-back—precisely where she always leaves them. Outside, rain tapped a gentle rhythm against stained glass.

For a heartbeat, I believed I was home.

Then she turned.

Behind the counter stood a girl—me, but not. Her blonde hair was pulled into a neat bun I hadn't worn since tedious job interviews. She wore the lime-green sweater I'd donated months ago, still faintly scented with lavender. Her eyes, though—tired in a way I'd never let mine be.

"Welcome back," she said, voice warm as wool. "Long shift today?"

I tried to answer, but no sound came. She nodded toward the window. "Rain's letting up. You'll be late."

"Late for what?" I found myself whispering.

Her brow arched. "For the rest of the story," she said, as if I should have known. Her hands—my hands—clasped a battered copy of *Through the Looking-Glass*.

I stepped closer. "This isn't real."

She offered a gentle smile. "Then remain here. It's safe.

That's what matters, right?"

A tremor ran through me. No puzzles. No danger. No Theo and his ill-fitting top hat that somehow made him look handsome. Just routine. Predictability. Safety.

She held out a tarnished brass key, its teeth carved like tiny runes. "Stay. Lock the door. Forget Wonderland. Forget her."

Her. The Queen who watched me, who wanted me to surrender.

I stared at the key. It wasn't mine—not the one etched into my blood, pulsing beneath my ribs.

"No," I said, voice trembling. "I can't."

She blinked, her form flickering like candlelight in a draft. Then she vanished.

The bookstore collapsed around me, pages curling and soggy as if doused by rain. I stood amid the ruins, lungs heaving, heartbeat roaring.

Then the path reappeared—this time paved with mirrors, each reflecting a thousand versions of me, waiting for the next step.

The mirrored path beneath my feet shimmered like liquid glass, each step echoing loudly, as if I were treading across the fragile surface of someone else's memory. There were no clear reflections to greet me this time. Only warped images. Distortions. Glitches. It was me, but not me. My smile was too sharp, like a blade glinting in the sun. My eyes were unnaturally still, like a painting frozen in time. My silhouette unfolded, stretching and bending as if it wasn't quite meant to hold a human shape.

Then—another door emerged from the haze. It was a deep, sinister crimson, seemingly carved from bone and bark interwoven, a living tapestry of the forest's ancient secrets. In the center, a symbol was scorched into the surface: a key, but it had been twisted and contorted into a crown, a sign of power warped by ambition. I reached out and touched the symbol—and the door dissolved into nothingness.

Inside, the air was oppressive, hot and dry, with a metallic tang that clung to my throat. The room was circular, its stone walls etched with runes that I didn't recognize yet inexplicably understood. At the far end, a throne loomed, hewn from black stone, its base entwined with roots that coiled like serpents, whispering of ancient power.

She was there, waiting for me. Or rather, I was waiting for myself—the version of me that had seized the key and wielded it. Not for liberation. Not for truth. But for power. As I entered, she rose. Her form was cloaked in shadow, a crown of roses resting on her head, her eyes lined with kohl and indifference. She resembled a nightmare brought to life, stitched together from the darkest threads of my instincts.

Her voice was a honeyed blade, smooth yet cutting. "I wondered when you'd show."

"Here I am" I quipped, though the words felt hollow, like echoes in an empty chamber.

"I am your inheritance," she declared, stepping forward with deliberate grace, the room throbbing with an unbearable heat. "I am what happens when you stop flinching. When you stop caring. When you realize Wonderland doesn't need a savior."

She halted mere inches from me, her presence overwhelming. "I am what you become when you stop losing."

I trembled, a shiver of fear and recognition coursing through me. I could feel it—this version of me was all wrong. She was weary, yes, but also untouchable. Terrible. Free. And deeply, achingly alone.

"I don't want to be you," I whispered, my voice barely audible.

She smiled, her teeth gleaming like daggers. "You say that now."

Without warning, she seized my wrist. Fire surged through my veins, white-hot and searing. A sigil burned itself into my skin, right over the rhythmic pulse of my heartbeat. A key. Split down the middle. I cried out, but her grip was unyielding.

"You don't get to walk away from destiny," she hissed, her words a venomous promise. "You carry it. Whether you want to or not."

Then she shoved me back with unexpected force. And I fell—

I awoke in bed, drenched in sweat, my lungs stubbornly refusing to cooperate, each breath a struggle. The room was cloaked in silence, the kind that felt heavy and oppressive. Moonlight streamed through the window, its silvery glow casting a gentle, comforting aura across the room, as if trying to soothe my racing heart. I pushed myself upright, my hands trembling uncontrollably, fingers twitching with an unspoken anxiety.

And there it was, unmistakable in the dim light—the mark. It was etched into the tender skin of my wrist, like a burn that refused to fade, its edges raw and slightly raised as if freshly branded. A key, split cleanly in two, its intricate details catching the moonlight like a mysterious symbol from a half-remembered dream.

In that moment, a torrent of visions surged through my

mind—not everything, but fragments, vivid and haunting. A throne, majestic and imposing, loomed in my thoughts. A choice lingered, heavy with consequence. A betrayal, sharp and cutting, left a bitter taste in my mouth. And then, a man with shifting eyes emerged from the shadows of my mind, his gaze steady and unwavering. He handed me the key, his voice echoing with quiet urgency as he said, "We need you."

18

Her Majesty Observes

The moment the sigil burned into Alicia's skin, the Queen opened her eyes. She had not been asleep, of course. Queens do not sleep. They simply wait.

She stood in front of the mirror that wasn't a mirror—an ancient pane of stilled water framed in living thorns. Alicia's image still shimmered on the surface, curled in tangled sheets, eyes wide and wild with knowing. So, it had begun. At last.

The Queen's reflection did not show in the glass. It never had. Reflections were for the uncertain. She smiled. Not kindly. It was a vicious kind of smile that promised a slow, painful death.

The tower behind her moaned with the sound of shifting gears and heartbeats that did not belong to her. The throne room above was empty—for now. Let the court sleep. Let the Red Bishop count his pawns. She had her eyes on the Key.

A servant knelt behind her, cloaked in feathers and silence.

"Alert the Knave," she said, voice smooth as sugared poison. "Summon him to me." The servant bowed lower. "Yes, your Majesty."

He slid away, gliding with a thief's easy grace, his shadow stretching and snapping back in the candlelight. Footsteps echoed through the stone marrow of the castle. Beneath the Queen's skin, an itch of memory surfaced, then sank.

The Queen's nails, lacquered the color of arterial blood, drummed against the rim of the water. The ripples trembled outward and shuddered the memory of Alicia's face into something fractured and strange—her mouth a jagged red crescent, her gaze a smear of blue accusation.

Without the sound of footsteps, the Knave appeared in the archway: tall, imposing, eyes eclipsed by the mask he wore made of what looked like flayed smiles and broken hearts.

He knelt, not out of respect, but to keep the old rituals from rotting further. "Majesty," he said, voice rough as grave-dirt. She did not turn, but the thorns behind her coiled inward, eager to close the door. "The Key is ready," she said. He nodded, one hand pressed to the floor, the other absently palming the hilts hidden in his sleeves. "Do you want her dead, or merely broken?" The Queen considered. Her tongue flickered, serpent-soft, at the corner of her lips. "If she is clever, dead is of little consequence. She must suffer. She must wish for death, again and again, until the wishing is all she knows."

The Knave's mask creased into a suggestion of a smile. "She is in the hands of the Hatter now. Shall I make it to where she will be in none at all?"

"Not yet." The Queen ran a finger along the rim of the mirror, and the water bled. "She must see wonder first. Wonder, then terror. It is the proper order." He bowed again, more deeply before turning on his heel and exiting the room, off to break the Key.

The Queen reached out once more, trailing one red-gloved finger across the water's surface.

It rippled. Alicia stirred in her sleep.

"She thinks she's beginning to understand," the Queen whispered. "But she hasn't even begun to break."

The air pulsed. A low, strange rumbling sound echoed from deep within the tower. Not machinery. Not wind. A heartbeat. Old. Patient. Hungry. The Queen turned away. "She has the coin. The mark. The map," she said, her voice silk-strung steel. "Let her run."

She walked away from the vision, red silk trailing behind her like spilled blood. "She'll come to me in the end." A pause.

Then, with a voice softer than ruin: "They always do."

19

The Knave's Visit

Alicia

My night of eerie dreams continued as I found myself in a room I've never seen yet somehow remember. The ceiling stretches impossibly high, like a cathedral made of smoke and mirrors. The walls breathe. No, really—they *breathe*. Each inhalation sending long velvet curtains rippling in an invisible wind.

I try to sit up. I can't. My limbs are heavy, threaded with something thick and buzzing. Magic. Or sleep. Or fear. A single candle burns beside me, tall and dripping with wax that pools like blood. It casts flickering light over the walls, revealing painted faces that move when I'm not looking directly at them. One sobs. Another screams. One stares at me, wide-eyed and silent.

Then the air changes.

Someone's here.

He steps from the shadows as if they belong to him. Tall. Crimson. Masked. A presence I somehow recognize even before he speaks. "Knave," I breathe.

The mask was different then. Or maybe it wasn't. His eyes are hidden behind slits. But I feel them. Watching. Reading. Judging. "Shhh," he says, and it's not unkind. Just final.

His voice is rough velvet, the kind that scrapes when it soothes. "I came to see what kind of story we're dealing with." He walks closer, slow and deliberate, like someone who's never had to rush because the world will always wait. "You're dreaming," he says, "but not deeply. You left the door open." "I—I didn't mean to." "No one ever does," he replies, crouching beside the bed. He doesn't touch me. But his presence is like a pressure on my chest. Heavy. "And who invited you in?" I ask, indignant and a bit emboldened by the fact that this is a dream and he most likely couldn't hurt me. I hope.

He laughs—not a bark, not a chortle, but a learned simulacrum of laughter, like he'd been taught what it was supposed to sound like and practiced every note and interval. "Oh, Alicia," he says, savoring the name like a rare fruit, "invitations are so overrated."

He plucks the candle from the bedside and holds his palm out. The flame leans toward him in a way no fire should, stretching like a tongue toward its master. Orange light dances over the mask, and for a split second I glimpse a seam running down the middle, stitched with what could only be hair. Human? Impossible. I look away.

"Is she watching?" I whisper. My voice is smaller here, but less alone.

He tilts his head in a hears-you-in-your-bones sort of way. "Always. You're the Key, love. She'd be a fool to blink, and our Queen is many things, but never that."

I try again to move—a finger, a toe, anything. But the magic, or whatever it is, has me iron-bound. I wonder if he sees the panic flicker through me. I wonder if he cares.

He sits at the foot of the bed, uninvited but inevitable. "You've been dreaming dangerous things," he says. "Maps, doors, little riddles tucked under your tongue by the Hatter. You should be more careful with your mind. It is a delicacy in these parts."

"The Hatter's harmless," I say, only because I can't stop myself, and because I want to watch him react. And he does: his masked head cocks, just enough to suggest a fox smile, something knowing and full of teeth.

"Oh, now, is that what you think?" The Knave drums his lacquered fingertips along the empty length of blanket. "The Hatter is many things, darling, but harmless is not one of them. He simply prefers to break you in more creative ways."

"And you don't?" I say, the words come out sharper than I mean. The Knave's mask splits at the seam—an illusion, a flex, a hunger—and closes again. He shrugs, as if centuries of accusation have worn him down to this gesture. "My methods are efficient. The Queen appreciates economy." There is a silence then, but it's not empty; it's teeming with all the things neither of us will say. I can feel his gaze drop to my hands, limp on the coverlet, and for a moment I am aware of every scar, every uneven knuckle, every line that never quite healed straight. He sees them all. He catalogs them. He reaches out a hand, softly grasping my wrist and pulling me to my feet. My movements become my own once more, but I don't run.

He holds my hand in a way that is almost gentle, leading rather than dragging, until my feet touch the black marble floor and the cold licks up my bone. He stands very close. If I wanted to breathe, I'd have to do it around him. He smells like smoke, maybe, or something rawer.

"In stories, when the monster visits your dreams, it's to frighten you into sense," he says. "But sometimes it's just to see if you'll flinch." He lifts my wrist to the candle's light, studies the sigil burning faintly beneath my skin, and lets a sound escape—not disappointment, not approval, but something like recognition.

"So," I say, my mouth dry, "are you here to frighten me or see if I'll flinch?"

He tilts his head. "Why not both?"

The darkness pushes forward from the corners, and I have to focus—really focus—to keep my eyes from inventing faces in the swirl of shadow. I shudder anyhow, and the Knave notices everything.

"You're afraid," he says. "Good." He leans in, and I see his mask is not just stitched, but scored with faint, tiny words. Names, maybe, or memories. "Fear is honest, Alicia. It gives you purpose. A wake-up call if you will." He tilts his head, as if amused. "You wear hope like it's armor. It's not. It's a tether. You'll drown with it wrapped around your throat."

"I'm not afraid of drowning," I lie.

He hums, a low sound that vibrates through the floor.

"You should be."

His hand hovers over my wrist, not quite touching. Just near enough that my skin tingles, like the air before a lightning strike.

"You're the Key," he says. "But even keys can be broken. Or used." His head quirks to the right. "Do you know which you are?"

I shake my head. I hate that I don't.

He leans closer, his voice a whisper on my neck.

"Wonderland doesn't need a savior. It needs a storm."

And then, softer: "Be careful who teaches you how to turn the page."

The Knave straightens, releasing my wrist, as my blood rushes back in a river, throbbing beneath the sigil. He watches the pulse, eyes hidden, and I sense the calculation. "What do you mean by that?"

"It means you're not the hero," he says. "Not yet. Maybe not ever. But you have something none of the rest do: an ending the Queen hasn't read." I want to laugh, but my throat's too cold. "And you're here to warn me?"

"Oh, Alicia." The Knave's voice is velvet again, a little sad, as if he already mourns me. "I'm here to watch you fall. Maybe to catch you on the way down, if it's a good story."

He leans over and plucks a knife from somewhere in his coat—long, silver, and wickedly sharp. With a practiced twist, he slices the candle's wick, smothering the flame. The darkness that follows isn't absolute, but writhes in shades of indigo and bruise. My eyes adjust. His silhouette is both there and not. "We all want to be irreplaceable," he says, rolling the knife between his thumb and forefinger. "But the wind will blow whether you name it or not."

Can you please stop talking in riddles for like two seconds. You're frying my brain.

"I could," the Knave agrees, "but what would be the fun in that?" He glides closer, so I am forced to look up into the mask's featureless shadows. "Do you know how many Keys find their way here?" he asks. "None. You are the anomaly, Alicia." The room shifts. A bloodred chessboard unfurls at our feet, seamless as if it'd always been there. Figures assemble at the edges—bishops bowing, Knights poised for slaughter,

Queens looming. All of it reflected in the glossy black of the Knave's standing shoes. "Every story wants a villain," he says, "but Wonderland wants a hero it can devour." A cold fingertip traces the line of my jaw, as if mapping what will soon be lost. "You should leave, before you learn what the Queen does to her bravest little toys." "But I can't leave," I say, voice rising despite myself. "I'm not even sure I know what leaving means anymore." He seems genuinely amused. "Good. You're learning." He gestures and the painted faces on the walls contort in unison, mouths agape—singing, maybe, or warning.

"Why me?" I ask the question in the way you ask the dark to keep quiet until morning, but sometimes the dark answers anyway. "Why anyone?" He shrugs, a ripple of leather and shadow. "Sometimes the world snaps. Sometimes it just wants to see what shape you'll make when you fall through it." He does not laugh at my next question: "Is there any way out?" The Knave considers, watching me like a scientist urged to mercy by habit, not feeling. "There's always a way out," he says.

"Why did you never leave if there's a way out? Why be the bastard that kills for the fun of it?"

He moves so fast the bedpost behind him cracks from the aftershock. When he speaks, his lips are an inch from my ear: "Here is a thing that isn't a riddle: The Queen will kill you if you fail her. She'll kill you if you displease her. She'll kill you if she's bored, and she's *always* bored." This is somehow more terrifying than all the poetry. "Okay, yeah, she's crazy. Got that." I say, slowly. "But why do you play the bad guy?"

He straightens, and for a moment I think he'll hit me, or laugh, or both. But his mask just goes quiet. "Because," finally he says, and the word trembles in the silence, "even nightmares need a shape. I was the first thing she ever broke, and she's kept me around so I can see how good she's gotten at it." He almost chuckles, and the sound is so sad it bruises the air. "You call us crazy, but what people call madness here is really just hunger with too many teeth."

A game piece slides across the chessboard at our feet—a pawn, red as arterial blood, dragging a streak behind it. The Knave looks down, amused, and nudges it with his toe. "It's not just a story," he says, voice lower. "You don't get to wake up unless you win. And almost nobody wins. They just get recycled, piece by piece, until there's nothing left but the Queen's voice in their head."

The weight of exhaustion is back, but it's lighter now. Like the world is giving me a fighting chance if I can just keep breathing. "You said you could break me," I say, "if I wasn't careful with my mind."

The Knave taps his temple. "You remembered to doubt. That's your flaw, and your shield. The Queen's dreams are sticky. They taste like honey but stick like tar. The Hatter was supposed to slow you down, but he likes you. I think he wants to see if you'll outsmart Wonderland." There's a strange, almost fondness there, buried under layers of bitterness and black humor. It's the first time I realize that the Knave, for all his menace, might be more than just another monster in the Queen's menagerie.

He lifts the pawn—its paint still wet, as if bleeding—and holds it to the candle's cold stub. "Most pieces only realize what they are after they've been moved a dozen times. By then, they have a taste for it." He presses the pawn into my palm, and it burns colder than any ice. I close my fingers around it instinctively. "What am I supposed to do with this?" He shrugs. "Hold on. Or let go. Your choice, Key." The chessboard underfoot begins to unravel, squares dissolving into smoke, the figures toppling and tumbling into the void at the room's edge. The Knave doesn't seem to notice, or else he's used to disintegration. He folds his arms, mask unreadable.

I shudder, and this time the Knave doesn't hide his pleasure at seeing it. "Just remember," he says, "every friend here will knife you with a smile, if the Queen asks it."

There's a creeping chill in my feet, like the marble is filling me from the toes up, solidifying me to this place. "If you're such an expert, why are you warning me?"

His hand finds my shoulder, cold and heavy like a coin pressed to a corpse's tongue. "Because I want to see if you can make it. The last Key was too slow. The last Key before that drowned in her own hope. The second and third Key, well, I killed. And you—" he raises my chin, finger rough with old scarring— "have a little bite left. Maybe you'll get farther."

The chess pieces twitch on the board. Some fall over, others fight amongst themselves. The faces on the wall begin to chant in low, hungry syllables. They say my name like it's a sin they want to taste twice.

The Knave leans close, breath smokey and sweet. For the first time I understand why men might follow him into their own nightmares. "You could run," he whispers, "but it's a long way down. And Wonderland is not kind to the cowards." He pivots away, the severed pawn clattering from my fist and spinning like a drunk at the edge of the unraveling board. I want to follow, want to scream, but the threads of sleep catch at my ankles. He is already half-shadow when he says, "The next door you open will not be the one you think."

I blink.

He's gone.

The candle snuffs out. The room fades and I wake—heart thundering, palms damp, the ghost of a voice still echoing in my bones, and the ashes from the pawn lingering in my hand.

20

The Mark, The Map, and The Madness

Alicia

After a night of dreams that felt way too much like drowning in secrets and choking on metaphors. My racing thoughts were interrupted by the sound of my mirror muttering about "split ends and self-sabotage." I tried to ignore it.

Mostly. Instead, I yanked on my boots, tucked the 'good luck' coin into my pocket, and stared down at my wrist. The mark was still there. Still pulsing like a heartbeat that didn't belong to me.

A key, split clean down the middle.

I grabbed the nearest sharp object—a hairpin with attitude—and pressed it to the sigil. It didn't budge. I tried a flame next. Then cold water. Then salt. Nothing worked. The mark didn't burn. It didn't blister. It just *thrummed,* like it was amused I even tried.

"Nothing says cursed chosen one like magical branding that

won't exfoliate off." I mutter on a sarcastic laugh.

When violence and denial failed, I defaulted to my natural state: **reckless research.** Which is how I found myself sneaking into the *Library of Leaves* before noon, armed with determination, a headache, and the growing suspicion that I might be a multidimensional weapon with boundary issues.

According to Cheshire—who mentioned it casually over tea like one might reference a hexed closet—the Library was off-limits to "intruders, keys, and unstable dreamers." Naturally, I took that as a personal invitation. Getting inside was easy. Getting past the whispering vines that tried to French braid my soul? Less so.

The library loomed like a cathedral swallowed by green. The front door bore a warning in silver script: *"ENTER KNOWINGLY OR NOT AT ALL."*

Cute.

Inside, the air smelled like lightning and another time. Books rearranged themselves like they were avoiding eye contact. A few hissed when I passed. I followed a ribbon of floating light deeper in, down a corridor labeled *"Histories: Redacted."* Oh yes. Definitely my section. The shelves closed in. My breath grew tight. Then—I saw it. A book.

Old. Bound in worn leather. Etched with a symbol that matched the one on my wrist. I reached for it. And the world exploded. Light shot from the pages—a cold, sharp, ethereal light. I dropped to my knees as images slammed into me: A girl—not me—in red. A crown shattered into jagged pieces. A king screaming. A blade. No, a key as sharp as a sword shoved into his back. A voice, whispering from everywhere and nowhere:

"The last Key failed."

"Can this one rewrite the story?"
"She'll break first."

I gasped, the images searing themselves behind my eyelids. Then—hands on my shoulders. I flinched. "Easy," Theo said. His eyes searched mine, too full of knowledge for comfort. "What did you see?" he asked. "What didn't I?" I wheezed. "That book just emotionally mugged me."

He helped me up. His touch lingered. I hated how much I noticed.

"You shouldn't be here." "Then stop leaving me alone in this nightmare jungle," I snapped. "Unless you want me to start hallucinating crown-wearing versions of myself again." His expression darkened.

"I saw her, again," I whispered. "The first Key. She was like me. She had to fix the story, defeat the evil, but she embraced it instead."

Theo's jaw clenched. "You're not her."

"You don't know that." "I *do*," he said quietly. "Because she chose power over everything. And you..." He trailed off.

And I hated him a little—for knowing me so well and hiding so much.

I stepped back, frustrated with him, with this whole Wonderland situation. I tried to gather the tattered rags of my composure, cinching them tight. It didn't help. "What happens if I break?" I asked, voice thin as the page of a cheap paperback. I watched the library walls edge closer, shelves straining at their leashes. Theo's shadow crossed mine. "Nothing good. For you, for Wonderland, for anyone who remembers this place." His fingers hovered at my shoulder like he might comfort me, then—no, decision made—he balled them at his side."Then tell me what I'm supposed to do," I hissed. "Everyone says 'save the story, restore the balance, change the ending,' but none of you say how. You all just… haunt me with warnings." He was silent for a long time. When he spoke, his voice was different: not soft, not barbed, but dangerous with the weight of truth. "Maybe it's because no one knows how. Or maybe it's because every Key has only ever gotten it wrong. Maybe Wonderland—maybe you—are meant to break the cycle, not patch it." "Cryptic," I deadpanned, because if I couldn't joke, I'd scream. "Is there a step-by-step somewhere? Key for Dummies?" "Only the story itself," he said. "Everything else is just noise." My wrist burned anew. I resisted the urge to scratch, or bite, or carve the damn thing right off of my skin.

He turned on his heel, ready to vanish again, but I wasn't letting him go so easily this time. "Not good enough," I called after him. My voice ricocheted through the stacks and came back sharper, hungrier, not entirely my own. "I'm not some magic eight ball you shake when things get weird. Every answer in this place comes with a threat and a side of warning. I want the truth." Theo's silhouette paused at the end of the aisle, shoulders braced like he knew what came next would hurt. For both of us. The library, for its part, was listening. The hush was too dense, too… anticipatory. I caught movement in my periphery—a wisp of shadow, a smile with its own gravity. Cheshire, leaned over a nearby stack, regarding us with the disinterested flair of a cat auditioning for Hamlet. He winked at me. "Careful what you wish for, Key." "Oh, butt out, Cheshire unless you have something useful to tell me." I all but growl. His giggled response was answer enough.

"You have no idea what you're asking." Theo says softly. I

looked down at the book, the one still humming faintly with the violence of memory. "She failed, didn't she? The first Key." "She did," Theo said. "She remade the world in her own image. It nearly broke Wonderland." A muscle ticked in his jaw. "She was supposed to fix things, but instead—"

"She became the Queen," I finished for him. The logic snapped into place, cold and clean as the edge of a well-honed blade. The Queen of Hearts was the first Key. The one who was supposed to save the story, not take it hostage. "That's why you all look at me like I'm a bomb with a smiley face sticker," I exhaled, steadying my hands on the living wood of the shelf. "I'm your fail-safe, aren't I." Theo didn't answer, which was answer enough. Cheshire's smile softened, just for a heartbeat, before he shimmered out of view. I wondered if he'd ever smiled for real, or if, like me, he'd spent his whole existence photoshopping his emotions for public consumption. "Every century a Key arrives." Theo's voice was low, resigned. "Some try to set Wonderland right. Some try to burn it down. Some just want out." He glanced sideways, a cold memory flickering in his pupil. "The Keeper designed the Key to bring balance to a world tainted by ego and evil. The Key is chosen for her ability to love—and to be loved," he finished, almost bitterly, like he'd bitten into a fruit full of worms. "But sometimes the Key loves the story more than the people in it. Sometimes she loves herself. She is picked not for strength, but for the spark she creates. The capacity to inspire, terrify, or destroy— sometimes all at once."

He drew so close I could feel the static tangle between us, but his eyes never left the mark on my wrist. "If you break, Wonderland breaks with you. But if you change, even a little, you might change everything."

It was all so on-the-nose I had to stifle a laugh. "What if I refuse?" I said, daring the darkness to answer for him. He didn't flinch. "You can try. But the Queen will hunt you down. She can't bear the thought of another Key—even now, she feels you here." He caught my hand before I could shove it back in my pocket, thumb brushing the outline of the sigil. "She'll send the Knave. She'll send worse."

I yanked free, clutching the book to my chest. "Why are you helping me, Theo? Or are you just another set of handcuffs with therapy skills?"

He gave a lopsided, haunted smile. "Maybe I'm hoping for a better ending, this time."

I couldn't hold his gaze. The book in my hands was still vibrating, bleeding fragments of someone else's terror through the cover. The Queen—The First Key—she'd burned this place into the shape of her own damage.

"How old are you?" I ask, realizing he said a new Key comes every century.

He blinked, confusion flickering through his features like an uninvited guest. "No one's ever asked me that before." I waited. He waited. The silence between us crystallized, sharp and heavy. "I remember the first Key," he said, finally. "I remember the world before the Queen. I remember… everything, I think. I don't know if it counts as age, here."

The answer carved a pit in my stomach. "So, you're a prisoner, too," I said. Not a question. He hesitated, then nodded once. "Something like that." I let that hang for a minute, watching the motes of dust swirl in the pale green vault where the light dared. I wondered if my own world was watching me just as patiently, waiting for me to break or choose or prove myself some statistical anomaly.

"There's got to be a way to end it," I said. "The cycles. The… curse. Otherwise, why did anyone ever write a story where the hero never wins?" He wanted to laugh, I could feel it in the set of his mouth, the way it kept pulling at the corners. "Wonderland doesn't care about heroes. Only endings." I crossed my arms, hugging meself, feeling the pulse of memory echo through the mark on my wrist. "Tell me how to break it."

Theo regarded me in a way no one ever had: with something like hope, but also with the steadiness of someone who'd watched every candle burn out in a thousand nights. "You rewrite the ending," he said simply before walking away.

I turned to the book still glowing on the floor.

Its title had changed.

THE KEY'S FALL

And beneath that, in shimmering ink:

"All things break.

Some just break louder."

Sick and tired of all the cryptic bs I was being fed, I decided enough was enough and it was time to bail on Hatter and his fancy estate. I snuck out past midnight, when the shadows puckered and crawled. I scaled the outer wall with more determination than grace, skinned a knee on a rogue gargoyle, and landed awkwardly in a patch of trilling violets. They clapped. That's not a metaphor—the violets literally clapped.

I flipped them off and limped through the moon-soaked garden.

I passed through the gates unnoticed. Or so I thought. Cheshire materialized, smug as a cat in a sunbeam, at the intersection of two impossible hedges.

"Finally had enough of royal mind games?" he drawled, all sass and irritation.

"I'm not anyone's pawn," I snapped, then realized how much it sounded like something a pawn would say. "I'm… I'm just over it."

He lazily examined his wrist, making a show of not caring. "Of course. Shall I guess where you're heading?"

"Don't bother," I said. "I don't even know."

He grinned wider. "You're doing that thing, Alicia. The one where you run straight toward the next disaster and hope it's the last."

I glared. "If you're going to be cryptic, at least buy me a coffee first." He offered a low, rumbling chuckle. "You're so close, you know. To the heart of all this. But you're still playing at not choosing."

I felt the mark on my wrist twitch, like it agreed with the obnoxious trickster. "Well," I said, "if you have any grand advice, now would be a great time to—"

But he was already gone, leaving me alone with the slow, cold itch under my skin and the sense that the path ahead was less a path and more a test. I wandered. The night pressed in, thick with the kind of silence that meant someone was definitely watching. The trees whispered in binary, leaves flickering on and off, and the grass underfoot seemed to pull me forward—toward a clearing rimmed with thorns, moonlight boiling in the center.

Waiting there was Theo.

He stood at the edge of the clearing, every muscle held tight against the moon's compulsion. The world was silver and glass, so sharp it could split you end to end. The key-mark on my wrist thudded, syncing to some private clock inside his chest. He watched me with that same old ache—like he was already mourning what I'd become.

He stood without his hat. He looked taller without it: shaved raw, stripped of pretense. His silhouette was a vertical line through the lunacy, the only thing not bending or writhing.

I stopped just short of him, folding my arms to hide the shiver in my hands. "I need to end this Theo. I have a life to get back to."

He smiled, and this time it wasn't the practiced one. There were cracks in it, and something reckless underneath. "You're not ready, Alicia." He said, voice mournful. "You're not ready to face her, yet. Come back to the estate, let me help you prepare."

His hand hovered between us, a tremor betraying the calm in his voice. Like one touch would send us both straight into the static that glued Wonderland together and risk it all cracking apart, just to see what would emerge at the seam.

I stared past him, at the boiling moonlight, at the hedge walls that curled tighter the longer I stood still. "You keep talking like this is some boss battle I get to gear up for, Theo. But every time I blink, someone's rearranged the board. And you're always two moves ahead."

"Because I have to be." He ran his other hand through his hair, knuckles white. "I'm not trying to hurt you, Alicia. But the Queen—she's not like the others. If you go to her now, she'll break you. And you don't get remade the same way twice. Every time, something gets lost."

"Maybe I want to see what's on the other side," I said. "Maybe breaking is the only way out." He stepped forward, and the air thickened. "There's no out. Not for me. Not for you. Only through." His eyes searched mine, and for a moment he looked so nakedly desperate I almost didn't recognize him. "Let me help you."

The truth hung between us, thick as honey, impossible to ignore. I could go with him, let him 'prepare' me, play along until I found whatever power everyone was so terrified of, or I could cut and run—straight into the arms of the world's most homicidal monarch and hope I landed the first punch.

"Just tell me what's at the center of this," I beg, voice shaking but steadying with each syllable. "No more riddles. No more 'it's for your own good.' I dream about her every night. I see her when I'm awake. If I'm the only one who can stop her—if I really am the Key—then let me be. Open the door." He reached for my hand, but I flinched away. "She'll consume you," he warned, desperate and breaking. "You don't know what she'll do to you."

"Maybe not," I said. "But I'm not the girl who hides in the fantasy aisle anymore."

He frowned, and for a moment his face was just a man's, not a myth's—tired, bruised by too many sleepless nights and too much hope burnt down to the stub. Then, softly: "There's a mirror, deep in the forest called the *Glassless Gate*. It will transport you to the Queen's castle. But, be forewarned the journey to the gate is a treacherous one."

"Aren't they all?" I said. It came out braver than I felt, but that's the thing about Wonderland: the only way to survive is to keep bluffing, even when the cards are all wild.

He half-turned, the moon shadowing his face to a silhouette. "Alicia, please, please be careful. I can't bear the thought of something happening to you."

"Then, come with me. Guide me. Help me with more than

riddles."

His mouth worked around a protest, but the words withered before they breached the air. Instead, he only nodded—one abrupt jerk, like it cost him something to agree.

We set out together, two silhouettes breaking the night along a path that sometimes existed and sometimes didn't, depending on how long you kept your eyes closed. The forest pressed in tighter, the trees gnarling overhead in knots that spelled out unspeakable warnings. Theo walked half a pace ahead, never looking back, but I could feel his attention tracing me constantly, as though he were measuring the moments before I'd decide to vanish or turn on him.

He didn't speak. Not the way he had back at the estate, where words tumbled out like amusements. Now, he looked more like someone walking to their own execution, even as he moved with the same reckless elegance as before.

21

The Orchard of Echoes

Alicia

The trees transformed gradually, their leaves bleeding from vibrant green to rich gold to shimmering silver. We stepped into a clearing that was almost unnervingly symmetrical, with rows of apple trees stretching endlessly in every direction like soldiers in formation. Each apple glimmered like polished glass, some pulsing with a faint, ethereal glow from within. The air here hummed softly, as if it held the remnants of an ancient melody.

Theo halted beside me, his presence a steadying force. "We're close," he murmured.

"To the Gate?" I asked, hopeful but wary.

He shook his head slowly. "To something that remembers what many have forgotten."

Does anyone in this world speak directly? Before I could inquire further, one of the apples spoke, its voice soft yet piercing.

"You're the Key? We're all doomed." it whined.

152

I blinked in surprise. "Did… did that tree just sass me?"

Theo didn't smile, his expression grave. "This is the Orchard of Echoes. Each fruit holds a memory. Some belong to you. Some to others. Some are hers." "The Queen?" I ventured. He remained silent, his eyes shadowed. More apples shimmered, their surfaces alive with a kaleidoscope of colors. More voices rang out in a haunting chorus:

"She let the world burn for a crown." "He wanted to protect her."

"You will become what you fear most." "Where does his loyalties lie?" The trees pressed in around us, their branches a living cage. Theo moved to shield me, his proximity a barrier against the growing dread. "We need to keep moving. The longer you listen, the harder it is to leave."

Without thinking, I reached for his hand, seeking comfort in the chaos. He flinched at the contact but didn't let go, his grip firm and reassuring. "Why does everything in Wonderland want me to doubt myself?" I asked, frustration lacing my words.

"Because you're the only one who can right it," he replied, his voice low and steady. We walked quickly, urgency propelling us forward, but the trees twisted around us like a maze, reshaping and reforming as we moved. Branches arched overhead, heavy with memories that had yet to be lived. I stumbled, my foot catching on an unseen root. Theo caught me before I fell, his arms too close, too warm. His gaze intense, knowing.

"Stop doing that," I breathed, my heart racing.

"Doing what?" he asked, his gaze steady and unsettling.

"Looking at me like you know how this ends." He swallowed hard, his Adam's apple bobbing. "I don't. That's what terrifies me."

We continued onward, our steps quickening, until we confronted a final tree looming in our path. Its fruit was an ominous black, its surface absorbing the light around it.

A single apple pulsed, its rhythm slow and steady like a heartbeat.

Theo grabbed my arm, his grip urgent. "Don't touch it."

But it was too late. My fingers brushed the skin, and the world fell away beneath me.

I was thrust into a vision—a throne of bones, a river of mirrors. The Queen stood there, draped in red, clutching a heart that might have once beat in her own chest.

She turned, eyes bottomless and burning. "I was the first. I will be the last," she intoned, lifting the heart for me to see. I tried to move, but the throne-room's gravity pressed me flat, my arms leaden at my sides. In the mirrors—dozens of them stretching up the throne's sides, forming a funhouse pyramid—I caught glimpses of every girl who had worn the mark. Some had my face. Some didn't. All looked wild with terror. I watched as they met their ends. Either with violence or despair, never peaceful. The Queen beckoned. "Alicia. Come closer." I obeyed. Not out of will, but because the orchard's magic had me on strings, marionetting me down the aisle of mirrors toward the dais. She wasn't what I expected. Not monstrous, not overtly cruel. Her features were razor-sharp and ageless, her skin translucent as rice paper, blue veins painting fangs and branches beneath its surface. The heart she cradled—was it mine?—wept thin lines of gold that sizzled when they hit her palm. She held it gently, almost tenderly. "My poor, persistent Key," she murmured, pressing her lips to the heart's surface. "Did he tell you how this ends?"

I heard Theo's voice echoing through the scene: "Alicia,

come back! Please, don't get lost. We need you."

I gasped and collapsed back into reality, my breath coming in ragged bursts. Theo cradled me gently, his presence an anchor. "You're okay. You're okay."

"I saw… me. Her. A throne," I whispered, the images still vivid and raw. He didn't ask what it meant. Instead, he pulled me close, his embrace warm and unyielding. And—for once—he didn't let go.

Light cracked through the branches, slowly, then all at once, as if Wonderland itself had exhaled in relief. The trees retreated, their trunks straightening into stately columns, their leaves fading from argent to a fragile, translucent gold. The orchard's song softened to a hush, only the memory of its melody lingering at the edges of thought.

"Is it over?" I asked, blinking against the sudden brightness, unwilling to leave the shelter of Theo's arms. He nodded, though his jaw was set and his eyes tracked every movement in the grove. "For now. But—" He hesitated, running a thumb along the back of my hand as if he could memorize me by touch. "I don't know what happened in there, but you've changed the story once more. This place was a black hole of despair, now look at it. I glanced around, the apples now a vibrant red, the clearing all sunshine and literal rainbows, a stark contrast to moments before.

I tried to stand but my legs quivered, unmoored. I let Theo guide me; my shoulder tucked under his as he led us through the thinning trees. Each step away from the orchard was a step closer to the Gate. Or to the Queen. I wasn't sure anymore which was more dangerous.

Beyond the trees, the ground sloped gently into a valley, its surface glittering with lavender heather and shards of glass, as if a thousand broken windows had been laid into the soil, reflecting the battered sky above.

We stumbled out of the orchard just as dusk began to swallow the sky, our breaths ragged, our limbs aching. The trees stood silent behind us, but their whispers clung to my skin like cold dew, threading through my hair and settling on my neck. Theo said nothing. He slipped his hand into mine—gentle this time, as though I were carved of glass and sorrow—and guided me through a bramble-choked corridor of oaks and thorn. At last we emerged into a small clearing where a stone cottage lay half-embedded in the hill, its mossy roof bowed as if the earth itself had coaxed it into a long, weary slumber.

"Safehouse?" I asked, my teeth rattling.

"An outpost for travelers," he replied. He pushed open the heavy wooden door, which groaned in protest, and we entered a single, twilight-lit room. Faint shafts of dying light sifted through dusty windowpanes, illuminating cobwebbed corners. A cold hearth yawned against one wall, and crooked shelves bowed beneath the weight of well-worn books whose spines smelled of cinnamon and secrets. The floor was patched with an old quilt, its fabric faded but still warm with hidden stories.

Theo knelt by the hearth and, with a quiet snap of his fingers, coaxed a spark to life. The flame trembled for a heartbeat, then blossomed, sending tongues of amber light curling against the walls. A gentle heat unfurled through the room, wrapping around my bones like the sigh I hadn't realized I'd been holding in. I slid to the floor beside the fire, the quilt soft beneath me. Theo settled across from me, shadows dancing over the sharp planes of his cheekbones. His jacket was damp, the fabric heavy and dark; a few stray strands of his hair had escaped his clasp, coiling around his ears. His eyes—too candid—kept flitting back to me, as though he were memorizing the rise and fall of my chest. After a long moment I broke the hush. "I saw her on a throne. Her hands dripping with blood."

He didn't blink. "You aren't her."

"I could be." My voice trembled.

"You aren't. You won't make the same mistakes she did."

I looked away. "You say that like you know me."

"I do," he whispered. His words settled over me like rain on glass, cool and immutable, as my throat tightened. "You're always so careful with what you know," I murmured. "As if you're holding back… everything. Why?"

He made no sound. Instead, he rose and pulled a woolen blanket from a shelf, the fabric worn soft by time. He draped it around my shoulders, the wool warm and fragrant, then sat down again, closer this time—our knees brushing. My heart stuttered at the contact.

"I'm careful," he said finally, voice low, "because if I let myself say everything I want to… you'd never look at me the same."

My breath caught in my chest. I turned my face just enough to trace the tension in his jaw; the slight parting of his lips as though poised on the verge of confession.

"Try me," I whispered. The fire crackled, and he leaned forward a fraction, the glow illuminating the earnest urgency in his gaze.

"I want to tell you everything," he said, voice gentle as embers. "But some things are better left unsaid. At least for the moment."

"Is that another riddle?" I asked. "Because I am all out of

patience and patience-adjacent products."

A shadow of a smile passed over his lips—gone before it could settle in. "Just an apology." He reached to brush a loose strand of hair from my face; his fingertips lingered at my temple, almost unsure if I'd let him. The touch was as light as the sigh of an old book closing, but it sent every nerve in my body flaring with static. I didn't look away. I did not flinch.

Outside, the wind rose, pelting the windows with flecks of rain so fine they sounded like computer keys chasing the punchline on a deadline. I pulled the blanket tighter, swallowing the sudden, desperate ache that I might never feel this safe again.

"Are you going to disappear again in the morning?" I asked.

He shook his head. "I'm not leaving you alone," he said, so softly it could have been the voice of a memory. "Not tonight. Not for anything."

We lingered in that silence for what felt like an eternity, the only sound the gentle crackle of burning wood. Then I took a reckless step. I rested my head against his shoulder. His breath caught, yet he remained beside me. Gradually, he lifted his hand to cover mine, starting with a hesitant touch that grew more assured. In that moment, for the first time since Wonderland had upended my life, a profound calm seeped into my being. I felt... still.

22

The Staircase That Wasn't

Alicia

The next morning, pale mist slithered between ancient trunks, as if Wonderland couldn't decide whether to keep us trapped or finally spit us out. The air tasted of dew and moss, the scent of pine heavy under the linen-gray sky.

We walked side by side in a silence that thrummed with unspoken things. Every time Theo's shoulder brushed mine, a current sparked through my ribs—I told myself it was just the early chill. I told myself a lot of things.

At last, we emerged into a clearing ringed by silver-spined mushrooms that glinted like lanterns and cobalt ferns whose feathery fronds sighed softly, exhaling tiny clouds of spores when you drew too near. In the center hovered a staircase, its alabaster steps spiraling upward into the heavens, defying gravity and common sense alike. The rails dissolved into nothingness, as if carved from air before reforming once more. Theo halted, brow furrowed. "This wasn't supposed to be

159

here."

I rolled my shoulders. "Oh good—spontaneous sky stairs. Exactly what I needed to shake up my Tuesday."

He cocked his head, eyes narrowed, as though he wanted to lecture the staircase itself. "It's a test. One of the Queen's."

I scoffed. "Let me guess—I climb, something tries to kill me, and you brood meaningfully at the bottom." A ghost of a smirk tugged at his lips. "Roughly. If you fall, you fall forever."

My mark pulsed on my wrist, warm and insistent. I squared my shoulders. "And if I refuse?"

"She'll send worse."

I drew in a breath scented with damp earth and resolve. "Well then. Let's make bad choices." He offered his hand. "We climb together."

Step by shimmering step, we ascended. Each tread wavered in a wash of pearlescent light, then winked out behind us—no turning back. Beneath, the emerald forest collapsed into a watercolor haze. Around us, the sky thickened into molten opal, streaked with rose and storm-gray clouds that pulsed with unseen energy.

Halfway up, the entire spiral lurched beneath our feet, tilting wildly. I yelped as vertigo snapped at my stomach, but Theo's arms shot around me—solid, warm, his palm pressed flat against the small of my back. He hauled me in so close that his heartbeat thundered against my ear. Our faces hovered inches apart—too close, yet not nearly enough. "You alright?" he murmured, voice low and rough.

"Fine," I whispered, though my gaze locked on his mouth as if it held some ancient answer. He didn't let go immediately, but when he finally released me, his fingers lingered like a promise.

At the summit stood a single door—fierce crimson, freestanding, its surface lacquered so deeply it looked wet. I reached for the handle and recoiled; it burned with a cold so pure it felt like ice sliding over my bones. Theo stepped forward. "Let me go first—"

Before he could, the door throbbed like a heartbeat and then inhaled us both in a silent, terrifying gulp. We plunged through a starless void and landed with a clatter on smooth stone. All around, mirrors rose floor to ceiling, thousands of them: tall, narrow, oval, fractured. Each reflected a different me—wide-eyed and trembling; fierce and snarling; one with blood crusted at her lips; another crouched, weeping beside a body too dreadful to behold.

Theo planted himself at my side, fingers drifting to my wrist. His gaze flicked among the reflections, wary. "They're not real," he said. "But they could be," I breathed. He turned to me, sincerity shining in his eyes. He took my wrist in his hand. "Then you must decide who you want to be."

"I don't know," I admitted.

"Then let me help you." His grip tightened, and as if in answer, cracks spiderwebbed across every mirror's edge— just enough to slip through. The glass fractured, not into a thousand dangerous shards, but into doorways leading onward. He gave my hand a reassuring squeeze, and together we stepped through the fractured reflections into whatever lay beyond.

We emerged from the shattered mirror room, stepping cautiously onto the edge of a cliff that hung high above a sky filled with upside-down constellations. The stars twinkled backward, casting an eerie glow that illuminated the vastness of the heavens. Theo stood beside me, silent, his eyes locked on the celestial patterns as if the stars themselves owed him some profound revelation.

I brushed the fine, glistening glass-dust from my jacket, adrenaline still weaving through my veins like a second skin, pulsing with the remnants of our recent escape. "Okay," I said, my voice slicing through the quiet sharper than I intended. "No more riddles. Why do you care so much?"

Theo blinked, startled as if pulled from a deep reverie. "What?"

"You keep saving me. Warning me. Throwing yourself into collapsing magical architecture for me. Why?" I stepped closer, the wind from the cliff's edge tangling my hair. "I'm just a girl who runs a bookshop and collects bad decisions. I anything but special."

His gaze dropped to the mark etched into the skin of my wrist, a silent emblem of something unknown. "That's where you're wrong."

I waited for him to continue, but the silence stretched between us, thick with unspoken truths. Of course, he didn't elaborate. He just looked at me like I was already transitioning into someone else—someone he feared, even if I didn't understand why.

"I'm not her," I whispered, the words carried away by the breeze. "Whoever you see when you look at me. Whoever or whatever—you need to let her go."

Theo's jaw tightened, his expression hardening like stone. "I'm not saving her. She was never worth saving."

A tense silence expanded between us, fraught with unspoken tension and danger.

"I'm saving you."

After hours of walking, no creepy apples or stairs to nowhere in sight, we finally find a place to sleep in the ruins of an old house that had clearly lost an argument with time—and possibly a dragon.

Theo ignited a fire effortlessly with a flick of his fingers, his casual display of magic as natural as breathing. I huddled close, wrapping my arms around my knees, absorbing the fire's warmth, yet acutely conscious of him sitting directly across from me. His coat, warm and heavy, was draped over my shoulders—a silent gesture of kindness after he noticed my shivering.

Theo's gaze fixated on the flickering flames, as if expecting them to reveal some hidden truth. "I always thought," I began, my voice a quiet murmur laced with fatigue, "that if magic ever found me, it would be whimsical. Like talking flowers, enchanted pocket watches, or cake that imbues you with confidence."

"No cake?" he inquired, the faintest trace of humor glimmering in his voice.

"Oh, there's cake. Just with a side of storybook nightmares and wardrobe changes," I replied, a wry smile tugging at my lips. His own lips quirked slightly in response, yet the smile never fully formed. "Wonderland's not a place of whimsy. Not anymore."

"Was it ever?" I asked, curiosity tinged with a touch of melancholy.

He remained silent, offering no answer. I leaned closer to the fire, the warmth seeping into my bones. "What was it like? Before it broke?" Theo's eyes gleamed with a distant light. "It was a story that believed in itself. Now it's a story trying to rewrite the ending."

I studied him across the dancing flames. "And you? What are you?"

His lips parted, hesitated, then closed again. "I'm what's left when the story forgets the hero." His words struck with the force of a thunderclap, leaving me momentarily speechless. I offered the only thing I had—quiet companionship and presence.

A moment stretched between us. Then he looked up, a soft intensity in his gaze. "You're changing it, you know. The story. Just by being here, surviving whatever Wonderland throws at you."

The fire crackled between us, casting flickering shadows that accentuated the lines of grief etched on his face, like ash stubbornly clinging to remnants of what once was.

I remained still, my silence profound. Yet within me, something shifted—slow and seismic. It wasn't because I was falling for him.

It was because I already had. The fire had started to die down, its light flickering low and gold. Shadows danced on the broken marble walls behind us, shifting like they knew we were holding our breath.

Theo leaned forward, elbows on his knees, watching me like I was the story he wasn't allowed to read but couldn't help skimming.

"You're cold," he said softly.

"I'm fine." I wasn't. But I'd forgotten how to ask for warmth without sounding like I wanted too much.

His coat was still around my shoulders. His scent clung to it—smoke and something wild, like thunderstorms and secrets that hadn't picked a side yet.

"I shouldn't have brought you this far," he said. "It's

dangerous, you could be harmed or worse." I grabbed his arm, trying to calm him as if he were a spooked animal. His gaze dropped to my mouth, and for a second—just one heartbeat too long—we weren't sitting by a fire in a cursed land. We were something else. Something inevitable.

Theo reached out, fingers grazing mine where they rested on my knee. Not a full touch—just a breath of contact, the world contracted to that sliver of space. He exhaled, low and ragged. "You have no idea," he whispered, voice barely there, "how I wish things could be different." That line landed like a cryptic blade wrapped in velvet.

My breath caught when he stood, suddenly, as if the confession had broken something in him. "I'll keep watch," he said without looking back, his voice steady now—too steady. "Try to sleep."

Then he turned and walked into the darkness, leaving the fire to burn alone and my chest hollowed out like someone had rearranged the furniture in my ribcage. The moment he disappeared into the shadows; I counted to ten. Then said screw it. I shoved the coat tighter around me and followed.

The space beyond the fire was colder, quieter. The ruins creaked and sighed like they remembered being something more. I found him standing at the edge of the porch, his back to me, head tilted to the sky like it might offer absolution.

"You don't get to drop that line and vanish," I said.

He didn't turn around. "You should be resting."

"I should be a lot of things. But here we are." Silence. I stepped closer, arms folded tight across my chest. His shoulders were hunched, like every word was a pebble in his shoe and the walk had been long. "Some consequences are written in before you know you've started the story." I scoffed, more bravado than belief. "If that were true, what's the point of living through it?" This finally wrung a half-laugh from him. When he turned, the starlight etched his cheekbones in silver relief. He looked at me, really looked, with eyes the color of deep winter sky. Not sympathy—solidarity. "You rewrite it. Even if it hurts." A wind kicked up. His hair, those jagged little wings of it, found their own orbit around his brow. He rubbed his neck, mouth twisting. "I thought I needed to keep you at arm's length. That the only way you'd survive was if I stayed a monster in your periphery."

I shivered, not from cold this time. "I don't want a monster."

He stepped forward, hands open at his sides. "Then what do you want?"

I almost lied. That would've been easier. Instead, I met his gaze and let the truth tumble out. "I want someone who fights for me. Even when it hurts. Especially when it's inconvenient." Theo's mouth parted, then closed. He had no defense against that. Maybe he didn't want one.

The wind tasted different all of a sudden, like the air right before a summer storm. He closed the gap, each step measured, until he was close enough that I could count the constellations in his eyes.

He reached out, finally, and tucked a wild strand of my hair behind my ear. His thumb traced the edge of my jaw, rough and stuttering like he was learning the shape of his own regret. My pulse skittered. Somewhere in the darkness, a nightjar called, startled into flight by the audacity of human touch.

"It's not convenient," he said, voice lowered into a trembling place between apology and reverence. "But you aren't convenient, either."

I laughed, sharp and small, because what else do you do

when someone says exactly the thing you never said back? "I'm famously difficult."

He smiled, real this time, the corners of his mouth lifting like dawn over a horizon neither of us trusted. "You're brave."

I wanted to believe him, wanted it so hard it made my teeth ache. But the mark on my wrist burned colder. "If I'm so brave, why am I terrified right now?"

"Because you've finally got something to lose," he said, and in that moment, he kissed me. It wasn't a shy, half-hearted thing, but a crash—the storm he'd promised in the marrow of every word. His hands framed my face, careful, steady, as if determined to prove that even in this world, something could be held without breaking. My own arms banded around his waist, pulling us together until the chill and fear and loneliness pressed out between our bodies, melted down and away by heat and momentum and wanting.

The kiss lasted just as long as it needed to: several intense beats where, impossibly, nothing else in Wonderland moved.

When his lips left mine, I tasted rain and regret and the possibility of something so bright it could raze the ruins of this world to nothing.

For a long moment, Theo kept his forehead pressed to mine. Our breath mingled in the blue-dark night, painting shapes in the cold until it was impossible to tell where he ended and I began. Something had shifted, tectonic and unstoppable, and I wasn't sure if I should run from it or build a city in its shadow.

He pulled back—too soon, always too soon—and tucked his hands in his pockets. "This changes nothing," he said, not meeting my eyes. "If anything, it makes the next part worse."

"Because we have to go to the castle," I guessed, the words

tasting like the aftermath of a dare. He nodded, jaw set. "The Queen is waiting for you."

I wanted to say something brave and clever, maybe a joke about baking her a cake laced with arsenic or staging a coup with nothing but sheer will and bad ideas. Instead, I just nodded following him back inside.

23

The One Who Came Before

Alicia

I didn't remember falling asleep. One moment I was tracing the stars through the leaf-laced ceiling of the forest; the next, the world pitched sideways, and I landed in a garden that time had forgotten. Vines choked the stone pathways, and black roses—shriveled as burnt paper—oozed thick, inky sap onto the cracked marble. A humid hush pressed against my skin, as though the air itself was holding its breath. Above, a bruised sky churned in slow, roiling swirls, the clouds taut and electric with unspent thunder. Even the cicadas seemed too afraid to sing.

At the garden's heart, a pool lay mirror-still. Its obsidian surface glinted with ripple-less precision. I stepped forward, each footfall muted on damp moss, and peered in.

My own face stared back—then warped into someone else entirely. This woman carried centuries of struggle behind her eyes. Her hair tumbled in red and black streaked coils crowned by a fractured halo of rusted gold. Thin cracks ran along its spiked arches, as if some hasty hand had tried to mend it with molten tears. Her skin was pale as bone; her lips curved into a razor's smile.

"You came back," she said, her voice a blade drawn slowly from its sheath. "You always do." The words echoed across the water with the weight of a challenge.

I opened my mouth, but the silence swallowed me.

"I was the first, as you know by now," she continued, the soft hiss of her tone like silk dragged over stone. "The Keeper chose me. The mark burned for me. And I opened it—but you will fail. This is my kingdom." She smiled again, the coldness of her promise singing through my veins.

"Not for long," I whispered, my voice small in that vast hush.

Her laugh rippled across the pool, thin and ageless. "Foolish girl."

Behind her, shadows quivered. A tall figure lurked at the edge of the dream, shoulders hunched. My heart thundered in my chest. "Theo?" I called, breath catching.

The woman's lips twisted. "Yes, our *dear* Hatter." She angled her head, and moonlight struck her wrist—there, etched in skin, was the same twisting sigil I wore on mine. Older. Fractured. Faint sparks traced its jagged lines.

Her voice softened to a whisper thick with menace. "And you're the one still pretending that makes you different. We share blood, the same fire—and when the world burns again, he won't save you."

I staggered back. Theo stepped forward, the darkness parting enough to show a flash of his eyes—her eyes, cold and unblinking. With the exception of their hair color, their features were similar. Then the garden shattered: stones, roses, the pool—all swallowed by a void so silent I could hear my own heart clawing for sound.

I woke with a gasp, clutching the coarse canvas of the blanket as if it could tether me to reality. My surroundings spun in smoky half-light. The acrid scent of campfire and pine resin filled my nostrils. My pulse pounded like a war drum. The dream clung to my skin: the Queen's cracked crown, her blade-sharp smile, the mark, and him—Theo—looming like a ghost.

I threw back the blankets and yanked on my boots so hard the leather groaned. My legs trembled, but anger steadied me. He sat by the fire, shoulders hunched, gaze lost in the dancing embers. "Did you think I wouldn't find out?" I snapped, stepping into the ring of firelight. Sparks spiraled upward, and his face flickered in and out of flame. "Alicia—" he began, but I cut him off.

"The Queen, Theo! She's awful." I crossed my arms, feeling the ache of betrayal. "And you—" My voice broke. "You're her brother."

He stayed silent. The crackle of burning wood and our ragged breaths filled the night. "All this time," I said, voice trembling with hurt, "every warning, every cryptic clue—you never once told me she was family?" He lowered his gaze to the glowing coals. "I lost her, to power," he whispered. "I'm terrified of losing you the same way."

The fire popped, and a shower of orange sparks lit the tears gathering at my lashes. "Why didn't you just tell me?" I demanded, though my throat burned with exhaustion. His eyes lifted, haunted and raw. Shadows carved hollows into his cheeks; an old scar traced his jaw like a dark river. He touched it absently, as if seeking its memory.

"I tried to stop her once," he said, voice breaking. "When

they crowned her, when the door flared open—I begged her to run. But she believed this was our legacy." He laughed—a hollow, broken sound. "And now it's yours."

The wind stoked the flames, and I felt the heat on my cheeks. A fresh knot coiled in my gut. "So, I'm just a replacement?"

Theo shook his head, eyes flicking past me into the woods. "No. The Key isn't meant to repeat history. It's meant to end it. I hoped, if I guided you, you'd choose differently." My throat tightened. I stared at him, at the brittle set of his shoulders, the way his hands hovered as if reaching for something he couldn't name. The fire cracked between us like an unspoken promise.

"And if I can't?" I whispered. He met my gaze, the flames reflecting in his dark eyes. "Then the world burns."

He said it without flinching, as if he'd rehearsed the line for centuries, his entire existence reduced to the inevitability of catastrophe. The silence after was a living thing—it prowled the circle of firelight, gnashing its teeth, hunting for what little hope we'd left unscarred.

I turned from him, unable to bear the sincerity in his wounds. My boots dug furrows through the dew-laced grass as I paced the edge of our makeshift camp, listening to the tremor in my own breath. In the stories, the hero always rallies here, stands taller, finds the right words. But I was fresh out of speeches, and the only thing I felt worthy of raising was my pulse, thundering more with terror than purpose.

"Do you think she remembers?" I asked the dark, my voice clipped and sharp, breaking just enough to let the wind through. "The Queen. Who she was before all this?"

He didn't answer. Maybe it was rhetorical. Maybe he didn't have anything left to say. But the pause stretched so dangerously long, I almost thought he'd faded off to sleep. "She remembers," he said at last. "She just doesn't care."

The answer landed like a stone in my gut. I pressed my palms to my face, willing the sting in my eyes to evaporate. The cold did the rest for me.

"For what it's worth," he said, after a stretch of quiet that spanned galaxies, "I didn't know you'd come this far." There was real awe in his voice, wounded and reluctant. "She's not the only one who remembers."

24

What She Doesn't Know

Theo

She turned away before I could shatter once more. The fire behind me crackled and hissed, its warmth contrasting sharply with the chilling silence that seared my very soul. Alicia—my sister's natural foe, my undoing—stood at the edge of the clearing, her silhouette rigid and storm-bright, desperately trying to piece herself back together with nothing but raw anger and racing adrenaline as her tools.

I couldn't hold it against her. She had every right to despise me. I just hadn't grasped how profoundly it would feel like being erased from the inside, like a shadow dissolving in the sun. I lowered my gaze to the earth, pressing my fingers deep into the soil as if I could anchor myself to something solid, anything real. For a fleeting moment, I allowed myself to feel it—her voice still resonating in my ears, sharp as shattered glass and trembling with emotion, demanding truths I wasn't yet able to give her.

Not yet.

The Queen had once been the Key, and I, her brother, had been a powerless witness as she surrendered to the intoxicating embrace of power.

Alicia didn't know the entire story. She didn't know what I had become in the aftermath. What Wonderland had forged out of me. Out of all of us. I gazed into the flames yet saw her face flickering there regardless. Not the Queen's. Hers. Alicia—wild, furious, and impossibly alive. And something within me fractured once more. Because I didn't know how to shield her without losing her. And I wasn't certain I could endure the loss of either possibility.

I rose and walked into the darkness, careful not to let the fire's glow outline my retreat. In this world, night is never black—always prismatic, always humming with the audio-visual static of stories that refuse to be silenced. The trees scrawled their twisted shadows over the forest floor, spelling out warnings in a language older than either of us. It wasn't always this way. Once, I could have simply followed her and said what needed to be said, no more, no less. But the world had made a liar of me, and now every word was a riddle, every confession a curse. The bottle of regrets in my pocket clinked as I moved, a deliberate sound—one I kept close, because sometimes you had to remind yourself why you weren't allowed to want things. Not even hope. Not even her. I joined her at the edge of the water, the pool slick with moonlight, her reflection painted upon it not as she was, but as she could have been. The face was softer, not yet carved out by anger or haunted by the burden of impossible destiny. My heart ached in recognition, a pulse I'd long ago trained myself to ignore. "Alicia," I called. My voice was gentle, but the night caught it and bent it, so that it landed at her feet as a plea or a dare. She didn't turn. Not right away. But her shoulders dropped, just enough, as though she'd let go of one of the thousand weights she carried. "Is this where you tell me I'm being unreasonable?" she said. It was almost a laugh. Or maybe a threat. I'd never learned to distinguish the two in her.

"No," I said, "this is where I admit you're right."

She still wouldn't face me, so I moved closer—slowly, so as not to spook the tension coiled around her spine. The moonlit pool mirrored us both, but in the glassy hush it was clear we hadn't shared a single past, only collided by accident in the turbulence of other people's stories.

"You should have told me, "she said finally, her voice a careful monotone. "You should have told me everything."

"You deserved more than the script they buried in you," I replied, which was not an apology, but the closest I'd get.

She snorted, a sound that cracked the night like a stone through thin ice. "You all act like I'm going to split in half at the first piece of bad news. Wonderland's not the only one with calluses, you know."

Even with her back to me, I could see the raw hurt in her posture. The way grief shimmered behind anger like heat behind glass. It was harder than I imagined seeing her so upset. I cautiously reached my arms out drawing her into me and, for a moment, she resisted. Then, with a shudder, she collapsed backwards against my chest. Not forgiveness; something more desperate, more temporary. A truce struck in the marrow. We stood there on the bank, her anger dissolving into shivers, my arms a poor substitute for all the things she'd lost.

"I wasn't made for this," she whispered, voice an echo the pond refused to claim.

"None of us were," I murmured.

She shook her head hard enough to scatter droplets from the ends of her hair. "Then why did you let me believe it? Why did you wait until... till now?"

The straight answer trembled on my tongue, too raw to surface. "If you knew, you would have run," I admitted. "And if you ran, she would have killed you by now."

25

The Ones Who Wait

Alicia

A heavy hush settled over the forest as we started on the path once more. Not peaceful—never that—but quiet as a held breath, taut and coiled, as if the trees themselves were bracing for a snap. Fingers of mist curled at my ankles; every bird and insect had gone still, leaving only the pulse of my own heartbeat in the hush.

When the trunks thinned, the gloom fractured, revealing a clearing that couldn't be natural. The ground leveled into a perfect circle, edged by stones hewn so smoothly they looked carved by something inhuman. Emerald leaves clung to them in intricate, repeating spirals, each tendril folding into the next like living mathematics. The air above the circle quivered, rippling like a heat-haze, as though reality was uncertain how to uphold itself here.

At the center hovered a massive portal, broader and taller than any door—its surface gleaming with a cruel flatness. No frame, no backing, just a flawless sheet of glass like energy suspended in midair. It reflected... nothing. No sky, no trees, no hint of us standing before it. The clearing felt hollow, as if the mirror had swallowed its own reflection along with everything else.

"The Glassless Gate," Theo murmured at my side. His voice was low, tense—like he'd packed every cautionary tale he'd ever heard into one syllable. Before I could ask what the catch was—there was always a catch—a voice purred from some impossible angle. "Well, well, well. Look who finally remembered which way is forward."

Above the mirror, Cheshire blinked into being, sprawled across an invisible hammock of air. His signature violet magic rippled in the dim light, as his grin shone like polished silver.

I hardly had time to scowl at him before someone hurtled into my side. "ALICIA!"

March Hare let me have it in a tackle-hug that reeked of burnt cinnamon and wild impulses. Pine needles scattered underfoot as he pressed me close, his laughter trembling against my ear.

"March?" I gasped, staggering. "You're here?"

He spun away with a flourish, ears tumbling to opposite sides. "But of course, fair Key. I wanted to come along on your grand adventure. Hatter never takes me anywhere with him."

"Probably because you start fires," Cheshire drawled, his smile sharpening, "in both the literal and metaphorical sense." March Hare drew up straight, hand to breast. "Metaphorically, if something doesn't burn, how do you know it's real?"

Theo gave March a wary half-smile that didn't reach his eyes. "How did you find us?" March pointed a thumb to his chest, lips puckering in solemn offense. "Why, I followed the unspeakably tragic smell of doubt and fear, naturally." He sidled between us and the Gate, his face falling serious for just an instant, furrowed in a way I'd never seen before. Then he blinked, and it was gone, replaced with his usual madcap brightness.

A low hiss of blue smoke unfurled from a third figure's fingertips, drifting like calligraphy in the air. Caterpillar stood with arms crossed, taller and leaner than I remembered, every edge of his silhouette sharp and deliberate. His eyes flicked over me, then Theo, then back again, cool and calculating.

"So, Alicia, are you ready for the next leg of the adventure?," He asked, voice flat as stone.

I took a careful step back. "What are you all doing here?"

Caterpillar lifted one perfectly arched eyebrow. "Guiding you. Watching you. Betting on whether you survive. Take your pick."

Cheshire dropped from his perch in a lithe arc, landing on his feet with a muted thud, then straightened until he was at his full height—limbs elongated, grin widening. "You've come farther than the last one," he said, voice layered with secrets.

A cold prickle ran down my spine. "I am obtusely stubborn in the face of certain doom."

He only smirked and leaned in but said nothing. Of course.

March nudged my shoulder, expression softening until his eyes were almost warm. "This is the part where we either wave goodbye or follow you through." My throat tightened. "Follow me through?"

"At your discretion," Theo said, jaw clenched. "The Gate only responds to the Key. Anyone else who steps across risks... warping."

"Or worse," Caterpillar added with impossible calm.

I studied them all—Cheshire, grin and riddles; March, fierce heart and cinnamon scars; Caterpillar, ancient stillness. They were my friends (sort of), my allies, my ragtag family in this fracturing world.

"You don't have to come," I told them, voice steadying. "This part's mine."

March shrugged, shoulders loose. "Maybe. But some battles aren't fought with swords. They're fought by standing together when everything tilts sideways." Theo's eyes met mine, searching. "Are you sure?"

I swallowed. "No," I admitted, "but I'm going anyway."

I lifted my hand; breath caught in my throat—

And pressed my palm against the Glassless Gate.

The instant my fingers brushed the glass, the world shuddered beneath my touch—not a tremor, but a shiver, like a spine pressed against ice or a memory clawing at your bones. The mirror's surface bulged and rippled outward in a slow-motion shockwave, each widening circle dissolving my reflection—and the familiar forest beyond—into something far older, something that watched with patient hunger.

Then reality flooded back all at once: colors bled sideways across my vision, gravity forgot its rules, and my body stretched like molten taffy before snapping back with a silent pop. My lungs burned as they remembered how to draw air.

I landed on scorched earth with a hollow thud, choking on ash that danced in the wind like ghostly motes. Gasping, I scrambled upright. The sky above was a bleached ivory webbed with angry red veins. Around me, the land gaped open in jagged black rock and the shattered trunks of obsidian trees—each shard pointing toward a distant crown-shaped peak. At its summit loomed a fortress carved from charcoal stone, smoke trailing from its tallest spire.

This was the Queen's domain.

Behind me, the portal shimmered like spilled oil and shattered promises. Theo stepped through next, his stride unwavering, as if he'd always belonged in that static haze. A heartbeat later, March Hare dropped in beside me with a triumphant whoop and a hat-flourish. "Ten out of ten, would travel by nightmare portal again," he announced, voice crackling with manic glee.

Caterpillar drifted through a curl of violet smoke, skin mottled emerald and indigo, his many-limbed silhouette disapproving. "Charming," he drawled, "if you enjoy trauma for decoration."

Last of all, Cheshire materialized midair—an invisible sigh that solidified into form. He landed softly, grin already in place. "Well. She's redecorated since last I trespassed."

I turned slowly, eyes sweeping the dead landscape. Not a leaf stirred, yet everything seemed to thrum with hidden awareness.

Theo's voice dropped low. "We need to keep moving. This place listens. It learns."

I swallowed against the dry wind. "And if we wait too long?"

Caterpillar's heavily lidded gaze flicked toward me. "It sends dreams stitched from teeth and silk. They burrow into your mind, feasting on the pieces of yourself you pretend not to miss."

Cheshire's grin widened. "Then the Queen unleashes her real pets."

My heart twisted at the thought. I didn't want to imagine my own personal nightmare. Instead, I squared my shoulders and faced the distant fortress, its jagged silhouette imprinted against the horrid sky.

"And, if you survive all of that," Caterpillar says, voice taking an ominous tone, "She sends in her worst weapon of all. The Knave."

The name hit me not like a drumbeat but a cold whisper, a trap laid in the only corner of my mind not yet claimed by fear.

"I don't care how many monsters she throws at me," I said, voice steadier than I felt. "Her hold on Wonderland ends soon."

Theo slid to my side, expression unreadable beneath the ash-gray light. "Then we'd better make it there alive."

Together, we stepped forward—five dark shapes cutting across the bleached horizon, threading through a realm of ruin and secrets bound for the Queen's crown.

26

Where Shadows Learn Your Name

Alicia

We followed the jagged road, if you could even call it that, deeper into the Queen's treacherous territory. The path wasn't made of stones or dirt, but of memories—fragments of voices and thoughts stitched together into ever-shifting cobblestones. I watched as my name flickered across one stone, and a moment later, I heard the ghost of my mother's laughter echoing faintly from everywhere and nowhere at once. Before I could fully react, Theo's boot crushed it, scattering the memory into the ether.

The wind here didn't simply blow; it whispered, weaving through the air with an eerie softness. It didn't speak in words, exactly, but rather in the subtle fears you didn't realize you still harbored within.

We moved through a grove of trees, their bark resembling cracked porcelain, their leaves shimmering like shattered glass. One branch extended toward me, murmuring in a haunting tone, "You don't belong anywhere." Without hesitation, Theo sliced it off, letting the taunting words fall silent.

Every few feet revealed a new landscape: obsidian dunes that shifted and pulsed like living, breathing entities; a silver lake whose surface reflected futures instead of faces; a field of thorned lilies that wept crimson when plucked from their stems.

The March Hare hummed a jaunty, almost discordant tune to push back the oppressive silence that threatened to envelop us. Meanwhile, the Caterpillar indulged in something that smelled suspiciously like dreams marinated in honey and despair. The Cheshire flickered in and out of existence, his watchful eyes taking in everything with a mischievous gleam.

Theo stayed close. Too close. Just enough that I could feel the heavy weight of everything he left unsaid, hovering like an unspoken promise. We didn't speak. Not until we reached the fork in the path.

Two trails diverged before us. One led ominously toward the Queen's palace, now looming ever closer—its form a blurred silhouette, as if the world itself refused to fully acknowledge its existence. The other path curved into a narrow glade of twisted, ancient oaks.

Theo halted, his eyes fixed ahead.

"We're taking a detour," he announced, his voice steady.

Cheshire raised an incredulous brow. "Sentimentality? From you?"

The March Hare sighed with theatrical flair. "Ah, yes. Our brooding hero's tragic backstory interlude. It was bound to happen eventually." Ignoring their banter, Theo looked only at me, his gaze intent and unwavering. "There's a place," he said. "Off the Queen's radar. We'll be safe there. For the night."

I nodded without asking for more details. I didn't want to imagine what a night in this surreal landscape would be like without shelter.

The path wound tighter, forest pressing in on all sides. Eventually, the trees gave way to a clearing—and at its center stood a small stone cottage, overgrown with ivy and draped in the stillness of forgotten things.

It looked… untouched by the rest of Wonderland. As though the Queen's reach stopped just short of its walls. Theo hesitated at the threshold. "This was your home," I said, softly, somehow knowing it to be true. "Once," he replied. "Before everything changed."

Inside, it was dust and memory. A half-burned candle sat on the mantle. A cracked mirror faced the hearth. A blanket still rested on a chair like someone meant to come back. Theo moved through the space like he didn't dare touch it. March Hare immediately found the liquor cabinet. Caterpillar discovered a cupboard full of expired tea. Cheshire phased through the wall and disappeared to "check the perimeter."

I remained by the hearth, staring at a faded photo on the mantel. It was hand-drawn—charcoal outlines of two figures. A girl with a crown of thorns. And a boy beside her. Eyes sharp. Smile sad.

I didn't ask, I already knew.

Theo was already kneeling beside the hearth, lighting a fire that sparked too easily for such old wood.

"Why bring me here?" I asked finally. "To show me the ghost of who you were?" He didn't turn around. "No. To remind myself."

I moved to sit across from him, the flickering light stretching our shadows into giants across the walls.

"You've spent this whole journey trying to protect me," I said. "But not once have you told me *why* I matter. Why *you* care."

He looked up, firelight caught in the angles of his face. "Because if you fall... she wins. Again." I swallowed. "The Queen?"

He nodded once. Slowly. "What did she do to you?" His jaw flexed. "More than I'll ever admit. And less than I deserved."

Silence.

Then—softly, tentatively—I reached across the space between us and laid my hand over his. He froze.

"Whatever you're trying to carry alone," I whispered, "you don't have to anymore." He looked at our hands, then at me. And for one raw second, his mask cracked. Not physically. Not like the masquerade. But something *in him* loosened. He turned his palm under mine, fingers brushing—*clasping*—just for a breath too long.

"Alicia..." he said, voice fraying at the edges. But whatever he was going to say died on his tongue. Because outside—the wind changed.

It hissed. And somewhere not far beyond the clearing, the Queen's pets began to howl. It went on for what seemed like hours but could have been less.

As the distant howl died away, its echo clung to every beam of the old cottage, setting its timbers humming with unease. Candlelight danced across the walls, throwing tall, twitching shadows at the windows as though they were leaning in to catch every secret.

Theo, by this point, stood rigid by the heavy oak door, shoulders coiled like drawn springs. His hand hovered over the hilt of a slender blade—one I'd never seen before—its steel catching flickers of the firelight. He hadn't spoken since the first eerie cry split the air, and neither had I. I was terrified that if I broke the silence, I'd break entirely. My emotions a turmoil of chaos, terror, and budding feelings.

Instead, I occupied my hands with meaningless gestures: prodding embers until they flared, shifting a stack of chipped pottery from one corner of the hearth to another, brushing lace curtains into perfect folds. All the while, the pulsating emblem on my wrist throbbed in time with my racing heart.

At last, I forced the words free. "You were going to say something back before the howls." Theo's shoulders tightened further, but he didn't look at me. "No, I wasn't."

"You were." Heaving out a breath as if expelling the night itself, he murmured, "I changed my mind."

"That's not how feelings work," I shot back, voice sharper than I intended. He turned then, slowly, so that the firelight sculpted his face with dark angles and half-hidden sorrow. "And what would you know about feelings like mine, Alicia?"

The question stung. "Try me."

His breath caught for the merest fraction of a second. "You think you want the truth. But you only want the parts that fit neatly into your picture of this world."

"Show me the rest," I whispered, my voice cracking. "I can take it."

He shook his head. "No." He leaned forward, closing the scant space between us. I held my ground.

"You are so damn stubborn." He blinked, as though I had upended the very ground. Then his voice dropped to a hoarse, fragile whisper: "I shouldn't care this much. I didn't mean to."

My throat tightened. I exhaled, bridging the last inches of distance. "Then stop pretending you don't."

His hand rose, hesitating just beside my cheek—so close I could feel the warmth radiating from his skin, yet unmoved by his fingers. They trembled in the charged stillness between us.

"This place—this world—it warps us," he breathed. "Turns us into reflections of our worst fears. You think I'm immune?"

"No," I said softly. "I think you're fighting it."

A sigh, rough and broken. "I'm losing."

Without thinking, I laid my palm against his chest, feeling the frantic hammer of his heart beneath my fingertips. "Then let me fight with you."

His eyes fluttered shut, as if the weight of that promise threatened to crush him. When they opened again, pools of grief stared back at me.

"You don't know what you're asking."

"Maybe not," I admitted, leaning forward until I could taste the ghost of his breath on my lips. "But I know why I am."

His mouth parted as though he would speak a confession, something dangerous and true, but the instant shattered.

Outside, the howling returned—closer now, threaded with a hungry urgency.

Theo jerked back, tension coiling at every joint. "Rest," he said, voice rough with regret. "You need it."

He turned away as if the motion pained him, and I let him—only because I knew that next time I reached for him, I wouldn't let go.

27

RSVP to Your Own Doom

Alicia

The morning light slanted through glass windows as I settled onto a high-backed chair at the breakfast table. It was a bizarre scene as I took in my companions, a hodgepodge of wannabe heroes.

March had commandeered the end seat, legs sprawled, powdering the remains of a scone into his tea while narrating the history of his scandalous footrace with a pack of badgers. Caterpillar regarded an omelet with the suspicion of a bomb technician, dissecting it bite by bite with the tip of a silver fork. Cheshire hovered in a liminal state, little more than a disembodied grin and a set of sly, slitted eyes, his body flickering in and out of definition like static on an old television.

We ate. Or pretended to. I let the flavorless bread turn to paste in my mouth, more interested in the way Theo's knuckles whitened around his cup than in the food. He'd said nothing since sunrise. Even after last night—even after the

190

way he'd reached for my hand as the dark pressed in, like it might keep him from dissolving—he'd retreated again behind the same old wall. The way he kept his face turned away from mine told me more than words ever could.

Outside, the wind had stopped. Nothing moved beyond the window. Not even the birds dared.

Then the scroll arrived.

It wasn't borne by owl or raven—or one of those punctilious postal pigeons. No. It drifted down from the shadowed rafters, a coil of blood-red fabric unfurling behind it like a ribboned wisp of menace. The air filled with the dark, heady perfume of wilted roses and something far colder: the promise of slow decay.

It touched the tabletop with a barely audible sigh—a silk-gloved caress that sent a tremor skittering down my spine.

Cheshire sat across from me, unblinking, his eyes slitted and curious as polished amber. The unnecessary candlelight danced in his grin but never reached those still pupils. Caterpillar, hunched at the end of the table, emitted a guttural rumble that rippled through five languages—and sounded suspiciously like an oath. His many-jointed fingers tapped the edge of his teacup.

Theo froze mid-sip, porcelain teacup halfway to his lips, as though stone had claimed his heart. I poked at the scroll with the tip of my silver fork. "Is this cursed? Poison-tipped? Whispering dread spells in Latin?"

"Definitely don't open it," Cheshire replied, voice smooth and low.

"Absolutely do not," Caterpillar agreed, eyes narrowing.

Theo didn't answer. Didn't even look up. He only murmured, "Too late." Because curiosity got the best of me and I'd already peeled back that ribbon.

The parchment was as fine as dragonhide and yellowed with age, its edges curled like drying petals. Gold embossing traced arabesques along the margins, glinting when the light hit it just so. The handwriting was impossible—serpentine loops, precise yet savage. It read:

Dearest Alicia Hightower,

I hope you're settling in nicely. It's always such a delight when one of my pieces returns to the board.

You've made quite the impression already—wandering my kingdom, disturbing my histories, dreaming of knives.

I find myself... intrigued.

Consider this a formal invitation to the Knave's Ball.

Come. Bring your questions. I so enjoy breaking things open.

—R.Q.

Beneath those curling initials lay the faint, trembling imprint of a blood-red kiss. I lifted my gaze. "So. That's not ominous at all."

"It's a trap," Theo said with quiet certainty.

"Obviously," I deadpanned.

"She doesn't send invitations," Caterpillar added, voice

hushed. "She sends lace-dressed warnings."

"And if you refuse?" I pressed.

"You live longer," Cheshire offered, voice like velvet.

"But I learn nothing."

Theo's eyes met mine—dark, unreadable. "You're not ready."

"You keep saying that," I said, heart thudding like a war drum. "But the dreams are worsening. The books shift on their own. The Queen reaches from behind her fancy throne. I'm not ready because—no one will tell me what I need to do."

His throat tightened. A flicker of something raw. "You know what she meant by 'pieces.' What does that make you?"

He turned away. Effectively dismissing the rest of the conversation.

That night, I found a second scroll tucked beneath my pillow. No fragrance. No flourish. Just black ink smeared with something red—blood, or sorrow, I couldn't tell:

Don't trust what you see.

Only a heavy parchment bearing a single heart, its edges inked in a deep crimson that seeped down in rivulets like fresh blood. A fault line cracked the symbol exactly in half, the two lobes parted as if torn by invisible hands.

I held the paper before me, eyes stinging from the firelight's glare, focusing until the room spun. That heart… it pulsed on the page. A familiarity stirred within my ribs: the weight of a confession. Each letter must have been scratched out in agony, the ink infused with the writer's tremors and unspoken sorrow.

Theo? The thought hammered in my mind, refusing to be quiet. It couldn't belong to him. He was too cautious. He would never leave something so bold in the Queen's reach. And yet. Theo had changed. His smiles were lopsided these days, his silences prolonged, as though something inside him was splitting open.

I glanced at the edge of the scroll and ran my thumbnail along its fibers, half-expecting a nip, a trick. The parchment didn't flinch; it lay still in my palm, humming with unsaid warnings and raw intent.

Gingerly, I folded the note, the crease snapping sharply in the hush, and tucked it beneath my thin mattress: close enough to cradle, far enough to deny. My heart thundered, but sleep slipped beyond my grasp.

I drifted down the hallway on restless feet, the floorboards cool beneath my bare soles. The kitchen lay ahead, draped in the rose-gold glow of embers. There stood Theo, his sleeves rolled to the elbows, forearms dusted with ash, shadows pooling in the hollows of his shoulders as if reluctant to let him go.

He stirred the coals with a poker, eyes averted as I stepped in. The hearth crackled, sparks swirling upward like fireflies.

"You couldn't sleep?" His voice was low, a soft rasp that settled in my chest.

"Too many cryptic messages," I admitted, leaning into the lintel. "And borderline poetic death threats." I shot him a wry glance. "Your contribution?" He paused, brow furrowed. "Dreams?" he asked.

"No, goth notes."

At last, he turned. Moonlight glinted on the silver shadow

along his lids. His lashes stretched long and dark, as if they were curtains concealing everything he felt. But still, he said nothing.

Between the crackle of flames, we exchanged a silence thick enough to taste. I broke it at last. "If this ball is a trap, we need a plan to spring it, not waltz into the lion's den."

"The Queen wants you," he said, his words soft as ashes drifting on the wind. "Every version of you. Especially the one you fear."

"The one in my visions," I breathed.

He said nothing, but his jaw worked, muscles taut as steel cables.

I stepped closer, firelight tracing the angles of his face. "You act as though I'm already lost," I said, voice softer than I felt.

He shook his head, shadows dancing in his soulful eyes. "Not lost. Just… in danger."

I reached out, fingertips trembling as they hovered near his chest. "Then anchor me. If I slip—if I become her—stop me. You keep saying I'm not her. Prove it."

His lungs drew in a ragged breath. "I can't," he said, voice cracking like thin ice. "If I hold on too tightly… I'll drag you under with me."

I held his gaze. My pulse pounded. "You're not the man I thought you were," I said, the words a tight knot in my throat.

His eyes flickered with something like regret. "And yet you follow anyway."

"Because part of me still trusts you."

He closed his eyes for a breath. "That part might be wrong."

I crossed the space between us, each step a defiance. "It might also be the only part that's right."

He reached for me then—slowly, hesitantly—the lightest brush of his fingertips against mine made me catch my breath. But before there could be more, he drew back as though the touch stung him. "Sleep, Alicia," he murmured, voice laced with warning. "The Queen's games begin at dusk." Against the hush of the night, he slipped away, leaving the last echo of his footsteps to fade—and the moment untouched, like a secret locked behind his retreating back.

* * *

The hallways in my dreams looked the same—too polished, too quiet—but something had shifted. The air smelled sharper now, like ozone after a lightning strike. In one of the tall windows, I caught a glimpse of my reflection—and froze.

It moved a half-second too slow.

I didn't look again, too afraid of what I might see.

Up ahead, the corridor curved into shadow. No torches. No moonlight. Just a stretch of velvet black so thick it swallowed the sconces on either side.

I hesitated.

Then I stepped forward.

One pace. Two.

My footsteps stopped echoing.

Then a voice followed me.

"You're late."

I whirled around. Nothing. The dark thickened, pressing against my ears like water.

"Don't worry, Alicia. Everyone runs late to their own undoing."

My breath fogged in the sudden cold. The voice came from

everywhere and nowhere—like it was *stitched into the walls themselves.*

"Still wearing hope like it's armor, I see. Careful. You'll rust before the Queen even touches you."

My fists clenched. "Show yourself."

Silence.

Then:

"I already have."

Something brushed past me—cold and invisible. I staggered back, heart hammering.

"Do you think he'll tell you?" The Knave again, his tone almost fond. "Your Hatter? Do you think he'll warn you before the end?"

"I trust him," I said. Shaky. Stupid. But true.

"Then you've already lost."

I turned again—faster this time. There—just beyond the reach of the candlelight—a shape. Tall. Still. Watching.

I took a step forward.

It vanished like smoke drawn into a breath.

"Enjoy the masquerade, Key. Masks are so very… *revealing.*"

"Yeah?" I ask, "So are you coming over here or what? I'm too tired to chase you around right now."

The Knave stepped into the edge of light, movements fluid but off, each limb articulating in ways that suggested he had learned how to be human by watching mannequins dance. He wore a crisp suit the color of old blood, and around his right wrist, a ribbon—a twin, I realized, to the one that had bound the invitation from the Queen. "Better darling?" he asked, tilting his head, so the crack in the mask aligned with the line of his mouth, making it look like it was full of teeth.

I took two steps back, but the hallway didn't lengthen. The

Knave took two in tandem, neither closing nor widening the air between us. Balance, even in menace. "You're good at this," I said, voice thin but steady. "The looming. The cryptic threats. You could teach a master class." "I've taught many," the Knave replied. His smile sharpened. "But few students last. Most lack your… resilience." He advanced, that slick marionette grace, until we could have reached out and exchanged heartbeats. I flinched, but stood my ground— if there was ground to stand. He circled me, head canted as though examining a specimen beneath glass. "You're different than the last one." I shivered. "Does that make me more dangerous, or less?" "Neither. Just more interesting." He stopped at my shoulder, close enough that I caught the salt-and-metal tang of his cologne. Close enough that if I turned my head, I might brush my lips against the fine seam of his mask. His voice was silk over razor wire. "What is it, Alicia Hightower, that you want most?" A mirror-flash of Theo's hand, warm and shaking in mine. The sharp certainty that I would never belong anywhere, not even in my own skin. But this, too, was a test. I shrugged the memory away. "I don't know."

"Try harder," he said, and the mask's lips stretched wide. "The Queen wants you shattered. The Hatter wants you whole. I want to know which is more beautiful at the breaking point."

I laughed—brittle, but alive. "You'll be waiting a long time."

"Patience is my only inheritance," the Knave replied, eyes glittering behind the fissure of porcelain. "That, and a singular talent for opening doors." He leaned closer. "You know, I could help you. If you asked, very nicely."

"Is that another trap?"

"Of course it is. But wouldn't Wonderland be dull without

them?" I shook my head. "You're not half as clever as you think." The Knave's tone slithered into a whisper. "That's where you're wrong, Alicia. We're all exactly as clever as we think—just never in the ways that matter." He straightened, lapels crisp, and offered a shallow bow. "Enjoy the ball, Key. I'll see you there."

He vanished. The hallway, suddenly ordinary, looked smaller, shabbier. I leaned against the wall, breath rattling. I hated that he'd made me doubt—even for a second—what I wanted from all this.

28

A Face for Every Lie

Alicia

I sat perched on the edge of the cushioned window seat, the faded brocade beneath me warm to the touch, my fingers nervously twisting a ring I didn't remember sliding onto my own hand. Its metal was cool and smooth, an otherworldly silver threaded with pale blue veins that glowed faintly—the same phosphorescent hue my mark took on when it burned too bright, too loud beneath my skin.

Somewhere behind me, a floorboard groaned underweight. Theo's presence was a quiet gravity in the room. When I finally looked over my shoulder, he stood just inside the doorway, framed by the gilded morning light. He was still wearing that deep midnight-green coat from yesterday—the one that draped over his shoulders like royal velvet, making him look part fallen prince, part dangerous mystery.

His eyes, dark as wet moss, traveled over me in a slow sweep: the rumpled fabric of my dress, the restless twist of my fingers, the pale bruise of dawn beneath my eyes. "Couldn't sleep?"

he asked, voice low and steady, as if testing the room's fragile calm.

I let my shoulders slump. "Kept dreaming I was drowning in rose petals and riddles. Not exactly spa vibes." I gave him a half-smile that felt more like scraping blade.

He moved to the far wall, planting his back against the plaster as if bracing himself. Arms crossed, jaw clenched, he watched me with a tight restraint. "Tonight," he said at last, words low and measured, "everything changes."

I raised an eyebrow. "Wow. Vague and ominous. You're really leaning into the brand."

His eyes flickered. "I'm serious."

I folded my arms over my chest. "So am I."

Between us, the air grew heavy—stilled like a spider's web trembling in the hush between two heartbeats. Dust motes drifted in the sunbeams, tracing invisible lines from past to future.

My heart hammered as I rose to my feet, skirt whispering against cool floorboards. "You've been keeping things from me," I said, voice cracking under its own weight. "About the Queen. About this whole twisted prophecy."

He said nothing for a long while—didn't deny, didn't look away. Just held my gaze, shadows pooling beneath his eyes. "I had to," he whispered, too low for certainty to leave his throat. "You needed time—to grow into this."

His words came out as a half-truth wrapped in concern.

"Into what, Theo?" My voice rose despite the tremor. "A weapon? A puppet? Some enchanted lock-picking tool meant to unleash Wonderland's darkest horrors?"

His jaw twitched. The green of his coat looked almost black in that moment.

"You're not a weapon," he said, but his voice lacked conviction. "You're… you."

I stepped closer, anger sharpening my tone. "Then why do you look at me like you're waiting for me to shatter?"

His gaze softened, pain flickering in those green depths. "Because I'm worried about how the story ends."

The confession struck me in the chest like a stone.

I opened my mouth to say something—anything—but the words caught in my throat. I thought of his sister, of the sweetness she once was, and the ruthless monarch she'd become: the Queen of Hearts. How he'd watched her slip away and feared the same fate for me.

Before I could sort through the tumult in my mind, he straightened, the shift in his posture all crisp lines and distance. "There's a gown being delivered," he said, voice clipped. "The Queen will expect you dressed appropriately. Refuse, and the consequences won't be kind. I have hired help to assist you and prepare."

I blinked, heat rising in my cheeks. "So that's it? Another ball I never asked for, and you slip back into cryptic bodyguard mode?"

He turned away, shoulders very still. "I have been summoned by my sister, a demand I cannot refuse. I'll see you before you leave," he promised, tone unreadable. But something in his eyes was already retreating. Already letting go. Before I could stop him, he turned and disappeared down the hallway—swallowed by golden morning light and too many secrets.

* * *

The palace emerged from the fog like a surreal fever dream, its ethereal presence both haunting and mesmerizing. Obsidian spires reached skyward, laced with intricate thorns that gleamed with a golden hue beneath the eerie glow of a sickle moon. Fireflies swirled in spiraling constellations, their trails of flame weaving through the air with mesmerizing grace. The music—a low, lilting melody that seemed slightly off-tempo—drifted from unseen strings, winding its way through ivy-draped archways like tendrils of smoke curling through the night.

As I stepped out of the carriage, an almost reverent hush settled over the world. The gown they had chosen for me shimmered like moonlight cast upon the surface of ink, its fabric clinging to my form as if spun from the very essence of shadows and stitched together with whispers of secrets. The sleeves hung delicately off my shoulders, as fragile and daring as an unspoken challenge. Silver embroidery swirled along the hem in intricate patterns, like stories written in a language I could not yet decipher. A mask—crafted from carved silver and veined with obsidian—rested lightly across my face, transforming me into someone I barely recognized.

Caterpillar extended a hand to help me descend, his expression unreadable. March offered a two-fingered salute, his eyes uncharacteristically sharp and devoid of his usual irreverence. Cheshire materialized at my elbow, his grin wide but not reaching the depths of his eyes.

"Theo?" I inquired, hope tinged with uncertainty.

Their silence told me everything. Words were unnecessary. He wasn't here.

A pang of disappointment tugged at my heart, but it quickly rose again, buoyed by anger and a stubborn refusal to break for someone who habitually walked away.

With a dramatic flourish, a crimson carpet unfurled before me as the grand doors of the ballroom creaked open, their sound like the exhalation of a held breath. Inside, a world of sparkling opulence awaited—glass chandeliers cast shimmering light across marble floors, while dancers moved with grace, wrapped in silky finery, and the tension of unspoken secrets. A thousand masks. A thousand mysteries.

And somewhere in the midst of it all, the Queen of Hearts herself awaited.

I lifted my chin defiantly.

Let her wait.

The ballroom yawned open before me, a cavern of excess that threatened to swallow me alive. Carmine velvet drapes hung in heavy swaths from towering windows, their folds dripping like fresh blood. Ivory marble pillars gleamed under the chandeliers, veins of gold streaking across their polished surfaces as though sunlight had been poured too thin and left to harden. Everywhere, color bled and blended—scarlet, cream, gilded yellow—so vivid it felt like walking inside a fever dream.

Dancers spiraled across the inlaid floor in impossible arabesques, their masks glittering with sequins and filigree. Their laughter pinched the air, too sharp and measured—as if joy itself were an actor reading lines. Every note of music, every rustle of silk, echoed unnaturally, as though the room itself refused to believe in celebration.

I stepped in. The air was warm with the scent of rosewater and burning beeswax, sticky under my skin. Caterpillar melted into the shadows by a rosewood pillar, murmuring something about surveillance sigils. March slipped away toward a table heavy with silver bowls of spiked punch, the crimson liquid catching the candlelight like molten rubies. Cheshire vanished altogether in the flick of a grin and the scattering of card-paper wings.

And suddenly I stood alone at the head of a broad marble staircase, watching the maelstrom below. A page in red drifted toward me, bowing so low his cloak nearly brushed the steps. His voice snapped when he spoke—like glass cracking in winter. "Your arrival has been noted. The Queen will be… delayed."

Delayed? I arched an eyebrow against the glare of candelabras. "Delayed from her own ball?"

He did not answer. He only bowed again, the hem of his crimson coat swirling, then disappeared into the throng like smoke drawn into a chimney.

I began my descent, each footfall muffled by the carpet but heralded by the soft whisper of silk against marble. All around me, eyes turned—just a fraction too late—like actors pretending not to watch the star's entrance. My gown, pale as moonlight, whispered its allegiance with every step, betraying me in murmurs of rustling fabric.

At the far end of the hall I stopped. There was no throne. No dais. No Queen. Only a bare stage, its crimson curtain drawn shut, the emptiness behind it more foreboding than any ornate chair.

I let the hubbub wash over me. The glittering masks and polite disorder, the clink of crystal and swirl of satin—it all felt tailored for me. They didn't need to speak the truth: this was no ball. It was a performance. And I was its star, destined to unravel under the bright glare of expectation.

A passing server offered a flute of champagne. I lifted it to the light, watching pale bubbles drift like stranded fireflies. I inhaled the crisp tang of yeast and sweetness, but it offered no salvation—only the promise of bad decisions.

The orchestra swelled, drawing dancers into the next measured waltz. Still no Queen. A tight ache seized my chest. Was she mocking me? Or —was she afraid of me? The thought struck like a flensing blade: if she wouldn't show herself, perhaps she couldn't face what I'd become.

Then the music stuttered. The dancers paused mid–twirl. Every masked head tilted, turning in unison toward the grand entryway.

A figure appeared in the doorway, alone. Clad in black leather that swallowed the light, moving with the hush of midnight.

His mask covered most of his face, but the intensity of his eyes told me everything I needed to know about him. And though my heart didn't want to believe it…

…it already knew.

The Knave of Hearts. My stomach dropped like a blade.

No.

No, no, no.

It couldn't be.

But it was.

I've met the Knave before, how could I have not seen it?

He walked like smoke with a spine. Confident. Controlled. Dangerous in that quiet, deliberate way I'd only ever seen in one other person. But it couldn't be Theo. Could it? The ballroom froze as he sauntered to the center, the crowd parting like he was a celebrity arriving at a red carpet event. His coat was the color of midnight cravings, trimmed in silver that sparkled like a cocktail party under the stars. A heartshaped mask obscured most of his face, but his eyes— those eyes. Now the color of chocolate. Dark. Familiar enough to haunt my dreams like a bad hangover.

The same ones that had tracked me across fires, through impossible forests, in moments when he thought I wasn't looking. Theo. And yet not Theo. He didn't look at me right away. He didn't need to. I could feel the gravitational pull— like the universe had just decided it was time for us to tango. My insides were reaching for him like a drunk reaching for their last drink.

When he finally met my gaze, it was like watching a mirror shatter from the inside, leaving me with shards of betrayal. It was a gut punch, realizing that Theo, the man I had foolishly started to trust in this crazy Wonderland, was actually my biggest enemy. I felt like a clown at a funeral.

He moved through the crowd with the slickness of a cat who'd just found the cream; every inch the dashing villain. His gaze locked onto mine, unreadable behind the mask. I was frozen, breathless. This wasn't a plot twist—it was the punchline to a joke I'd always been on the wrong side of.

He approached, gliding over the marble with an elegance that made the other guests pale by comparison. Even the music seemed to hush, shrinking from the sudden weight in the air. The world had been holding its breath for this reunion, every eye in the room darting between us, hungry for spectacle.

His eyes never broke contact, not even as a parade of elegantly masked nobodies tried to intercept him. They wilted under that stare: withered, bowed, gave way. When he reached the foot of the staircase, he stopped and swept a bow so perfect I could hear every muscle in the room clench in envy. Laughter rippled through the crowd, but it was edged with teeth. I hated that I immediately knew how to return the gesture—chin high, lips curled in something that could almost pass as regal amusement.

I felt exposed.

Naked in a masquerade of monsters.

He was everything I feared. And everything I wanted. And suddenly, none of it made sense anymore.

He reached me and bowed once more, the picture of villainous charm. "You look stunning tonight, Alicia," he said so casually, like we hadn't just had the big villain unmasking.

His voice was smooth and violent all at once, a caress that dared you not to flinch. "I almost didn't recognize you out of context."

I swallowed, pulse a slow-burning fuse. "That makes two of us," I managed, fighting to keep my hands steady at my sides. "New part in the play?"

The smile that lingered on his lips was private—full of secret wounds and pleasures. "Not a new part. Just a different mask." He extended a gloved hand. "Will you dance with me?"

"Will I dance with you!? Are you insane?" I hissed, voice low enough to make a snake jealous. "I don't think so, Knave. Or should I say Hatter?"

He chuckled, extending his hand as if this was all some delightful misunderstanding. "Let's not make a scene. One dance. Then we can chat—like civilized adversaries."

I glared. "I'd rather you send me to the dungeon."

"Too crowded," he murmured near my ear. "Besides, you

clean up too nicely for chains."

His hand hovered, expectant and patient, while the entire room vibrated with anticipation. Every mask in the ballroom flickered with hungry glee. On a lesser day I might have played coy, or gone limp and forced him to drag me, or just kneed him in the shins. Today, with the weight of a thousand stories watching, and ignoring every ounce of common sense such as my inner alarm bells were wailing like a siren, I turned my back on the dangerous predator and began to walk away.

I heard him trailing after me, the measured cadence of his boot heels swallowing the waltz's downbeat. The guests—my audience—tilted in their orbit, waiting for a punchline or a scandal or for me to shatter right there on the mirrored floor. I would not give them the satisfaction.

Cheshire materialized in my periphery, all sly approval. "Never meet your heroes, darling. Especially when you're written to outdo them."

I ignored him, but not the heat creeping up my neck as Theo's shadow overtook mine at the edge of the ballroom. I spun on him—sharp, sudden, the skirt of my dress arcing around my ankles like a blade. "Why?" I demanded, every syllable cold as crystal. "Why pretend?"

He faltered. For the barest second, the mask slipped, and I saw the man behind it—the one I'd kissed in a ruined garden. A flicker of regret. A tremor of hope. Then, just as quickly, it was gone. Replaced by the cold Knave once more.

"You played me," I whispered.

"Did I? I never denied being the Knave. You assumed."

"That's called lying by omission, you smug, mask-wearing, tea-addicted—"

"Charming rogue?" he interrupted, grinning like a cat with

a canary.

I really should've ground my heel into his foot. Or given him a slap. Or maybe both, just to drive the point home. Instead, I settled for personal insults. "You absolute asshole. You said you'd help me. You let me— You said—"

"—what, Alicia? You said a lot of things, too." He lifted his hand, fingers splayed, as if to cradle the air between us. "You asked for the truth. This is what it looks like, raw and unsweetened." His voice, steady and strange, lapped at my anger until I wasn't sure what I felt. "I told you," he breathed as he grabbed my hand, drawing me to a less crowded area of the ballroom, "I'd get you to the queen. I keep my promises, even when they're inconvenient."

"I've never been an advocate for murder," I snarl, "But, you're kinda selling me on the whole deal, you arrogant demon." I stomped the arch of his foot with my stilettos just to see if he'd flinch. He only smirked and squeezed my waist tighter. "There's the heroine I've grown so fond of." The orchestra reached a rattling crescendo. Masks whirled past us, all hollow eyes and painted smiles. As I tried to cling to dignity, spitting venom in a whisper.

"I swear, Theo, if you so much as try to sweep me into a romantic dip, I'll rip out your throat with these fake nails." He leaned in—dangerously close—so only I could hear.

"My darling, you're about to rewrite the end of the story. If you want, you can start by breaking my heart."

"Too bad you don't have a heart." I say, emotion raw enough to slice through steel. His mouth twisted in a grin so brittle it threatened to crack the mask. I wasn't sure if I wanted to scream or kiss him again—maybe both, preferably in that order. "All this time," I hissed. "Everything. Was it just a joke to you?"

I jerked away, pulse skipping, but he followed—never closing the space fully, just orbiting, always within reach. The music changed: a slow, deathly thing, a melody to eulogize illusions. "Stop following me!" I snap, voice a whip.

He did not. "Come, love. I know you're upset. Though, a little gratitude would be appropriate. Most adversaries never get to see me in formalwear."

I shot him a glare so sharp it nearly cut through the lacquered surface of my mask. "I liked it better when you just haunted me in my nightmares." He steered us expertly through the spiraling mob, drawing more than a few spiteful glances from the bystanders—envy, fear, curiosity. "Oh, Alicia. I haunt you in daylight, too. That's the part you always forget." He was closing in, until even the air between us was so alive with charge I thought it might ignite. "I mean it," I hissed, barely moving my lips. "You could have warned me. Any time, any place. It didn't have to be—" "A masked ball? The most dramatic possible setting?" His hand shifted up to me, fingers splaying wide across the perilous territory of my back. "You, of all people, ought to appreciate the narrative economy."

"How long have you been working for her to double cross me?" He tensed, the tiniest quiver, then spun me to face him once more. "That depends," he said. "Does it count if you never see the checks?" "You're not funny." "Technically, I'm hilarious."

He backed me up against the wall, then; his hands caging me in, palms flat against the marble, heads turning from every quarter. "Is this the part where you brutally expose my villain monologue?" He whispered, just loud enough to blend into the waltz's sweep.

I tried to break his grip, but he only let go when I stilled, and then he slotted his body so close I could count the flecks of colorful prisms in his eyes. "You think you're the only one who's been played?" he asked, voice suddenly, savagely raw. "We're all puppets here, Alicia. Some of us just get nicer strings."

The orchestra fell away, leaving only the tick of my furious pulse. "What's the plan now?" I demand after a moment of hush. "March me up to the Queen? Hand over the Key and collect your reward?" Something flickered in his eyes; pain, maybe. But the mask stayed. I wasn't finished. "I had no idea you were your sister's little lap dog." I say giving him my best unaffected smirk. "Her little subservient creature." I will not let this man see how badly he has broken me. I will wear my snark like a suit of armor.

"I prefer the term 'loyal,' but thank you for the revisionist history," he said, voice even but with a tremor beneath.

"I trusted you," I said quietly, venom nearly swallowed by the rawness underneath. His grip softened, just a fraction, as though he'd heard the tremor in my voice and wished he could rewind.

"I know," he replied, and the honesty in his tone was sharp as broken glass. His fingers stroked the inside of my wrist, just once, fleeting, as if seeking forgiveness but finding only skin. In the hush before the next musical phrase, he murmured so low only I could hear: "I wasn't supposed to—" but the words shattered, dying somewhere behind his mask.

"You lied," I repeated, louder now, for the benefit of the bloodthirsty gallery. "There's not a single thing about you that's real, is there?"

He flinched. Just enough to see. I resented him for it, hated that I wanted to pull the truth through the cracks.

"You'd be surprised," he said, voice hoarse. "Most of this is as real as it gets." Still caging me in—like if he didn't, I'd slip right out of reality and be lost to the black velvet between the stars.

And maybe I would. Maybe that would be easier.

"I should stab you. Actually, I think I might."

He almost smiled, but it was sad, unconvincing. "You won't. Because you're still hoping for a way out of this."

"I don't really care how this plays out to be honest. As long as I get back to my world, Wonderland can burn in the fiery pits of hell for all I care." Shrugging my shoulders in a nonchalant gesture.

His expression clouded with a look akin to panic. "You've come all this way to chicken out now?"

"I'm not chickening out." I jabbed a finger into his chest, and it landed on the breastbone like a dull punch. I leaned in, low and mean. "I'm just not interested in being another pawn in your sister's game. Or yours."

"And you'll, what?" He asks incredulously. "Go back to your world and let Wonderland implode?"

"Absolutely." I say, not caring in the least what happens after this evening's revelations. "Wonderland has been the worst experience of my life. I don't care what happens to it. Or you."

I expected him to argue. To sharp-tongue me the way he always did, to parry my rage with cynicism and half-truths polished to a shine. Instead, he just stared—a look so long and bare I wanted to turn away but couldn't. His mask fluttered at the edge, something desperate underneath peeling through.

"You would," he said finally—voice strangled. "You'd really

let it all burn?" Not a challenge. Not even an echo of his usual sarcasm. A plea, maybe. Or an accusation with nowhere else to go.

"I'd light the match myself," I said. "After all this? After the lies, the games, the—" My voice trembled, so I swallowed the rest.

"Liar," he said, barely audible over the orchestra's rise. For the first time all night, something about him fractured. His hand slackened at my side, the heat in his eyes was unmistakable: not rage, not even wounded pride—anguish, naked and raw. "If you didn't care," he went on, "you wouldn't still be here."

"Save the melodramatics, Theo. Or do you prefer 'Knave'?" His lips barely parted. "Names don't matter. Only outcomes."

"Spoken like a true coward," I spat, twisting out of his grasp. My arm ached where his hand had been, the phantom pressure blooming with heat and—disgustingly—longing. The ballroom spun on, dancers whirling around us, but their laughter sounded shrill, staged. All eyes tracked us, savoring the spectacle. Theo didn't chase. He only hovered at the perimeter, mask inscrutable. But the muscles in his neck pulsed with tension, the thread tying him together pulled taut to snapping.

29

Time Is Fake, and So Is My Ally

Alicia

I stormed to the outer edge of the dance floor, snatching a flute of champagne—or absinthe, for all I cared—from a passing tray. The bubbles scratched my throat, a sharp little violence I welcomed. Cheshire reappeared at my side, not quite corporeal, the air around him buzzing with static. "So," he drawled, "how goes the lovers' quarrel?"

"Go fuck yourself," I snapped. Cheshire winked, unfazed. "Most certainly, but I must say, I am enjoying the show." March sidled up behind, a bright carnation between his teeth and a bloodied handkerchief at his cuff. No idea. "Strong entrance, Alicia. Ten points for dramatic reveal, fifty for the stomp on the Knave's dignity." I eyed the dance floor for a heartbeat, unable to quell the tremor in my wrist—the mark pulsed with a feverish glow, as if it fed on my anger. "If either of you knew about Theo," I said, low and dangerous, "I will personally see to it that your afterlife is spent in a room full of malfunctioning smoke detectors."

215

Cheshire's eyes glinted behind his smile. "No one can know the other side of a mask, my dear. Isn't that the whole point?" March hummed agreement and offered me the handkerchief, presumably for emotional purposes, though frankly I was more inclined to use it as a tourniquet if necessary —or possibly as a weapon, if the opportunity presented itself.

I brushed his hand away and squared my shoulders, barely noticing the way the crowd's attention orbited around me now, the entire ballroom watching for what I'd do next. They were vultures, every one of them, feathered in silk and gossamer, faces folded behind their own false selves. They wanted blood, or spectacle, or both. I flipped them off causing a wave of gasps of horror to reverberate around the room. Grinning, I turned back to the idiots I was stuck with in this half-mad fairy tale. "If the Queen wants me as her showpiece, she's going to get a performance," I growled. March clapped. "Break a leg, darling."

I didn't get more than two steps before Theo appeared at my side again. "What?" I snap, not even bothering to look at him.

He didn't answer at first, but his sleeve brushed mine—an accidental touch, or the closest thing he allowed himself to an apology. "We need to talk. Outside. Alone."

"No, we don't."

He flinched at the acid in my words. Not visibly, not in any way that the mask-and-gown crowd could see, but I felt it—a ripple, a tightening just under the surface of him. "Please," he said, softer, and it gutted me more than a thousand sharp words could have.

"Absolutely, not." I say, doing my best to channel what I hope is indifference.

It must have worked because his voice became a low hiss. "Out. Side."

"No. Go away."

His hand found my elbow—soft, persuasive, and absolutely infuriating. Before I could resist, he steered me through a set of terrace doors, the night air licking at my bare shoulders. Above, the sky was stitched with trembling blue stars, like someone had splattered paint across a velvet canvas. The garden below was more shadow than shape, a maze of trimmed hedges and marble statuary glistening with dew. I yanked my arm loose as soon as we passed the threshold. "If you're here to gaslight me, at least bring snacks," I spat, folding my arms to hide the tremble in my hands.

"Your cooperation could use improvement."

"Bite me."

A silence grew between us, wide and sharp as a battlefield. In the glow from the ballroom, Theo's mask caught the light and threw it back at me in shards. He seemed taller out here— less a young man, more a shadow cut loose from its moorings.

"I never wanted this," he said finally. His voice was raw, scraping up from somewhere deeper than lungs.

"Oh, please," I snapped, "don't act like a martyr now. You could have told me at any time. About her. About you."

He looked away, watching the stars. "I tried. You kept seeing what you wanted to see."

I laughed, breaking with a sound closer to a sob. "So, this is my fault. Classic."

"No, Alicia." He turned, urgent. "It's not your fault. It's—"

"Spare me the tragic backstory." I cut him off with a slice of my hand. "I'd rather die a fool than another pawn in her game."

"You are so aggravating." He complained, exasperated.

"You're not exactly a ray of sunshine yourself," I shot back, defensive. He hesitated, just a moment's pause, then closed the gap between us, every step slow and deliberate, like he was approaching a wild animal at risk of bolting. Even in the mask, I could see it—the struggle in his jaw, the tight set of his shoulders. "I didn't come here to hurt you." Every atom in him was focused on me, and it was terrifying, how much I wanted—needed—for it to be true.

"The Queen told me to keep you alive," he said, the word *alive* trembled, unsteady on his tongue. "But she said I had to break you first."

"So, this is what you do? You break the Key, and Wonderland wins?"

A humorless smile. "Wonderland always wins. You know that by now." I thought…" I start, but my voice falters. "I trusted you. I believed in you. I thought you were falling for me, too, instead, you were plotting my downfall. That's the cruelest betrayal of all." To my utter embarrassment, tears began welling in my eyes as the knife of his betrayal cuts worse than anything his sister could ever do to me.

His hands trembled at his sides—hands that, only a night ago, had gathered mine in the hush of firelight. He tried to look away, to retreat behind the battered dignity he wore like a threadbare coat. But then—slowly—he drew off his mask and held it in his fist, baring the delicate agony of his face to the night.

"My sister is dangerous," he said, voice hoarse. "You know that's not a metaphor." I laughed, short and sharp. "Okay, so that gave you the green light to pretend you cared." A muscle flickered in his jaw. "I never faked my feelings, Alicia. I knew you would be a problem from the very beginning. I wanted to hate you, it would have made my job easier but it didn't work. Every step I took away from you, I ended up right back at your side."

The words slashed through the dark, crueler for their softness. I found myself blinking, disoriented by the sudden collapse of the world into just this: a guy and a girl, and the cold gravity that kept them from touching.

His honesty made me furious. It would have been so much easier to hate him if he'd just lied, or laughed, or swept the whole thing clean under the elegant rug of villainy. Instead, Theo just stood there—hurt shining in his eyes, mask dangling from one hand, the silver and black filigree catching the moonlight between us like an apology.

I tried to look away, but anger and longing pulled my gaze back. "You know what I don't understand?" I spoke. "Why you? Why did the Queen pick you for this? Why not do it herself?" He started to answer, but I barreled on: "Is it because you're good at pretending? Because she wanted to see if I'd fall for a pretty face and a tragic story?" "She wanted you broken, not dead. That's my specialty."

"Well, gold star for commitment," I spat, blinking away hot tears. "But save your pity. I'm not your project, or your failed redemption arc. This isn't my world. I have a home, a life, a guy (I didn't), back home."

"And yet," he said quietly, "you never talk about it."

"Maybe because I've had other things on my mind like this traumatic sycophantic circus," I snapped, but the bite had gone out of it. Just exhaustion, and the ghost of a longing I'd never want to name.

The air grew sharper, colder. Wind chased a flurry of petals past our feet and sent the torchlight guttering. The hush that followed was not empty, but full of words we'd both left unsaid.

Theo's voice splintered the silence: "If you could go back, would you?" "In a heartbeat." I said, meaning it with every fiber of my being. "My life there maybe was not as adventurous as here, but it sure was better than this nightmare of betrayals and blood feuds." I scrubbed a hand under my nose, feeling the telltale burn of embarrassment, but I held his gaze. "Where love betrays you in the blink of an eye. And lies are layered so thick you doubt your own bones." My voice shook but I forced it to carry. "You think you're a master of masks, Theo? I wore mine every day before Wonderland ever noticed me." His lips parted, maybe to argue, maybe to ask what I meant, but he thought better of it. For once, he let the words belong to me. I pressed on, grasping the iron rail of the terrace so hard the cold bit through my skin. "You know why I read? Why I lived half my life in stories? Because if I screwed up in fiction, the only casualty was a plot twist. Out here, you screw up and someone gets their heart ripped out. Sometimes literally." He watched me in silence. "My world," I said, "was about as glamorous as mildewed carpet and overdue bills and the occasional rats in the walls. But it was real. There was never any question who the monster was. You didn't have to wonder if your best friend was going to betray you with a smile or if your boyfriend was plotting to shatter your mind like a chandelier." I paused, chest heaving. "I never wanted to be the hero, Theo. I just wanted a reason to keep turning the page."

He shoved a hand through his hair, wild and dark and furious.

His laugh took on a low and cruel, sound but with an undercurrent of anguish. "You silly little girl. You don't understand anything. You're naive, reckless. Too free with your emotions." The venom in his voice was such a change from his earlier tone, it caught me off guard. "Better than freezing yourself to death and hoping you forget how to feel," I fired back, my voice warped thin and sharp by misery. "But go ahead. Tell me how much smarter you are than everyone else, Theo. Explain away everything I saw in you for the sake of a neat little ego trip."

Something in me wanted to claw at him, unravel him, wrap my hands around the truth and shake it loose. Instead, I stood with my arms welded to my chest, more armor than gesture now.

He advanced on me so suddenly I flinched—a single step shrinking the distance until our faces were almost level. "You think this was easy for me?" he hissed, close enough that I could taste the bitter heat of his breath. "You think I didn't try to warn you? Every damn turn, I tried to give you an out."

I flinched. Not because he was wrong, but because he was exactly right. He did try to stall me, but I was reckless and naive and too free with my emotions—but even now, even after all the lies, I wanted to believe some part of him regretted every moment of this. Some desperate spark inside me wanted to rewrite this whole scene—make us two stupid lovers bumbling through a masquerade, not enemies on the verge of mutual destruction.

I shoved the feeling down. Dug my fingernails into my palm until the sting anchored me in place. "If you're going to stab me in the back, at least have the decency to not lie."

He was silent a long moment—so long I nearly spat my

demand again, louder. But Theo just watched me, the night pressing close, as the moon drew a ring of bone-white light around us as if to keep us from running. His silence heavy; intense. "The hour grows late, Knave, I do believe I am going to call it a night." I say, beginning to turn around. "Be sure to give your sister my regards."

I didn't get three steps before his hand caught my wrist—gentle, but unyielding. "Alicia," he said, and I stopped not for the grip but for the way he said my name: with apology, with resignation, with a hunger that frightened even him.

I didn't turn, stubborn to the core. "If you want to monologue, at least let me face away. Makes it easier to roll my eyes." He exhaled sharply—somewhere between a cynical laugh and a bitter sob. "You don't understand, do you?" he taunted, his voice dripping with derision. "I am your adversary, not your romantic ideal. Do you truly crave the truth?" His words were clipped, jagged, raw, and for a fleeting moment, I glimpsed the shadow of the man I had woven from illusions and deceit.

He drew me back—not roughly, not in a way that would bruise, but with a quiet insistence that made me want to scream. In the violence of the stars above, I thought, let them see us. Let Wonderland stand witness. Let every mask and monster feast on my humiliation.

My mask slipped, skewed along my cheekbone, the silver filigree biting into my skin. I locked eyes with him, unwavering, as he held me there, as if this solitary confrontation could sear shut the chasm between us. "The truth is you weren't the only one who cared."

The confession landed like a slap. My breath caught; I could feel my pulse in every extremity. For a long fragment of life, I was just silent, staring at the angles of his face, how the light gathered in his eyes—uncertain, desperate, undone. I'd been ready for blame, maybe for rage. This was worse. This was the one thing I never prepared for. "I don't care," I said, except my voice trembled and the words felt hollow before they even left my lips. "That doesn't make it right."

"I know it doesn't make it right. And you can say you don't care, but that's a lie."

We stood in that suspended moment, bare as nerves. The hush between us had the unsteady weight of a collapsed cathedral, the kind you tiptoe through so as not to disturb whatever faith once built it. The moon hung low, plump with secrets, casting our twin shadows across the frost-dusted terrace. Somewhere inside the ballroom, the tempo swelled, the music frantic with its own decay.

He turned me to face him, a smirk on his face. "Tell me you don't," he said, daring me to draw first blood.

I wanted to. I did. It could have been heroic, the stuff of legends: the girl who spat in the face of heartbreak and walked away. I wanted to laugh, to cut him down with a single word— but my throat locked up. You don't get to break me and then ask for the pieces, my mind screamed, but what came out was soft, a sigh barely strong enough to stir the air: "I, do. I love you, even. But, I wish I didn't."

For once, he didn't sneer. He just stood, chest tight, gaze snagged on mine, like he was waiting for me to punch him or kiss him or collapse. Instead, I yanked my hand back and knuckled away the tears, furious at myself for making this any easier on him.

I turned to the railing, fingers white-knuckled on cold marble. The world below was a chessboard of cultivated hedges and mirrored pools, every path leading back to the looming palace and its secrets. My reflection peered up from the black water—a rippled ghost of a girl in a borrowed face and borrowed courage, drowning in a night stitched for her humiliation.

He stepped closer but didn't touch me. His shadow merged with mine, taller, darker, a mirror image warped by regret.

"I know you want to hate me," he said, voice low, each syllable chipped from somewhere ancient and exhausted. "Even though I can't give you what you want— what you deserve. Know this: I do love you. I have since the moment I first laid eyes on you. If I could give you a way out, Alicia, I would. But in Wonderland, the only way out is through."

"Oh," I said, two letters that contained enough heartbreak to drown a city. He shrugged, helpless. "I'm not the only one who slipped through the cracks between stories."

I wanted to scream at him. I wanted to shake him until something—anything—gave way. But the look on his face stopped me. It was haunted. It was human. It was everything I'd hoped to find, and everything I couldn't forgive.

Breaking the silence at last, I looked into his eyes. "Here's the difference between you and me, Theo. I refuse to be a puppet for anyone. No one gets to rewrite my story but me. Go back to the Queen like the little lapdog you are. I will end her and if you get in my way, I'll end you too."

I shoved past him, the material of my gown hissing like an angry cat. For a second, I thought he might follow, or say something—a retort, a threat, a plea. But he only slid down the wall, folding in on himself the way people do when the world is too much and nothing at all.

30

Hearts, Lies, and Shattered Masks

Theo

The door shut behind her with a hiss of silk and salt. I didn't follow.

Couldn't.

The night air clawed at my throat like punishment. Each breath tasted of frost and failure. I let myself sink against the cold marble wall, knees drawn up, elbows resting on them, hands tangled in my hair like they were the only thing holding my skull together. Alicia's voice echoed—still fierce, still trembling with betrayal. I could feel it in my bones, like her words had rewritten the very framework of me.

"Go back to the Queen like the little lapdog you are."

I grimaced again.

For a long while, I didn't move. I let the cold seep into my jacket. Let the silence swallow the sting. Only then did I dare whisper it aloud, the one truth I hadn't had the courage to say to her face. "I never wanted you to see me like this."

A soft scrape of footsteps on stone broke the stillness. I

didn't look up. "I was wondering when you'd crawl out from under your dignity," came a velveted purr.

I sighed. "Cheshire."

That grin—just a mouth and a pair of yellow eyes, sharp as broken promises—blinked into existence beside me. "That was quite the performance. Bravo. Brava. Bravissimo."

"I didn't come here for a review."

"No, but you got one anyway." His body followed at last, curling languidly along the terrace railing. "You do realize she would have forgiven you. Maybe. But now..." He tsked. "Well. That door's closed tighter than a Wonderland jury."

I let my head fall back with a hollow thunk against the wall. "I had no choice."

"Oh," Cheshire said, uncharacteristically serious for a change. "You always had a choice. You just didn't like the outcomes."

A beat of silence. Then: "She'll hate me forever."

"Probably," he said cheerfully. "But then, isn't that what you wanted? You are her destined enemy. The dear brother of the Queen of Hearts." he cut in. "What's next? Will you keep dancing on the strings until they wrap around your neck?"

I winced. "That's not—" "Don't insult me with half-truths, Theo." He examined his fingernails, eyes slitted. "You peddle in loyalty the way the Queen sells pardons: transactionally, and with more regret than you'll admit." He tipped his head, almost curious. "You ought to ask yourself whether you're a villain with a redemption arc, or simply a very bad hero." I drew in a shaky breath, knuckles whitening around my knees. "Says the man who's betrayed every ruler since the Spade Dynasty." Cheshire bowed, jagged grin splitting wider. "Consistency is a virtue. And unlike some, I don't pretend my stripes are painted on." He leaned in, voice dropping low, intimate as a confession. "You have stopped every Key since your sister. Never thought twice about ending them." He grins in a malicious way. "But this one, Alicia, you have protected every step of the way. So why is her ruin salt in the wound?" The accusation landed with a quiet finality. I pulled the words around me like a shroud, wishing for some revelation of self—anything except the shapeless ache inside my chest. "Because I knew she'd make me want to be more than this."

Cheshire drifted closer, all feline grace and threat, his gaze almost gentle. "She still does, doesn't she? That's the problem. You think yourself a villain, but you're a coward. Villains at least get things done. You just wait for others to decide your story."

I bit down on the urge to argue. The marbled sky above was starting to lighten, edges of dawn splitting the darkness apart molecule by molecule. In a few hours, the Queen would expect me at her side. I would stroll in, face scrubbed clean, voice oiled and ready. Pretend I hadn't shattered Alicia's trust and my own hope in a single, dizzying moment.

I felt Cheshire's hand clamp my shoulder, sharp nails digging through the fabric. "It's almost over, Theo. You know that. Whatever end she meets in the city—on your sister's blade or her own foolishness—it will finish you, too." He crouched, yellow eyes level with mine, and the mask of amusement fell away. "So, if you want her to live, you have to start lying to someone besides yourself."

31

Shatter Me Quietly

Alicia

The moment I slipped back through the terrace doors, the ballroom swallowed me whole. A wave of heat rolled over me like a wall of flames—stiflingly bright, thunderously loud, brimming with exaggerated laughter that clanged off gilded walls. The orchestra's strings and horns swept on without missing a beat, as if the world hadn't tipped sideways and ejected me somewhere between tragedy and absurdity.

I ached to scream, to shatter every crystal chandelier with the force of my rage. Instead, I curved my lips into a smile—dangerous and brittle, the kind a girl wears after hurling her heart off a cliff and waiting for the splash.

I descended the marble staircase again, this time measured, deliberate, each footstep echoing against the carved balustrade. No longer the wide-eyed outsider. No longer a pawn to be maneuvered.

Down below, the crowd turned toward me with fresh

hunger. Whispers curled through the air like threads of perfume; heads tilted as if they could sniff out the shift I carried. There she is, they thought. The girl who brought the Knave to his knees. Let them wonder. Let them choke on it.

I made a beeline for the punch table draped in satin. I snatched a crystal goblet—its rim cool against my fingers—and tipped it back without a second's hesitation. Dark crimson liquid slid down my throat; I didn't pause to test for poison. After the emotional ambush on the terrace, a mild attempt on my life might have felt downright invigorating.

Out of the shadows, Caterpillar materialized, tall and immaculately tailored, offering me the ghost of a nod. "You survived," he murmured, voice low and amused.

"More or less," I replied, wiping my mouth on the delicate lace of my wrist. He didn't press for details. I appreciated that.

Across the parquet floor, March lifted his glass in a toast I neither wanted nor deserved, the golden liquid catching light like captive fireflies.

From behind a curtain of gilded columns, Cheshire emerged—half in shadow, half in grin—twisting a martini between slender fingers. His eyes glinted with mischief. "So," he purred, "did you rip out his heart, or simply stomp on it with flair?"

I turned slowly, chin tilted high, letting the lantern light dance across the lace and silk of my gown. "Wouldn't you like to know?"

He only chuckled, clearly pleased by my reticence.

I slipped toward the edge of the dance floor, careful not to snag the hem of my gown on the stray thorns someone had scattered like dark confetti. Fitting, really—this entire night felt like dancing through a nest of vipers.

There was no throne tonight. No Queen to command this revelry. Only that heavy curtain, the color of fresh blood, hanging over an empty dais. She hadn't appeared—not even for the Knave's grand reveal.

And now I understood why. She wasn't ready for me. She expected me to crumble under betrayal, to fall to pieces once Theo's truth was laid bare. She expected me to be destroyed.

Wrong on both counts.

Behind me, the waltz continued—spinning dancers in silks and satins, oblivious to the tension rippling through the room. Yet I could feel it: a tremor beneath the floorboards, a charged crackle behind every velvet smile, a drumbeat down in my bones.

Something was coming.

And when that curtain finally rose… I would be more than ready.

* * *

The moon was cruel tonight. It watched from above like it had front-row seats to the unraveling of Alicia Hightower and had brought popcorn.

I slipped out through the side garden gate, no fanfare, no farewell—just the soft hiss of taffeta and the crackle of frost beneath borrowed slippers. The chill sliced straight through the layers of satin and spite I wore, but I didn't care. Let the cold bite. Let it hollow me out. Maybe then there'd be room to think.

The path to the cottage was burned into my bones, every twist and stone remembered in the quiet rhythm of rage.

I didn't look back.

I couldn't.

Not after the mask came off. Not after the words. The truths.

Theo was the Knave. And worse, he wasn't sorry—not in the way that counted. He said he loved me, maybe, in his own broken way, but not enough. Never enough.

The Queen had planned this. A perfect trap, sprung with silk gloves and sweet lies. She'd dangled her monster in front of me, dressed him up in tragedy and cheekbones, and I'd fallen like a fairytale idiot.

Not again.

I felt my anger take hold, something simmering and uncomfortable unfurling inside of me. Rage built up inside of me hot and wicked.

Let it burn, I thought, and pictured the flames carving me anew, bright and angular and impossible to ignore. Let me be dangerous, if I can't be loved. Let me be the storm, not the debris.

Wind clawed at the corners of the garden, rattling last year's leaves across ice-glazed grass. The path twisted, it grew narrow, stones slick and slicker with each footfall. I nearly slipped once or twice, and it almost made me laugh. Imagine, dying alone and unremarkable, dashed bloody on a garden pebble, out of sight of every ribboned and jeweled monster back at the palace. No tragedy or rage. Just a stain on the moss.

The wind grew frantic as my own emotions reached a tipping point. I watched in shock, or maybe horror, as a rose bush to my right went up in flames. Did I do that?

Did I want to?

The bush hissed and popped, thorn-shadows shriveling as the petals blackened. Light flickered gold on my bare hands, and for a split, wicked instant I thought: Yes. Let it all burn. The flowers, the garden, the whole rotten world. Let the Queen wake to smoldering ruins, find the neat geometry of her kingdom chewed by cinders and spite. I let out a cackling sound that was more manic than humor. It felt good to get even, it felt right to destroy instead of create.

I wanted the world to know exactly how much it had broken me. And yet, as I stood there—palms trembling with the aftershock of impossible fire—I realized that it wasn't destruction I truly craved. What I wanted was for someone, anyone, to see me for what I was: not a prophecy, not the Key, not the next Queen or the Queen's Pawn, but Alicia Hightower. A girl with no map and no compass. A girl with hands she no longer recognized. These perilous thoughts only enraged me further when a second bush, farther down the path, exploded in a sickly green flare. Then a third. The fire jumped, greedy, uncontained, and my stomach swooped with an acidic thrill that was almost, if you squinted, pride. The Queen, Theo, the whole damn civilization of Wonderland wanted to break me, well, let's see what happens when I break them first.

The blaze surged, consuming the hedgerow, curling inward toward the palace like a ribbon of apocalypse. Even here, in Wonderland, even now that nothing made sense and everything tasted of heartbreak, I recognized the sick pleasure of having ruined something beautiful. Why should the Queen have the monopoly on grandeur and disaster? Why shouldn't

I leave scars in my wake? I stood perfectly still. Leting the heat wash over me, lips parted as if drinking the pain. What would Theo think if he saw me like this? Would he laugh, or run? Would he pity me, or—unthinkably—take pride? For a moment that thought made me sicker than the smoke clawing my nostrils.

The flames spat and danced, licking up the latticed trellis in a helix of orange and blue. I watched, hypnotized, until the wind shifted and the smoke stung my eyes, making them water. Or maybe that was just me—maybe that was all I had left. This must have been what the Queen felt like as she embraced the darkness instead of the light. That thought was enough to stop me in my tracks.

The second I realized how far the fire had spread, I panicked. It was one thing to torch a rose bush in a fit of pique, another to set a blaze rolling through the Queen's prized gardens, coming for the statuary and topiary like a slow-motion avalanche. This wasn't me. The darkness, the violence, I am not that person. I don't want to be *her.*

I started forward, hands raised, as if my frantic apology could un-burn what already smoldered. But the blaze just laughed at me, mocking my nerve. I began to shout for water— like a total idiot, in a world where nothing obeyed classical logic. The flames flickered, then—like a ripple in a painted mural—hesitated. For a split second, they looked back at me, hungry yet uncertain. My breath caught. The roses, the night air, even the burning seemed to pause, listening for what came next.

I crashed to my knees among the spiny roots. My gown snagged, shredding the beautiful material, but I didn't care. I pressed my hands to the frozen earth, reckless, pleading.

"Stop," I whispered, to myself or the fire or both. "Please."

I tried to remember how the stories went. How did Alice put out a fire? With tears. Well, I had plenty of those. I clenched my jaw, squeezed my eyes shut, and let my shame and grief loose. The tears came hot and ungraceful, running down my cheeks in rivers.When I opened my eyes, the garden was a mess of steam and ash, the rose canes glistening with melted frost and the blackened skeletons of petals. It looked like the aftermath of a war, or maybe the beginning of one. My hands stung, raw and trembling, and the cold felt deeper now, almost alive in the spaces the fire had left. The flames drowned out, one by one, but still the tears came.

I wiped my cheeks with the heel of my palm, snotty and blotched, and managed a laugh so sharp it made my teeth hurt. This was who I was now: a girl who set fires she couldn't control, then tried to weep away the consequences. I knelt among the smoldering thorns, fingers finding one stubborn rosebud that hadn't burned, just caramelized at the edges, sticky with sap and possibility. I tucked it into my hair, a ridiculous crown for a ruined woman, and turned toward the cottage.

32

What Could Have Been

Alicia

The cottage loomed from the trees like a forgotten memory. Shadows clung to the eaves. One window still glowed, soft and gold like candlelight, and I knew—he was already back. That was the problem with people like Theo. You could run halfway across the world and still feel them in your bloodstream, humming like unfinished songs.

Sighing, I started towards the cottage, not ready to face him but knowing I had nowhere else to go. It's better the enemy you know, I suppose.

I eased the door open. No creak. No dramatic entrance. Just me and the old bones of this place and the faint scent of burnt tea and regret. The hearth was still lit. He hadn't gone far.

I didn't call out. Didn't check the bedroom. I moved to the worn velvet chair near the fire and sank down like something had cut my strings. I unstrapped my shoes and tossed them across the room. One hit the wall with a satisfying *thunk*. My hands shook. Not from fear. From fury. From betrayal and exhaustion and that sick, clawing ache of hope dying slow in your chest.

"I know you're there," I said aloud, not bothering to raise my voice. "Come on, Knave. Don't pretend you're not lurking dramatically in a corner somewhere." He hovered in the doorway, as if proximity might ignite something between us—a last-ditch hope or an explosion, either would suffice.

He'd changed clothes, I realized. The fine coat replaced by a thin linen shirt open at the throat. He looked younger like this, and more tired, but that didn't soften me. Not tonight.

"Nice of you to drop by," he said, voice gravelly, sarcasm clinging to it like a coward's aftertaste.

Anger flared, immediate and bright. "You don't get to do that," I spat. "You don't get to act all high and mighty like I'm the villain in your story."

He flinched—subtle, a falter of the jaw—but recovered fast. "You were always the hero, Alicia. That was the problem."

I snorted, bitter. "Right. Because heroes never get tricked by the people they trust." I stood, heat radiating from my skin, challenging the embers with the glow of my rage. "You could've given me a clue, anything would have been better than this."

"You want an apology," he guessed. "You think that'll fix something." "I want the truth," I said, and the words surprised me with their hunger. I wanted the truth from him, after so many layers peeled back and found wanting—wanted it like a blade, like a key. He crossed the room but stopped short of the circle of lamplight that limned the rug. "Everything I told you before," he said quietly. "It wasn't all a lie. I meant it about your heart." He gave me a sideways look, mouth twisted half into a sneer, half into a prayer. "But I was always going to sabotage you. You… you never really had a chance." I let that settle. Then I found myself laughing, a splintered, shocking sound. "God, you're terrible at this." "At what?" "Being a villain. You keep trying, but you never quite pull it off." He blinked, slow, like he was still learning my language. "What am I supposed to be instead?" "Human." He reacted at that—subtle, but it was there.

He licked his lips, brow furrowed in pain or self-loathing or both. "It wouldn't change anything. You'd still be here, wouldn't you? Still trying to fix what can't be fixed. Still giving the Queen exactly what she wants."

I wanted to hit him, to make him hurt the way I did. My hands curled into fists. "I'm not here for her." He raised an eyebrow. "No? Then why are you in my cottage, in my chair, burning through my tea like it's the only thing keeping you upright?"

He watched me with eyes that were too right, too hungry, like the only thing he wanted more than hurting me was holding me. I hated that about him, that I could see every twist of his wanting so clear and honest. There was a truth in cruel things that you never found in kindness.

"You're right, I should go," I said, "I shouldn't have come back here."

I shoved to my feet, nearly toppling the chair, and wiped my palms down the front of my ruined dress. But the entrance was further away than I remembered, the night outside thick with frost and merciless possibility. I hesitated, just for a moment, and that's all he needed.

"Stay," Theo said. Just that—husked and hopeless, a single syllable balanced on years of unshed confessions.

He rose to his feet, crossing the distance between us one step at a time. The floor groaned under his weight, or maybe it was the universe sighing at the inevitability. His shadow fell across my bare feet.

"You're trembling," he murmured.

"Leave it to you to state the obvious."

Still, he reached for the old tartan blanket slung over the arm of the love seat, shook it out, and softly pushed me down into the seat, draping the blanket across my lap. Even then, when nothing made sense, he couldn't stop himself from the small mercies. He sat next to me, tense, but protective.

We sat there like that for a long while, the hiss of the fire chewing through silence. Finally: "I thought it would be easier," he admitted, voice stripped bare. "Once you knew. I thought you'd hate me, walk out, never look back." I stared into the fire, watching flames curl and die. "You want me to hate you that badly?"

"It's safer." His knuckles went white on the edge of the coffee table. "For you. For me. But I keep forgetting how impossible you are."

I shut my eyes, so tired I could scream. "Why do you support her? I know she's your sister, but she's straight up evil."

His voice floated out, thinner than steam. "Because she's all I have left. Because without her, I'm a ghost in a deck of strangers. Because I owe her everything, even if she'll kill me for it someday." He chuckled, hollow as a bone. "The Queen of Hearts doesn't tolerate sentimental fools, but she collects them like rare coins. You, me, even Cheshire—she holds us in the palm of her hand and makes us think we're free."

I shook my head. "That's not love, Theo. That's sadism. She's going to burn Wonderland to the ground, and you're just—waiting to see if she leaves you a corner to stand in."

He ran a hand through his hair, mussed and sharp with static. "It's not that simple."

"It's always that simple." My voice cracked. "Either you help her break this place, or you help me fix it."

We sat in the flickering dark, the space between us a chessboard crowded with every move I'd never seen coming. The tea kettle whistled its shrill despair from the kitchen, but neither of us moved to silence it.

I turned, sudden and electric. "Why didn't you kill me when you had the chance?"

He blanched as if I'd slapped him. "Because," he said, his voice a rasped confession, "I've been the villain in everyone else's story. I didn't want to be the villain in yours."

I didn't respond, because there was nothing to say that wouldn't dissolve us both. We sat side by side, staring at the embers and the dying night. I wrapped the blanket tighter, letting it cocoon me, hoping it could squeeze out the ache. Above us, somewhere in the black sweep of sky, the moon kept its voyeur's watch.

"Tomorrow?" I asked, my voice a croak, "we are back to being enemies, aren't we?"

"Yes," he whispers in a hollow voice. "But, tonight we get to be honest." He reached for my hand. No demands, no sly seduction. Just his palm, scarred and shaking, offered like a treaty.

I curled my fingers into his, gentle and tight, as if we could anchor each other for one more hour.

The fire snapped. The air hummed.

"I don't think I know how to stop loving you," I said, and the words, once surrendered, didn't break me. Not like I thought they would.

He smiled, small and sad. "That's the worst thing you could ever do to me."

"I'm serious, Theo. You pretend as if I'm nothing. Maybe, I'm not to you and that's why it's so easy."

He shook his head slowly, like he was trying to dislodge a memory. "You have no idea what you are to me, Alicia. None at all." His thumb traced the edge of my knuckle, almost imperceptible, an apology in the language of touch.

"Then tell me!"

"What good would it do?" he asked, quiet as the old clock ticking on the mantle. "It wouldn't change anything. It wouldn't make you safer." I pulled my hand away, yanked, really. "I'm not a fragile thing, Theo. I never was." "I know," he said, and the way he looked at me then—like he'd learned every constellation of me by heart, but still didn't dare to wish on any of them—made something twist deep and sharp inside my ribs. "You're angry." The corner of his mouth twitched, bitter. "You should be." "I'm furious," I corrected, because 'angry' was for toddlers and people who stubbed their toes. "I'm so mad I could set this entire city on fire. I'm mad at you. At the Queen. At myself most of all, for wanting…" I let the sentence dangle between us, poisonous and sweet. He shook his head. "That's the thing about wanting, it doesn't ask your permission." "Don't make excuses for yourself." My voice was ice. "Own what you did." He exhaled, and it was almost laughter, the sound brittle as frost. "I do. Alicia, I have loved you in every possible way: as a liar, as a coward, as the Knave and as myself. I have loved you while planning how to destroy you, and after. Especially after." The words slid into the hollows left by everything he hadn't said, and I hated how well they fit. He leaned back, rubbing his eyes. "I serve the Queen. I have no choice. But if you want to hate me, really hate me, then do it for this: I let you matter to me anyway."

I stared at the tangled fingers of fire in the grate, squinting until it blurred. My heart pulsed like a wound stitched shut but still aching underneath. I wanted to throw the blanket in his face. I wanted to crawl into his lap, beat his shoulders with my fists, and beg him to not let the morning come. Instead, I settled for leaning into him, seeking comfort in the one place I had left, pretending for a moment that the world outside the cottage was not waiting to burn us both.

His arms folded around me, slow and cautious, as though he half-expected I might turn to vapor and leave him holding nothing but chilled air. I pressed my cheek to the slope of his collarbone, breathing in those colliding scents—wood, smoke, fear, and the faintest trace of desperation.

"Who are you really?" I ask instead, sitting up to look in his eyes. "What is your real name?"

He half-laughed, then stopped himself. "Theo is my real name. I'm the boy who watched the palace walls from the gutter and thought if he became indispensable enough, he could belong. Help bring change. I'm the guy who watched his sister become queen and then a tyrant." He traced the hem of my sleeve, slow and reverent.

I laid my head against his chest, desperate to be close to him for whatever time we had left. "I may hate you tomorrow, but I need you tonight."

He held me tighter, breath catching on my hair, and I let the world narrow to that circle of heat and grief and shared hunger. We sat in silence, the kind that's so thick it smothers every impulse to speak; I could feel his heart, frantic as a moth, through the thin linen and the bones of his chest.

I didn't let go, not even when the embers collapsed and the hearth filled with soft, ashen sighs. Even when the words dried up and we were left only with the ache of what we'd done to each other. Maybe it wasn't forgiveness, but it was something—some half-step toward understanding, or surrender, or simply not being alone. At some point I needed to be closer, I brought my face up to his capturing his lips in a kiss that was all desperation and heartbreak. It tasted like loss, like last chances, like a dare. He stiffened at first, as if unsure if this was a trap or a final mercy, but when my fingers wound into his hair, he gave in with a groan that rattled us both.

We kissed as if it hurt—and maybe it did, but I'd stopped caring about pain a long time ago.

His hands were careful, always careful, even when I wanted them rough. My hands, on the contrary, were everywhere. I ran them over every plane of his body like I could learn every secret he'd never dared to say. Over shoulder blades mapped in old scars. Down the taut shiver of his back and into the hollows at his waist, memorizing the topography of someone I could not, would not ever fully have.

When he finally broke away it was only to draw me tight against him, burying his face in the wild of my hair. We clung to each other on that battered armchair as if the fire might fail and leave us to freeze. Maybe we were already frozen— the world outside the cottage a glacier, glinting and deadly, refusing to melt for anyone.

"I never asked you to love me," I whispered, not as an

accusation but as a confession.

His chest rose and fell, uneven. "No. But I did anyway."

I pressed my lips to the hollow of his throat before working my way up his jaw, the curve of his cheek, his ruined mouth. I couldn't stop. The want was a fever: dangerous, mindless, pure.

He let me. Just let me consume him, like if he held still enough, I could claw the poison out of both of us through skin and heat and hunger alone. His hands slid down my arms, not restraining, just knowing, tracing every seam of me as if they ached to memorize even this: the disaster, the aftermath, the beginning of our end.

Before I realized it, he had lifted me onto his lap, blanket and all, until I straddled him, knees braced on either side of his hips. His breath was hot against my collarbone, hands tight around my waist. He kissed me with a gentleness that bordered on cruelty, so slow and thorough it felt as if he was trying to heal every wound he'd ever given me with his mouth, or perhaps leave new wounds on top of the old ones just to remind us both how we got here.

When my fingers found the buttons of his shirt, he shivered—not with fear, but with wanting, I think—and let me undress him. The shirt slid away, baring a chest carved to perfection. I ran my hands over every inch of it, as if gathering evidence, counting ribs and faded bruises. I wanted to leave new marks, proof that I had been here, that I was not some idle fantasy conjured at the bottom of a bottle. We tumbled backwards, not quite graceful, nearly upending the chair. He caught me with a startled sound and we both started laughing, a brittle, dangerous sound that threatened to spill over into tears.

It felt right, somehow, that we couldn't do this perfectly.

His hands found the laces at my back, working them loose with methodical precision. The dress slithered down to my waist, pooling in a defeated heap. I was half-naked, shivering, but I didn't flinch from his eyes. He looked at me like I was the first sunrise after a decade of storms, a miracle that arrived bloody and unapologetic.

My nails traced the map of his shoulders, the dip of his collarbone, the line of a scar I'd never noticed before. "Does it hurt?" I asked.

"They all do," he said. Then, softer: "But some are worth it."

I forced myself to meet his gaze, searching for the lie. There wasn't one. I almost hated him more for that.

I pressed my lips to the long seam of scar, a benediction or a dare, I didn't know. He shuddered. For once, I had the power. I relished it.

I felt his hands at my sides, trembling, uncertain whether to hold me in place or send me away. Maybe both. I leaned in, whispering, "If I stay tonight, you're not allowed to lie to me. Not even in self-defense."

His smile was a war wound, raw and shining. "Cross my ruined heart."

His hands cupped my face, cold and careful, and I realized he'd been holding his breath. When I kissed him again, I tasted the truth of it, un-sweet and un-pretty—just the raw salt of two people clinging to each other's wreckage.

The blanket tangled around us as we slid to the floor, neither quite letting go, neither quite giving in. The rug was thin and scratchy beneath my knees, the hearth's heat a halo around us. I straddled him, pressing his shoulders back with my palms, and he let me. "No matter what happens tomorrow, just know that you are the first person who's ever really mattered to me. That's how I know I'm already lost," I said. I heard the shiver in my own voice and let it stay. "You got under my skin so completely, I can't find the borders anymore."

He reached up, fingers trembling as they brushed clumsy and reverent against my jaw. "Then let's stop pretending there are sides left to pick."

We moved together, nothing gentle or soft about it, just raw, unfiltered need—the kind you only get on the far side of heartbreak. His touch was electric, greedy. Mine was desperate, bruising. Every gasp, every bitten lip, every whispered curse was an admission of guilt, a tally in the ledger of things we'd never be able to take back.

For the span of a few cruel hours, there was nothing but us: the heat, the hush, the strange grace of bodies folded around each other like letters never sent. I watched the way his face fell apart in the half-light, saw the places I'd broken him, and was surprised to find myself mourning them. I wanted him whole, but I wanted him flawed, too. I wanted the ache.

It didn't last. Nothing that pure ever does.

In the hollow before dawn, I woke with my cheek on his chest and his arms locked around me, so tight I almost couldn't breathe. I didn't move. His heart thudded beneath my ear, a slow, stubborn drum refusing to quit. There was a scar beneath where my palm pressed his ribs, a jagged ridge invisible in daylight. I mapped it with my thumb, gentle, thinking of all the other wounds the world had carved into us and the ones we'd made ourselves.

He stirred awake without speaking, just tightened his grip and let out a long, steady exhale. I felt his lips drift through my hair, the weight of the moment like gravity in the air. I wanted to say something cutting or final, some last barb to push us apart. Instead, I found only the ache of wanting to stay. I held still, clinging, as the cottage pale-lit and the world gathered itself outside the steamed windows, getting ready to tip us back into war.

He broke the hush first. "You could leave now," he whispered, voice a shiver at my temple. "There's time before the city wakes."

It wasn't a threat. Not even a dare. I propped my chin on his chest and gazed up at him, at the face I'd memorized down to its smallest flaw. "If I run, she'll hunt me. If I stay, she'll break me. Isn't that how the story always goes?" He ran his hands down my back, slow and reverent, as if smoothing the creases out of a life. "Not if you break her first."

33

We Are Still at War

Alicia

I must have fallen back asleep, because when I awoke once more, the morning pressed its heavy fingers through the cracks in the cottage walls, painting the wooden floorboards in harsh stripes of gold. I lay on the straw-stuffed mattress and felt hollow, as if last night's fire had burned out every ember in my bones. Sunlight battered the windows like an unwelcome guest—too bright, too hot, too arrogant—stirring motes of dust into a slow-motion storm that danced across the room like mocking confetti.

The hearth lay cold, its red embers reduced to gray ash that clung to the hearthstone like soot fingerprints. Ghosts of heat lingered there, a memory of warmth long since vanished. I was alone. The weight of absence bore down on me sharper than any blade.

Where Theo's body had curved beneath me, above me, beside me, there was only empty space. The rough wool blanket, still knotted around my ankles, clung to the scent of him—sweat, cedarwood, something uniquely his—and I hated how my fingers tightened anyway, as if I could trap that warmth like light in a jar.

I sat up, slower than pain should allow, each movement resonating through muscles still tender from last night's recklessness and regret. My dress lay crumpled near the hearth, a pale scrap of linen stained with burn marks, lavender oil, and half-forgotten kisses. Along my ribs and hips, I traced the faint ridges of his fingertips, as if mapping the geography of loss.

I didn't cry. Not yet. Not while his scent clung to every corner of this room.

A floorboard groaned behind me. I didn't turn.

"I didn't think you'd stay," he said, voice low and rough, each word soaked in what sounded like apology.

"You left first," I answered, each syllable deliberate, my tone a blade's edge.

His shoulders slumped, as though words had weighed him down. "I needed to think."

Finally, I turned. Theo stood framed in the doorway—shirtless, ribs half-exposed, hair tousled in dark waves, shadowed eyes betraying a storm he tried to hide. The pale morning light revealed the tension in his jaw, the slight tremor in his hands.

"What do we do now?" I asked, voice soft but urgent, as though the question itself might shatter us both.

He swallowed. His gaze fell to the hearth, where he crouched and stirred the cold ashes with a trembling finger, as if seeking a spark. "This doesn't change anything," he murmured. "We're still on opposite sides."

I felt the words settle in my chest like ice. "Last night says otherwise."

He met my eyes—really met them—for the first time since he'd stepped in. "Last night was real," he admitted, voice raw. "But it was also selfish. I wanted something I knew I couldn't keep."

"My heart isn't a trinket to be hoarded," I snapped, bitter as wine left to sour.

"No," he said, softer now, wounded. "You're a wildfire I couldn't resist, even knowing the scars you'd leave behind."

His confession silenced me. My pulse thundered in my ears.

"You said we could be honest," I whispered.

"We were," he insisted, but the walls of the cottage felt suddenly smaller, closing in on us.

"The battle is still coming," I reminded him, voice rising with a tremor of fear.

He nodded, pale determination flickering in his gaze. "When it does, we'll be enemies again. Worse—a memory we try to erase."

I rose, the blanket slipping from my shoulders like the last vestige of a dream. I stood so close I could feel the heat of his skin, the rapid beat of his heart—proof that I mattered to him. "Listen carefully, Theo. I'm not here to be saved. I'm not your redemption story. I won't be the pretty regret you tuck away when duty calls."

A crack appeared in his composure, tiny but real.

"I know who I am to you," I said, voice steady despite the tremor in my limbs. "So tell me—who are you to me? What am I supposed to do with someone who wounds me so precisely?"

He had no answer. Perhaps that was the truth we both needed.

I gathered my discarded clothes and walked toward the

washroom, shoulders straight, refusing to look back. Let him ache. Let him wonder how it feels to risk losing the one thing he never expected to care for so fiercely. Let him know that some fires, once ignited, change everything they touch.

34

No Safe Way Back

Theo

She didn't slam the door. She closed it so softly that it whispered against the frame—and that silent departure cut deeper than any outburst. A slammed door I might have tolerated—righteous fury flaring up and then burning out. But the way she turned, spine straight, shoulders trembling only once, left a jagged ache in my chest, raw and unhealed.

Alicia was never going to be mine, not in the way I'd dreamed. Not with the shadow of my choices looming over every promise. The hearth's last embers lay dull and gray, and I couldn't summon the will to coax them back to life. What was warmth worth here, where every wall held a memory I couldn't escape, every mote of ash carried half-truths I couldn't bear?

I drifted through the cottage like a ghost collecting souvenirs from my own life. I found my coat hanging by the door—heavy wool, midnight black—slipped my arms into its sleeves as though I could armor my heart. Gloves followed, lined in soft leather. I secured my twin knives inside the lining, their cold weight a reminder of obligations I couldn't abandon. Then I picked up my mask, its cracked porcelain facade perched on the table like a question I already knew the answer to.

Last night, in the hush between two heartbeats, I'd believed we could press pause on all this. Holding her beneath the low-burning candlelight had felt like salvation—like maybe I still had a choice. But dawn had come with its own reckoning. Alicia had breathed life back into me, made me feel human, and the Queen would never forgive that.

I stood in the center of the room, mask in one hand, my unmasked heart in the other, listening to the silence surrounding me. How many more lines could I cross before I forgot who I'd been? If I ever really knew.

The truth was simple. I belonged to the Queen. Service had never ended. But loyalty—loyalty had frayed beyond repair.

Outside, the wind had shifted. I felt its fingers through the floorboards and ribs, promising something ancient, something sharp and hungry on the horizon. The Queen was moving her pieces. And no matter how desperately I wanted to be something else, I was still her knight.

I glanced at the back room, where she'd stood moments before—her breath trembling with fury, her hair drifting in the silence she carried like a cloak. I almost opened the door, almost defied every rule to fall at her feet and plead for her to see past the monster I'd become.

But love does not save monsters. Alicia deserved more than a man shackled to her enemy. So I left without a word. No note. No excuse. Only a locked door and the faint, clinging scent of last night's perfume—sweet and sinful—burning on my skin.

Outside, the sky pressed down in a slate-gray warning. My boots cracked over frost-hardened earth and scattered regrets. In the distance, the Queen's castle loomed—towering spires carved from bone and shadow, windows like watchful eyes. It stood silent, eternal, waiting.

I set one foot before the other toward its gates, the weight of every choice pressing on me. I walked on, pretending I still had a choice.

And somewhere deep inside, I prayed that Alicia Hightower would be the one to stop me.

35

Calling the White Knight

Alicia

The cottage was empty when I came back out.

Not in the physical sense—Theo's scent still clung to the room like woodsmoke and old confessions, the blanket still draped over the chair, half-folded like he meant to return.

But I knew he wouldn't. Not yet. Maybe not ever.

Not until this was over.

Outside, dawn had crawled into the sky like a wounded thing, bleeding pink and gold across the treetops. I didn't stop to rest. I didn't let myself ache. Not yet.

They were waiting.

I found them exactly where I expected—sprawled in various states of chaos around the clearing behind the cottage.

March Hare was asleep in a tree, one boot hanging off a branch like he'd lost a bet with gravity. Caterpillar crouched by the old stone fire pit, boiling water in a chipped copper kettle over conjured flames, muttering to himself in a dialect even the grass seemed wary of. Cheshire lounged nearby, stretched across a crooked bench, his body twitching in and out of existence, eyes sharp and unreadable.

"You look like death," Cheshire greeted as I stepped into the clearing.

"Good. I'm hoping it throws the Queen off of her game."

"Speaking of, an official summons from The Queen came for you while you were in disposed." Caterpillar said holding out a heavy envelope, the wax seal fissured down the middle. "It bit March when he opened it." March, who had at some point fallen to the forest floor, groaned and rolled over, holding up a bandaged thumb. "It had teeth," he slurred, "and opinions." I took the letter. Inside, the words were hand-penned but unmistakably hers: neat, arching, almost cruel in their clarity.

TO THE KEY: YOUR PRESENCE IS REQUIRED AT COURT BEFORE THE FINAL TURN, AS DICTATED BY LAW. YOUR ENTIRE SUITE WILL ACCOMPANY YOU. YOU HAVE 24 HOURS. NO EXCEPTIONS. —Q

March , blinked like a drunk owl. "So, what's the plan then, General Hightower?"

"We go," I said simply.

That earned their full attention.

"We don't have an army," Caterpillar reminded me.

"No," I agreed. "But we have chaos. And we have allies."

Cheshire raised an eyebrow, curious. "Planning to wake the Dodo from retirement? Or perhaps trick the Tweedles into starting a revolution?"

"No." I stepped forward, feeling the wind shift around me like it, too, had decided to choose a side. "We summon the White Knight."

Caterpillar's brows rose. "He won't like that."

"He doesn't have to like it," I said. "He just has to fight."

March straightened, dusting his sleeves. "Well. If we're dragging out legends, we might as well go all in."

"He's loyal," Caterpillar said. "But unstable."

"So's Wonderland," I replied. "And if there's one thing I've learned here, it's that unstable can be weaponized."

Cheshire gave a slow, curling smile. "She's learning."

"Don't sound so surprised."

"We'll need a blood marker to summon him," Caterpillar warned. "And a map. He doesn't just ride in when the sky turns dark. He needs an invitation."

I held out my hand, already digging a knife from the folds of my skirt. "Take what you need."

March whistled low. "Remind me not to get on your bad side."

"You're already on it," I muttered.

As Caterpillar began the ritual—etching runes into the bark of a gnarled tree and muttering spells older than sense— Cheshire circled me, his grin smaller now.

"You still trust him?" he asked quietly.

"Theo?"

A nod.

I looked to the firelight, to the shadows of the trees, and finally to the blood welling in my hand. "No," I said honestly. "But I know who he is when he isn't hiding behind masks. That'll have to be enough—for now."

Cheshire's smile flickered, thoughtful. "Just be careful where you place your pieces, Alicia. The board's rigged, but the endgame's still yours to choose."

Before I could answer, a gust of cold air tore through the

clearing. The kettle shattered. The fire sputtered out.

A white horse appeared at the edge of the wood, steam rising from its nostrils like a dragon denied flame.

And astride it, armor gleaming and eyes full of thunder, was the White Knight.

He saw me. He didn't smile.

"You called for help in your battle against the queen?" he asked. His voice was forged iron. "While that is a valiant cause, I must ask, what's left to save?"

I stepped forward. "Everything."

The White Knight didn't dismount. He didn't blink either, which was mildly disconcerting. He sat astride his ghost-colored steed like a statue carved from winter, eyes fixed on me with the kind of silent appraisal that made my skin itch. His armor was brilliant—too brilliant. No scratches, no tarnish, no blood. Which told me everything I needed to know.

It wasn't that he hadn't been in battle. It was that he'd refused to let any of it show.

"Welcome back," Cheshire purred beside me, though he sounded more like he was welcoming a plague. The White Knight didn't acknowledge him. Instead, his gaze pinned me. "You're the Key." "Guilty," I said. "Though I'm starting to think that title is more curse than prophecy." He swung down from the horse with fluid, inhuman grace. Not a rattle, not a clink. Too quiet. Too precise. "The Queen has already moved her knights to the edge of the smoldering gardens," he said. "She expects resistance, not strategy." "Good," I replied. "Let's make sure she's surprised on both counts." That earned a flicker of something behind his expression. Approval, maybe.

Or recognition. "You're different," he said at last.

"We've met?" I asked. "No." His head tilted. "But I knew the First Key. The one who broke Wonderland open. The one who turned love into despair."

Ah. There it was.

I braced myself, but he didn't elaborate. Instead, he turned to the others, giving March a nod, ignoring Cheshire entirely, and giving Caterpillar the kind of side-eye you only earn after decades of magical beef. "I'll take the eastern flank," he said. "You'll need a distraction before you can breach the gates."

"Hold on," I said, stepping forward. "Before you go full-knight-on-a-crusade, she summoned us. Also, I need to know something."

He paused. "What did she do to you?" I asked.

For a moment, I thought he wouldn't answer. That maybe his silence was its own kind of defense. But then he spoke, voice quieter than before. "She gave me purpose," he said. "And then she made that purpose my prison." He looked down at his hands, gauntlets still pristine. "I was the first to kneel. I believed in her before the madness. Before the red crown stained her thoughts. I would've followed her to ruin." I swallowed. "And did you?"

His mouth twisted—not quite a smile. Not quite a scar. "No. That honor went to her brother, the Knave." Theo. My pulse stuttered.

"She always needed one of us to chase after," the White Knight went on. "One to prove she could be loved despite the rot. One to drag into her darkness and say, *Look, even this one broke for me.*" He glanced up. "That's the curse you're here to undo. It was never just about Wonderland."

It was about the pattern. The cycle. The game.

I felt cold, suddenly. The same chill that threaded Theo's words. The same hollow behind his eyes.

"She broke your heart," I said softly.

"No," he replied, and something in his tone made my breath catch. "She convinced me I never had one to begin with."

A beat passed.

"Don't let her do the same to him."

He didn't say Theo's name. He didn't have to.

Then, with a fluid motion, he turned toward his horse and mounted again. "When the signal comes, I ride," he said, already fading into the mist.

We watched him disappear into the trees, nothing left but hoof prints and silence.

"Well," March muttered. "That was cheerful."

Caterpillar lit a pipe with the tip of his finger. "Tragedy wears the best armor."

I didn't reply.

I was too busy thinking about the look in the White Knight's eyes—and the quiet warning inside it.

If Theo wasn't already lost… I might be the last one who could save him.

36

Through the Thorns, We Rise

Alicia

The Queen's castle didn't rise—it loomed. A thing of shadow-stained marble and velvet cruelty, wrapped in thorns so dense they bled darkness into the soil. Its towers sliced the sky like fangs. Every shuttered window, every curling spire, whispered *you shouldn't be here.*

Too bad.

We were already past the point of should.

"We go in quiet," I said, crouched beside the ruined bridge that marked the edge of her territory. Fog rolled across the stones like breath from something buried alive. "We find the throne room. I'll handle her."

"You'll *handle* the Queen?" March repeated, raising a brow. "What are you going to do, offer her a strongly worded review on her interior design?"

"She won't expect us to move first," Caterpillar cut in, unusually grim. "She thinks she's still in control."

"She isn't," I said. My fingers closed around the coin in my pocket. Cold. Steady. *Mine.*

The White Knight stood next to us, silent and as composed as any solider.

Theo hadn't returned since that morning.

He wouldn't.

He was doing what he always did—hurting alone, acting like his suffering was a penance instead of a choice. But I had to believe he'd be there when it mattered. He always had before.

"Ready?" I asked, scanning their faces.

Cheshire's grin flickered into view. "Born ready. Or possibly hatched in a vat of sarcasm. Jury's still out."

March cracked his knuckles. "I call dibs on punching someone smug."

Caterpillar only nodded once, sharp and certain.

We moved like ghosts—cutting through the briars that lined the castle's edge, slipping through side halls where chandeliers swung low and the wallpaper breathed. The Queen's influence was everywhere. Portraits of strangers watched us with eyes too human. Music whispered from walls that hadn't heard a note in centuries.

Inside, the castle pulsed.

It wasn't just a building—it was *alive.*

And it didn't want us here.

Every step was heavier than the last, the floorboards groaning with secrets. A mirror on the landing reflected only your worst mistake. The stained-glass windows rearranged themselves when you weren't looking, each a silent warning.

But we didn't stop.

Not when a dozen faceless guards patrolled the outer gallery—we slipped past in silence. Not when an entire room filled with red roses screamed as we entered—we didn't flinch.

It wasn't until we reached the corridor of blood red doors that I hesitated.

They stretched endlessly in either direction. Each identical. Each humming with power.

"She's close," I said, breath catching. "She's watching."

"She's *always* watching," Caterpillar murmured. "That's her curse. And her weakness."

I stepped forward.

The door in the center glowed faintly. Red and gold. A heartbeat of light. I knew this was the way forward.

No one argued. No jokes. Just the sound of drawn breath and the quiet of five people choosing to face something they might not walk away from.

I pushed the door open.

And walked into the lion's den.

The door shut behind us with a sigh, like the castle itself had exhaled.

The throne room wasn't empty.

Not exactly.

It *pretended* to be.

A cavernous hall of black marble and velvet shadows stretched before us, its only light coming from a fractured skylight high above. Moonlight poured through in jagged beams, slicing the darkness like silver knives. Dust hung in the air like suspended ash, and the floor beneath my feet pulsed faintly—as if remembering footsteps long since vanished.

"She's not here," March whispered. But even he didn't sound convinced.

"Not in body," Caterpillar murmured, "but something of her remains."

There was no throne.

Instead, at the center of the room stood a full-length mirror in a gilded frame so ornate it looked like it had been spun from blood and bone.

I stepped toward it.

The air shifted, electric and heavy with secrets. The others fell away from my awareness like mist. There was only me… and her.

Because the reflection staring back at me wasn't *me*.

It looked like me—same eyes, same mouth, same wild tumble of golden hair. But where my expression was cautious, hers was amused. Where I hesitated, she glided forward like she owned the world.

Her crown glinted black and gold, twisted into barbs that bit into her brow. Her dress shimmered with layers of red so deep they looked soaked in blood. And her eyes—my eyes— gleamed with the slow, decadent cruelty of someone who had stopped asking for permission a long time ago.

"Is that…" Cheshire's voice was faint, far behind me.

"That's not Alicia," Caterpillar said. "That's what she *could* be."

The reflection changed to me in the garden, torching the roses with an unseen power. Than manic look on my face sent shivers coursing through me. The Queen's voice slithered through the air like silk against skin, though her form never appeared. Only her shadow stretched impossibly long across the walls, curling around the mirror like vines.

"You look good in power, darling."

I didn't flinch.

But I wanted to.

"You *were* me once," she whispered. "Curious. Reckless.

So convinced you could win without becoming something terrible."

The reflection reached for me, her fingers brushing the glass. The mirror *rippled*.

I should've stepped back.

I didn't.

"You don't have to keep fighting with them. Let them kneel," she said, voice growing stronger, almost warm. "Theo would stay. He already *has*. All you need to do is take it. The crown. The control. The respect. You'd be magnificent."

The vision smiled—and gods, it was my smile, but twisted. Tired. Dangerous.

"Look what they've made you endure," she hissed. "Look how they betrayed you. How they doubted you. Even *he* did."

A flicker of Theo's face bloomed in the mirror. Beautiful. Broken. Gone.

My throat burned.

"Enough," I whispered. "I don't want to rule like you. I don't want to *break* the world to fix it."

The reflection tilted her head. "Then you'll lose."

I stepped forward, nose inches from the glass. My heart thundered like war drums.

"Maybe. But at least I'll still be me."

The mirror *shattered*.

Not with sound—but with silence. Each fragment peeled away from the frame like ash on the wind, dissolving before they could hit the floor.

Behind me, I heard March mutter, "Remind me never to get on her bad side."

Caterpillar exhaled like a held breath had just been released.

I turned away from the ashes of the mirror.

And for the first time in this cursed place, I *felt ready.*

Throughout it all, The White Knight remained quiet, steadfast. It was a bit eerie to be honest.

In the back of the room, was a corridor, door set ajar, an invitation of sorts that promised lethal pain.

I entered through the door, my cohorts just behind me.

My footsteps sounded sharp as dropped glass. At first, I thought we were alone, but then—at the end of a corridor arched with thorns—I saw Theo.

He was waiting for me.

His hair was slicked back, tailored coat buttoned to the throat, the whole look—if you ignored the soul-crushing heartbreak—criminally attractive. I slowed, expecting snide or smug or at least a scathing one-liner, but he just looked tired. Not the drowsy kind, but the kind that happens when you've worn out every story you ever believed in and found the ending wanting.

"Alicia," he said. Like he was testing if I was real.

I braced myself, every part of me on edge. "What do you want, Theo?"

His mouth twisted around the words like they hurt to say. "She'll kill you," he said. "You know that, don't you?"

I shrugged, aiming for nonchalance but landing closer to nihilism. "We all have to die sometime. Some of us just do it with more style."

He didn't find my joke funny in the least. "Sarcasm won't protect you from the Queen, Alicia." His voice raised in anger, or urgency, it was hard to tell. "Get out of here while you still can. Find a way back to your world, live your life, forget about Wonderland. Don't be stupid."

I blanche at that. "I'm not running so your precious Queen

can have another heavy-handed victory. I may go down, but she's coming down with me!"

Theo's jaw worked. "Are you really that stubborn?" His eyes flashed; I nearly believed the anger was for me, but I'd learned to read the layers. Underneath the barked words was—fear. Not for himself. For me. The revelation made my skin prickle.

"I'm done being afraid of her," I said. "Why are you warning me? Just let her kill me if you want it so bad."

He looked away, hands braced on the windowsill as if keeping the whole palace upright by sheer force. The silence grew thorns.

I realized then that Theo looked worse than I'd ever seen. Under the fine tailoring, he was gaunt, colorless, as if every day under the Queen's thumb had siphoned a little more of him away.

I refused to pity him. But God, I did.

As the silence stretched on, my question going unanswered, something in me snapped.

"You sold out your friends. Sold me out." I snarled. "You want me to believe you didn't have a choice? The truth of the matter is that you want me dead. You'll do anything to please her." My voice catches but I continue on. "What does she have on you? Explain why you would betray me? Everyone for that matter." My words were poison. My anger and hurt pouring out in waves of angry words.

His head snapped up—eyes wide and stunned, as if I'd slapped him. The next instant he was moving, so close I could feel the anger crackle off him. "Is that what you think?" he said. "You think I'm here because I want to be?"

He reached for me, then stopped himself—fingers curling

in the empty air. "I never wanted any of this," he said, the words dropping heavy between us. "Then why?" I hissed. "Why do you do it? Why follow her, betray me, all of it?" His face twisted, something savage and vulnerable wrestling just behind his eyes. "Because I am bound to her. Her prisoner," he said, but now there was no venom, just marrow-deep despair. "She is my sister. I watched the darkness consume her and didn't do a damned thing to stop it." He laughed, broken, and looked up at the ceiling like he was praying for lightning to finish him off. "I don't want that to be your fate. There are maybe three things in this world I care about, and you are the most important. And I ruined it." Suddenly I saw him for what he was—not some manipulator with a secret tragic beauty, but a man so desperate for meaning that even love was a punishment.

He looked at me then, really looked, and I realized that the flint of his anger had been beaten by rain and hunger—he was hollowed out by longing, not power. If the Queen had emptied him, she'd left just enough to notice what was missing.

"Your words are all tortured soul and doom and gloom, but let's not pretend you didn't take this path on your own accord." I say, letting my hurt propel my words. I guess some part of me thought after our night together, that he would choose me.

"You think I had a choice?" he asked, voice sanded down to the core. "You think I could have stopped it?" He laughed—a single, keening sound. "I tried to walk away," he said. "I begged her to leave you out of this. But that's not how any of this works. And I..." He swallowed hard. "I should've warned you. I should've done a thousand things differently. But I was a coward. I thought I could protect you from the inside."

I stared at him, something inside me splitting—clean and quiet.

"I don't need protecting, Theo. I needed the truth."

He nodded once, hollow. "I know."

A breath passed between us. The last, maybe.

"I still love you," he said, and his voice broke on the last word like a snapped violin string. "Even if you hate me forever. Even if you kill her and leave me behind. I will love you with whatever's left."

Before I could speak—before I could even decide if I was ready to believe or burn—Cheshire's voice echoed down the corridor.

"She's waiting."

The moment snapped. We were no longer two fractured people bleeding in the dark. We were soldiers again. Opponents, maybe. But aligned—for now.

"I wish it didn't have to be this way." I whisper to Theo, voice breaking.

He didn't answer. Didn't need to.

I understood then: this place was a trap for both of us. Even the guards and the grinning villains and the pawns were trapped, each of us performing the same desperate tricks for her amusement, hoping the Queen would finally clap and set us free.

But the show never ended.

I let my anger go, just for a heartbeat, and stepped closer, closing the space where neither of us dared touch the other. "I'm sorry we are on opposite sides. Motal enemies and all that jazz, but I am here to kill this bitch. Stay out of the way, or don't, it's up to you."

When I tried to leave, Theo caught my wrist—not tight, just enough pressure to say: wait.

"She'll kill you, and she'll make me watch," he said, and this time there was no mask at all. "Every time I look at you, it's the only thing I see."

"Then look away," I shot back, voice a sawblade. But neither of us moved, frozen in the sick gravity that pulled us together as much as it ripped us apart. For a second, he closed his eyes—like he'd already started mourning. He only nodded, once, like a man taking poison with his morning coffee. "I never wanted to be the villain in your story," he murmured, eyes lidded and far away. "But no one in Wonderland gets the ending they want." Then he stepped aside, letting me pass, as if to say: Go on, then. Write your own disaster.

37

The Exit Through The Madness

Alicia

The upper galleries were empty, a grand arcade stretching in a starburst of velvet ropes, moonlight cold as logic falling onto polished floors. I walked them with my head held high, though my heart was beating a panicked rhythm inside my chest. Somewhere, distant and echoing, the orchestra played a dirge disguised as a waltz. The scent of roses had curdled. My heels left phantom bloodstains in their wake.

When we came to the Hall of Portraits, I knew we were close. I took a look around at my small army of mad misfits, proud to have them at my side. The White Knight stood close by, his sword strapped to his hip, boots polished bright. He looked like a Renaissance painting designed to make old ghosts jealous.

March Hare was a disaster: double-cuffed at the wrists, ears askew, hair uncombed since God knew when. But his eyes had the crazed clarity of someone up all night planning the undoing of empires. "I brought the pebbles," he whispered. "For the windows. Like the old fairy tale." No one asked what he meant; he seemed content just holding a fistful of smooth river stones, like they might be the weapon to end all wars.

Caterpillar doffed his hat and rolled one cigarette to the other side of his blue-stained mouth. "We have reached the crescendo," he said, voice thick with smoke and irony.

Cheshire, for his part, was stretched along a brocade settee. Only his teeth were visible in the gallery dusk. "We lack only the final player," he said. "Or perhaps she's the prize, and we're just the entertainment."

I tried to find my voice, and when I did it was hoarse but sure. "We move now," I said. "The Queen's expecting a show—let's give her more than she bargained for." The White Knight's eyes kindled. "The guards will be thick, but most are ceremonial. The only real threat is the Hearts themselves— and Knave."

"I wouldn't worry much about him," Cheshire drawled. "He's already given you a head start." I ignored the throb that comment sent through me and focused on the plan.

Caterpillar eyed me with a look that was one part derision, two parts deep pity. "You look ready to kill something," he offered, producing a flask from who-knows-where and handed it over.

"Is it poison?" I asked, eyeing the label, which read DRINK ME, predictably.

"It is if you want it to be," Cheshire purred, doing nothing to reassure me. "But for now, it's just gin."

I took a swig, the burn a tiny mercy, and handed it back. Glancing around once more, I sighed.

If this was my army, we were in for a spectacular defeat.

Hare looked like he'd mugged a haberdasher, wearing a hat that was probably alive and definitely plotting. Caterpillar had a damp, fungal melancholy about him, like he'd overwatered his soul. Cheshire hung at the edge of the candelabra light, only sometimes choosing to appear all the way.

"My faithful misfits," I began again, trying for bravado. I think my voice only shook a little. "Are we ready?"

Cheshire grinned, teeth unsettlingly white. "We've been ready and unready so many times they've become the same sensation. If you're asking whether we'll follow you into suicide, then yes, and with bells on."

I smiled, despite everything. "I'd expect nothing less."

The White Knight leaned in, "the time is nigh," he said, as if a harbinger of doom. "We need to move fast," he explained. "Most of her soldiers will be at the feast. And we have less than an hour before the Queen closes up for the night."

The plan, if you could call it that, hinged on five contradictory impulses: speed, stealth, spectacle, unpredictability, and luck. The nearest secret passageway started behind a portrait of the Queen herself, in a corridor crowded with marble busts of her better-looking ancestors. We shuffled behind the knight, who picked locks and silenced alarms with the resigned air of a man who'd broken into this castle before, and probably not on official knight business.

Every forty feet, March Hare threw a pebble at something—lamps, windows, the walls themselves—and listened for the echo. I never figured out what, if anything, he was listening for, but his grim satisfaction each time made it seem essential to our survival.

Caterpillar muttered coded riddles under his breath, the way some people recite prayers: "The shortest path is a circle.

The Queen's heart is a pentacle. Find the star, and you'll find the blood." I tried to ignore him, focusing instead on The White Knight's steady stride and the reassuring pressure of Gin in my chest.

The further in we crept, the more Wonderland buckled around us. The carpet crawled with blooming violets; the ceiling warped into a checkerboard night sky pulsing with unfamiliar constellations. Sometimes the halls seemed to move as we did, switching direction or veering left when they'd run straight a moment earlier. Our sense of time unraveled, minutes and seconds chasing each other's tails until the only constant was the pounding in my ears.

At the end of one tunnel, we ran up against a pair of Heart Guards in full regalia: spikes and frills, axes and tartan sashes. They stood so still for so long I wondered if they were statues, then one slowly turned its jaw, the heart-shaped mouthpiece fluttering like a moth's wing.

The White Knight stepped forward, drawing his sword, but the guard raised a palm—a strange, almost gentle gesture. "She is expecting you," it said, voice like it had been ran through a meat grinder and polished with syrup. "The Key. The Knight. The Mad, The Drunk, and the Lost." Its eyes flicked to Cheshire, narrowing with a feline wariness.

The other guard produced a small velvet pouch and spilled it open: inside, a single black chess piece. A queen, scorched at the base. "A token from her Majesty," the guard intoned, and handed it to me with a rigid, unsettling bow. The pawn-to-Queen gambit was impossible to miss.

March Hare cackled under his breath, his nails digging crescents into Cheshire's arm (which he did not seem to mind). "Final move," he whispered, "and she already knows the outcome."

I pocketed the piece, trembling. "Let's keep disappointing her," I said, and we muscled past. The guards did not resist—instead, they watched us go, heads cocked at identical angles, the way birds looked at the world below.

The last corridor was endless, lined in stained glass and surprises. Our reflections flickered a second too slow. My feet smudged reality as I walked, and at one point I was certain I'd left my body and was only memory and hunger.

We reached the final antechamber, a red-lit vault where the temperature dropped twenty degrees and the silence was so absolute it felt like a threat. The walls here were slick with condensation, candlelight shivering in pools on the floor. There were no guards, only a sense of anticipation so dense I could taste it on my tongue: metal, ozone, something primal.

Cheshire faded fully into view and twitched his lips. "If you have a clever tactic, now is the time," he said. "Otherwise, we improvise—and Wonderland is very fond of improvisation."

March Hare pulled another pebble from his pocket and rolled it thoughtfully in his palm. "Doesn't matter," he whispered. "We're already inside the Queen's head. That's all the battle ever is."

Caterpillar blew a charge of smoke at the sealed double doors, watching the cloud spiral against the gloom. "Whatever happens," he murmured, "remember: The only way out is through."

The White Knight led, sword raised but steady. His footsteps rang on the marble, the sound making concentric rings in the heavy quiet, and for a second it felt like we weren't just breaking into a royal room—we were invading the heart of a world.

At the threshold, I stopped. The chess piece in my pocket throbbed, cold as a secret. I pried my fingers around it and realized, abruptly, what I had to do. "Wait," I said, and all of them turned to me—misfits, champions, monsters and broken things, the only family Wonderland had left me. "We don't go in as pawns," I finished. "That's her game, and I'm done playing it. We go in as ourselves."

It was March Hare who grinned first, a rictus that split his face ear to ear. "And if ourselves are fundamentally unfit for polite society?" he asked, squeezing my shoulder hard.

"Then we make it impolite," I said.

The White Knight sheathed his sword with a hiss that sounded like satisfaction. Cheshire flickered in and out of visibility so quickly it made my eyes hurt, a stuttering Morse code of approval. Caterpillar just nodded, as if the riddle had finally solved itself.

We pushed open the doors together, an untidy wedge of malcontents, and entered the Queen's audience chamber.

The room was a fever dream of grandeur. Crimson spilled down the walls in velvet and living vine; light fractured through stained glass, and the floor? A chessboard, of course, but the squares bled into each other here, black licking at white, all boundaries consuming themselves.

The air pulsed with a hush so immense it might have belonged to a cathedral, or an execution.

At the far end of the room, enthroned on a dais of bone and roses, sat the Queen.

She was beautiful, in the way of rot and rainbows. Her lips dripped silver and her eyes were bottomless, black but kindled with stars. Her dress was not fabric at all but a latticework of tiny, overlapping hearts—each one a living reliquary, beating softly, whispering to itself. She looked at us with the patience of a glacier and all the appetite of an avalanche.

Beside her, less a sentry than a shadow, stood Theo. His face was unreadable. His eyes were not. I held his gaze for one heartbeat, two, but there was nothing there now but the cool, calculated emptiness of a man who'd chosen his role, and chosen it absolutely.

He watched me like a scientist watches a test subject, or a wolf, a carcass—no malice, but no mercy, either.

The Queen rose, each movement measured and inexorable, as if her body were only the visible tip of some ancient submerged force. She spread her hands—not in welcome, but in a conjurer's sweep. "Alicia the Key," she said. Her voice was both honeyed and hollow, and it made my name sound like a curse. "Knight of Hope, Wraith of Cats, Dross of Hares, and the Vestige of Rebellion. Wonderland has not seen such a parade since the last dreamer met her end. I've been eager to meet you little Key."

Her eyes landed on Theo, then me, then flicked across my allies as one might inventory weak spots in an opposing army. "I suppose you think, in that short, feverish life of yours, that this is a contest you can win." She smiled, and it was the smile of a guillotine: sharp, unambiguous, and oblivious to mercy. "Kneel, or show me what you brought in your claws and teeth."

March Hare put pebbles in both fists and glared, trembling. Cheshire's grin slipped a notch wider—challenging the Queen where she stood. The White Knight and Caterpillar exchanged a glance, and in that look, I saw the flicker of nerves beneath their borrowed bravado.

"No," I said, lifting my chin with a defiance scraped raw. "No more theatrics. If you want a show, bring your lazy self off of that throne of lies and I'll show you what I can really do." It was all false bravado of course, but fake it to you make it or whatever that saying is.

She laughed—a sound that was neither cruel nor kind, but ancient. "You mistake me for a monarch who answers her subjects' summons."

I laughed right back in her face. "And you mistake me for a subject. Listen lady, I don't answer to you. And really, it says a lot about a "monarch" that you have to rule with fear and evil doings, rather than earn that loyalty. Must be a bitch knowing how utterly hated you truly are."

She regarded me for two entire heartbeats, as if deciding whether to strike me dead or simply let me wither under her stare. The tension in the room was a violin string stretched between us, singing a note only mad people could hear.

Then, she descended the dais, hips swaying, the floor rippling under her feet as if Wonderland itself bowed to her. Even the stained-glass windows seemed to lean in, hungry for the spectacle.

Cheshire drifted a step forward, but the Queen pointed a finger and he froze, mid-fade. "Careful, Cat," she intoned. "You never know when an observer becomes the observed."

Cheshire inclined his head, eyes slitting. "I am nothing if not a fan of paradox, your Majesty."

The White Knight's hand hovered over his sword hilt, but I touched his wrist: Wait.

The Queen circled me, the way planets circle a sun. Her perfume was red wine and rusting iron, her dress making the sound of whispers—each heart-shaped bauble murmuring in a different dialect of dread. When she closed the loop and faced me again, her eyes had softened—not with kindness, but with a new appraisal, as if I'd just failed or passed a test I wasn't even aware I was taking.

"This is good," she mused. "It's the ones who kneel that I have to watch. Wouldn't you agree, brother?"

Theo flinched minutely, as if shocked to be addressed. "You taught me that yourself," he said, his voice flat as a guillotine's edge. "Only the heads that stay up past the blade matter."

She gave a wintry smile. "A lesson you seem to have learned too well." Then, to me: "Up close, you're less than I imagined." She traced a finger down my cheek, a chill slick with power. Theo didn't move, but I saw it. A twitch in his hand, a flicker in his eyes—as if the man I knew was trying to claw his way out from behind the mask. But there was no need because that was when I snapped.

It wasn't my mystical key power or anything arcane, but rather my all-American bar fight persona, primed and eager for a brawl. I drew back, channeling every ounce of raw energy, anger and betrayal, delivering a punch squarely to her face. The impact resonated through my knuckles, sending a thrilling jolt up my arm. It felt incredible, a surge of adrenaline and satisfaction. I wagered that no one had dared to lay a hand on her in centuries, making this moment all the more electrifying.

The Queen staggered a half-step, and the room turned to ice in the breathless space between action and reaction. My knuckles stung and the hearts on her dress fluttered, pulses tripping over one another. She dabbed her lip, crimson smudging her silver lipstick, and looked down at her glove with a kind of clinical astonishment. Then she laughed—not the brittle cackle of a storybook villain, but a low, delighted rumble. "Delicious," she said. "No Key has ever dared."

March Hare began to clap in manic, arrhythmic bursts, eyes bloodshot with glee. "Brava! Brava!" he hooted, bowling a pebble down the gleaming marble like it was a ceremonial shot. Caterpillar exhaled smoke that briefly sketched my punch over again in blue, then shrugged as if conceding the point.

Theo showed no reaction at all, except that the line of his jaw softened by a fraction, and he blinked once—slow, deliberate, the way soldiers do when they're resisting the urge to salute an enemy.

The Queen stretched her face, feeling the impact. A dusting of blood glittered on her teeth. She regarded me not as one might a rebel, but as a new abstraction, a thing never before seen. "You've got more than teeth, girl," she said. "I'll have to decide whether to bludgeon or break you." Her gaze slid to Theo. "Remind me to try both."

I smiled then—an ugly, vicious smile. "Oh honey, you can't break me. You can try, but in the end, the only one who will break, is you."

Whether it was the sharp edge of my words or the intense gaze I was directing at her, it caused her to hesitate, a flicker of worry passing over her features like a shadow before the familiar, stone-cold expression reclaimed its territory. I couldn't help but notice the slight retreat as she took a step back, clearly unprepared for the unexpected side of me she was now witnessing.

I have her scared.

I pressed the advantage, stepping in, no space for her theatrics to breathe. "My friends and I," I motioned to the ragged squad behind me, "are here because we chose to be. What about yours, Queen? Tell me—how many of your loyalists are truly loyal, and how many are just too terrified to quit?"

Her hand dropped to her side, and the latticework of hearts on her torso began to pulse faster—panic, or rage, I didn't know, but I knew enough of power to see the tremor. "You think you know what keeps my house together, little Key," she said, and lightning skimmed the chandeliers. "You've spent one night in the halls of power and fancy yourself a revolutionary."

I shrugged. "I never wanted a revolution. Hell, I never wanted to come to Wonderland to begin with. I want out. But before I go—I want to see what happens when a tyrant meets the sharp edge of her own story." My eyes flicked to Theo, and I saw a fracture pass through him. Good. If I couldn't have his loyalty, I'd have his doubt. It was not much, but it was something.

The White Knight straightened, shoulders set. "Your reign is done," he called, voice clean and knightly, the kind that makes villagers believe in the old tales. Cheshire flickered, leaning against the banister, golden eyes slit with anticipation. Hare was crouched, humming, winding up for a sprint or a scream.

But the Queen just smiled, slow and terrible. "Have you ever seen what happens to a heart when it's split in two?" I met her smile with one of my own. "I have, thanks to you." I say in a dead voice that was creepy to my own ears. "Let's find out what happens when I do it to you." In that instant, I felt as though I had transformed into someone entirely different. The intricate sigil etched onto my wrist began to sear with an intense heat, while the coin nestled in my pocket—the very one Theo had gifted me "for good luck"—started to emit a radiant glow. A peculiar surge of energy coursed through my veins, racing up and down my arms and pooling heavily in my chest. It wasn't just light. It was a sound—a chord splitting the air like a scream turned inside out. Blue lightning spiraled from my palm, laced with silver veins that whispered in a voice not my own. A startled gasp echoed from somewhere behind me, but I couldn't discern who it came from, as my mind was consumed by a persistent voice urging, *"use the magic, Key."*

The coin in my pocket pulsed like a second heart. Wonderland was listening. I didn't plan to do it. But the air changed, thick with anxiety and inevitability. The sigil on my wrist burned like a prophecy. My right hand, adorned with the swirling blue sigil, seemed to move with a will of its own. It was as if every cell in my body had been meticulously prepared for this singular moment, with my simmering anger serving as the perfect catalyst. I watched in awe as raw power erupted from my fingertips, propelling her forcefully across the expansive room.

She hit the wall with a sound like a bell struck wrong. I should've been afraid. Instead, I felt electric. Alive. Maybe even a little dangerous. For a moment she just hung there, suspended a handsbreadth above the checkerboard tiles, held up by nothing but stolen majesty and stubbornness. The impact had ruptured her dress; the lattice of hearts went wild, beating in terror, in pain, in awe. Blood—or something more precious—leaked through onto the marble.

A raw, stunned hush.

Then, sound: the gasp of the March Hare, the choked thrill in Caterpillar's lungs, the faintest appreciative murmur from Cheshire. The White Knight stepped between me and the

Queen, blade drawn as if to finish what I'd started, but even from a distance I could see the Queen was not close to dead— her eyes burned, white-hot, fissures spidering through the black.

The real battle was about to begin.

38

Battle in Wonderland

Alicia

Theo started forward—just half a step, just a breath held too long—but it was enough.

The Queen's hand lashed out like a whip. She didn't touch him. She didn't have to. Her gaze pinned him in place with the elegance of a guillotine.

"Don't," she hissed, low and razor-sharp.

Theo's jaw tightened. "She's not—" he began, but the words crumbled before they could fully form. His voice—usually smooth as silk and twice as slippery—sounded frayed now, torn between the man he'd chosen to be and the one he used to be when he looked at me.

"She's not what?" the Queen pressed, venomous. The word stretched, taut, as if daring any of us to breathe.

He shook himself like a dog coming in from the rain, one hand hovering where his sister's gaze had struck him. "She's not yours to destroy."

The Queen let her arm fall, disappointed. "Oh, yes she is,

dear brother. But slowly. Pain is an art form. I'd never rush the final act." She advanced down the dais again, as if walking on water, each step a ripple of violence barely contained. "I spent years preparing Wonderland for this moment. And you—" she tossed a sneer at Theo, "you spent years sabotaging yourself for the hope you could change anything."

She snapped her wrist, and the floor split with a shriek like shattering stained glass. The chessboard beneath us writhed—black and white tiles curling into jagged blooms, razor-petaled flowers exploding in spirals of perfume and madness.

Out of the shards, the first wave of Heart Guards rose, summoned by her agony: faceless, gleaming, their axes made of cleaved regrets and loyalty. They advanced in ceremonial unison.

The White Knight moved first, cleaving the air with a shout the Queen's guards had to have been bred to fear; two peeled off to intercept, but he barreled through, each stroke all intention, all muscle, sending a spiral of red and silver arcing onto the white squares.

In the chaos, March Hare shrieked and began pelting the guards with his river stones. Each thrown pebble multiplied, fractal, a calculus of distraction. Guards slipped and stumbled as tiny impacts echoed through their hollow bodies. Hare cackled, ecstatic, his chaos more contagious than the Black Death.

Caterpillar, whose idea of a fight was usually waged with words or opiates, surprised absolutely everyone by blowing a lungful of blue smoke at the nearest guard. Where it touched the armor, it melted straight through, leaving a pitted, weeping mess of man and metal. The guard didn't scream—

none of them did—but the hiss of dissolving bodies was a sound I would never forget.

Cheshire simply vanished, but wherever a guard faltered, wherever one of their number raised a weapon high, a ghostly flash of a grin and a metal weapon shaped like a claw intervened: silent, efficient, surgical. The Queen watched this with an unblinking, reptilian calm, as if already imagining how she would have the mess cleaned up.

I should have been overwhelmed. Instead, I felt the inverse: an expanding clarity, the way an eagle must see the world in the clean updraft before a storm. The Key in me—it was more than just metaphor now, it was heat and direction, a line from my heart to every beating thing in the room. I didn't even need to gesture; with a thought the magic did my bidding.

And what I wanted, viscerally, was to break her game.

I locked eyes with the Queen—her hands already slick with the pulse of Wonderland itself—and forced her attention my way. I said nothing, just smiled the way a locked door smiles at a skeleton key.

She tried to speak, but her teeth rattled. "You think you can defeat me?"

The magic inside me surged once more, synthetic and blinding. The chessboard snapped inward, new seams radiating in the marble, and with them, the room itself began to twine and unfurl, brick folding into brick, air into air, until it was not a room at all but the memory of one—a recursive loop, a vortex. We were all being sucked to the center.

Guards were torn apart, reconstructed, then torn again. The Queen laughed or maybe screamed; the sound was both and neither, as if her voice alone could hold the castle together. I rode the current, feeling everything: the ache in The White

Knight's sword arm, the punctured pride in Caterpillar; the madness ricocheting through Hare's synapses; and, farthest away, a dreadful, glorious longing in Theo.

In the eye of that storm, the Queen went for me with viper speed, nails hooked and eyes afire. But I was ready. There was no finesse to her attack—just hunger. Easy, then, to sidestep and—almost gently—drive the heel of my palm into her jaw. She reeled, spitting blood and teeth like poppy seeds. Her smile was the kind born out of the nightmares of the darkest night. It wasn't just cruel—it was ancient. The kind born from nightmares that outlived their dreamers. It split her face with glee, sharp as glass, and sent a pulse of dread down my spine throwing me off my guard long enough to allow someone to sneak up behind me, arms like vices as they came around my body holding me in place. I didn't hear him approach. I only felt it—the sudden, crushing grip around my arms, the cold bite of a blade at my throat. Precise. Intimate. Familiar. The knife at my throat was a promise of instant death. I didn't have to turn around to know who it was. Theo, the Knave, the Mad Hatter, whatever name he is going by today. His breath ghosted over my skin. The tip of the blade rested just over my pulse, a lover's caress that promised murder. It trembled—but not from hesitation. From restraint.

He did not speak. His hand—steady, even tender—pressed the blade so precisely I could feel my pulse bounce off the edge. The queen cackled like a maniac as she saw the pain of Theo's betrayal reflected in my eyes. "You thought he would protect you, stupid woman? He's my brother, my blood."

She stepped closer, slow and delighted. Her perfume choked the space between us—dark wine and rotting flowers. Her bloodied smile glistened, catching the candlelight like a wound dressed in diamonds. Her tongue flicked over her broken teeth, collecting blood in a little goblet at the hollow of her lip.

"Do it," she said to him, fingernails glinting with a wet, terrible anticipation. "Spill her. End it."

Theo's grip didn't tighten. The edge pressed one heartbeat deeper, not enough to break skin—never enough. His chest hitched behind me, and for a moment I thought he would. Maybe he did, too.

Theo didn't move. But he didn't let go, either.

The knife kissed my skin. The line it traced was whisper-thin, just enough to sting. His voice was ragged when it came. "You never could do your own dirty work, sister. You just taught your monsters to kneel."

She arched a brow. "Then kneel."

He laughed—a sound like broken glass—low, hollow, the sound of a blade flexing inside its own sheath. "I'm going to disappoint you again, sister."

With a violent twist, he yanked me behind him. The blade scraped a shallow line across my neck—a souvenir—and then I was airborne for a heartbeat, spun away to safety.

For the first time since the brawl began, I saw what Theo was when he wasn't pretending to be human: all angles and fury, coat flaring like a crow's wings in a gale, his face wiped clean of anything but intent.

The Queen shrieked, a noise so sharp my vision swam. "You are choosing to stand against me, your own sister?" she howled at him, "For her?"

"She made me remember who I was before," he answered, raw. "Before I became your weapon." The Queen's face cracked—not a smile this time, but something deeper, an ancient wound reopening. "You think you're a hero? You're nothing without me. You always needed someone to tell you who to be." Theo bared his teeth, blood running down his chin from a wound I didn't see land. "I may not be a hero, but I'll be damned if I let you harm Alicia."

"You've become weak. A disappointment." She sneered, derision apparent in her tone.

Theo didn't argue. He didn't have to. He lunged. They hit together, Queen and Knave, claws and blade, brother and sister, the impact shaking the entire room to its bones.

Her hand caught him at the throat, nails piercing skin. It didn't stop him though, his knife was already at her ribs, sliding in just above the lattice of hearts, between her ribs, angled like he'd been imagining this moment for years. Blood welled, vivid and impossible, as the Queen bore down, lips pulled back and teeth like pearls in red wax. She whispered a curse or a name—it was hard to tell; the syllables were so twisted—and the breath that left her scalded Theo's cheek a dead white. Theo screamed as she used what was left of her power against him. His knees buckled, but he forced the blade deeper, teeth clenched, every nerve sparking. Her dress convulsed, the stitched-on hearts pulsing erratically, beating out a panic that shook the floor. His arm started to shake, then the rest of him, as if every nerve was being peeled from within. And yet he drove the blade deeper, until the hilt was flush against both their ribcages.

Time slowed. The chessboard beneath them rippled and went soft, the black squares draining upward into the wound at her side, or else pouring out as shadow onto the tiles. The Queen's fingers scrabbled at Theo's face, clawing a line down his jaw, but there was no triumph in her eyes now, only a bottomless bewilderment—like, in all her centuries of cruelty, no one had ever dared call her bluff before. Least of all her own family.

She tried to gasp one last spell, but all that came out was a slept-over memory of smoke and the taste of her own blood. She fell to her knees, clutching at Theo's lapel as if the right grip might let her take him with her to hell. The light in her dress flickered, then went out, the lattice of hearts nothing but hollow trophies now. For a moment he just stood, breathing her in, face expressionless. Then he let her slide from his grasp and, with an odd delicacy, wiped the knife on the hem of her ruined skirt.

All at once the air was different: As if a lens had snapped into focus, every edge too bright, every silence too loud. The Heart Guards rattled, spun, and then—stripped of will—toppled backwards onto the marble. One by one, their axes clattered from nerveless hands. March Hare hooted in triumph, leaping atop the nearest inert body and pounding his chest with both fists.

For a moment, no one else moved. Caterpillar stared, aghast, as blue smoke curled and died in the stagnant air. The White Knight sheathed his sword, staring at the body on the dais as if waiting for it to rise and demand a rematch.

I pressed my palm to the thin line Theo had left at my throat, half-expecting to find myself bleeding. I wasn't. There was only the faintest mark, a souvenir of almost-betrayal, almost-loss.

I looked up into his eyes, eyes that held unfathomable pain. "You saved me" I whispered, dazed.

He blinked, then he laughed, a ghost of himself, the sound empty but not mocking. "I owed you that much."

For the first time since Theo—since all of this started—I reached for him. Just two trembling fingers, barely enough to count as a touch. He didn't flinch. He just held my gaze, like he was waiting for me to tell him what part of him was allowed back into the world.

"Thank you, for protecting me, for not giving up when it mattered," I said, and my voice sounded brittle, not the heroine's final stand but the aftershock of all the stories that lived and died in the marrow of my bones.

He crumpled then, the sharp lines of his jaw and cheekbones dissolving into something messier and infinitely more human. Tears spilled down his face, bright as mercury. "I don't think I know how to be anything now," he said.

I reached up and touched his face, wiping away the tears. "You can be anything you want. The question is, what do you want?"

"You." He says softly, "Only, you."

He fell to his knees, still clutching the knife, his hands shaking so violently he nearly drove the blade into the tile. I slid down to the floor in front of him, knees colliding with his, arms drawing him in as if to knit the pieces back together by force alone. His head dropped to my shoulder, a shuddering release, tears soaking through the collar of my shirt. I held him, rocking us both in the middle of a battlefield.

His hand groped for mine and squeezed, almost a plea. "Don't leave," he said, and the need in his voice—the childlike, animal need—was so raw it made my throat close.

"Nowhere else to go," I promised, the only vow I had left.

39

Back to Boring… or Not

Alicia

Behind us, the others recalibrated to the new reality. March Hare was already leading a victory parade with himself as Grand Marshal, pelting fallen guards with leftover pebbles and inventing battle songs with all the subtlety of a marching band on meth. The White Knight approached the dais with caution, like the corpse might bite. Caterpillar slumped into a settee, eyes ringed with blue.

"You see?" Cheshire whispered. "Never trust a monarch for drama. It's always the minor characters who steal the scene."

I rolled my eyes, but kept my focus on the crown, toppled and rolling in slow, lazy circles across the floor.

March Hare was still howling atop a guard, now pounding out a drum cadence with the heel of his boot. "The Queen is dead! Long live… someone else!" he crowed, voice echoing in the shuddering silence.

Caterpillar slumped against a fallen candelabra, smoke curling around his head like a battered halo. "I had a bet she'd kill the Knave first," he said, as if this were a complaint instead of a lament. "Odds were twenty to one."

The White Knight bowed to the void where the Queen's spirit might still linger. "It's done," he said, more solemn than I thought possible for a man wearing four different shades of white armor. "You're free now, Alicia." He then turns to Theo. "You dealt the fatal blow, do you know what this means?"

Theo's head jerked, eyes rimmed with a newborn terror. "It means everything changes. Or nothing does." He wiped the blood from his chin, the gesture as precise as ever, but there was a slackness to him now—the puppet whose strings cut loose but who doesn't yet know how to fall.

I leaned into him, recognizing the panic within him. I could see the wound on his cheek, the gash left by the Queen's last, desperate claw. I wanted to touch it, to do…something. His arm circled around me almost reflexively, like he needed tethering to keep from floating away. His grip both desperate and grateful, as if reconciling the mechanics of embrace from first principles. "Is it really over?" he whispered into my hair. His voice was scorched down to the wick, barely a sound at all.

I looked at the Queen's body, its outline unraveling at the edges, red leaching out beneath her like someone had sliced the heart from the world itself. She was beautiful even in death—feral, unapologetic, legendary. I felt a complicated sadness for her, the way you feel for things that should never have existed, but once there, made the world stranger. She was the First Key after all. She chose power over peace and the echoes of her choice pulsed through Wonderland, shaping every nightmare and every rebellion since.

Her choices destroyed her just as surely as any knife could have. Maybe more.

"What the Knight means," Cheshire cuts in, sly and cool as ever. "You are now king, Theo."

All eyes turned to Theo, who looked as if someone had set a crown of spikes aflame atop his skull. For a long, glacial instant, he said nothing, just stared at his own hands as if he might drop dead if he moved them. The hush was awkward, then horrifying, and then, as so often in Wonderland, it curdled into farce.

March Hare slid off his dead rodeo and pirouetted. "Is there a coronation snack? I vote lemon tarts! Or those little jam pinwheels!" He fished a ruined cravat from a fallen guard, knotted it into a makeshift sash, and flung it dramatically at Theo's feet.

Theo did not so much as blink. "No," he said. The word fell like an atomic bomb, the kind that ends a dynasty—and very nearly a room. "I can't, I'm nobody's monarch."

"You are, Hatter," Caterpillar says softly. "That is the rules. Wonderland is now yours, I know you can already feel it's power coursing through your veins."

Theo stared at the circle of us, his inner war leaking out in the tremor of his jaw, the rawness in his eyes. He stepped back, nearly tripping over the Queen's cooling body, and pressed the heel of his hand to his forehead like he could squeeze out the headache of sudden sovereignty.

"I don't want it," he said, voice shredded but not soft. "This isn't what I... Alicia is the Key; she should be queen." His gaze slid to me, seeking confirmation or maybe contradiction.

"Alicia did her part, yes." Confirmed Caterpillar.

I stared at him in confusion, "I didn't do anything. Theo

took her out, not me." Cheshire's grin somehow grew even wider. "Oh, quite the contrary, my dear. You've done exactly what you were meant to do."

The White Knight stepped forward, his expression solemn. "The prophecy spoke of a Key that would unlock Wonderland's true potential. We thought it meant you would help us defeat the Queen, but it seems your role was far greater than that."

"You set Wonderland free," Cheshire finished. "Look around you, Alicia. You changed the story. You inspired change. You rallied the troops. You inspired love in the blackest of hearts. Can't you feel the change in the air?"

As he spoke, I became aware of a subtle shift in my surroundings. The oppressive atmosphere that had hung over the castle seemed to lift. Colors appeared brighter, more vibrant. Even the air felt fresher somehow. But something else was starting to churn. The others turned to me, as if they felt it too: the *magic*. The air around me shimmered like a heat mirage. Wonderland wasn't pushing me out. It was waiting. Listening.

"I didn't do anything," I murmured once more, bewildered.

"Oh, but you did," Cheshire crooned. "You *changed* everything."

Caterpillar nodded, smoke wisping into thought-bubbles. "You were never here to kill the Queen. You were here to rewrite our story."

"You inspired a rebellion," said the White Knight. "You altered the course of fate."

A gentle, electric tug in my chest, like the first unraveling of a dream before waking. Wonderland had shifted. But so had I. And now… something was calling me home.

Colors brightened. The weight of the world lifted. Wonderland, finally, was exhaling.

Suddenly, the ground beneath our feet began to tremble. The walls of the vault shimmered and blurred, as if reality itself was being rewritten.

"What's happening?" I cried, clinging to Theo for support.

"Wonderland is reshaping itself," the White Knight explained, his voice filled with awe. "Returning to its true form, free from the Queen's corruption."

As we watched, the dark stone walls of the vault melted away, replaced by lush greenery and vibrant flowers. The ceiling dissolved, revealing a brilliant blue sky dotted with fluffy clouds.

Where the Queen's oppressive castle had stood, a beautiful garden now sprawled before us. Fantastical creatures flitted among the colorful flowers, and in the distance, I could see rolling hills and sparkling streams.

I turned to Theo in amazement. "Is this... the real Wonderland?"

He nodded, his eyes shining with wonder. "This is Wonderland as it was always meant to be. Free, wild, and full of magic."

As we stood there taking in the transformed landscape, I felt a strange tingling sensation. Looking down, I gasped as I saw my body starting to fade, becoming translucent.

"What's happening to me?" I cried in alarm.

Cheshire materialized beside me, his grin softening into something almost wistful. "It seems your time in Wonderland is coming to an end, Alicia. You've fulfilled your destiny here."

Panic seized me as I realized what was happening. I was being pulled back to my own world. I—Alicia Hightower, reluctant bookstore heroine and chaos collector—was being written out of the story.

"No!" I reached for Theo desperately. "I don't want to go! I want to stay here, with you!"

Theo caught my hand, holding on tightly even as it began to slip through his fingers. His eyes found mine—panicked, pleading, so blue it made the world feel shallow by comparison. "Don't leave me," he begged, and his voice had none of the Knave's bravado, none of the Hatter's old cynical shield. Just a man being unmade by loss for the second time in his life. The second time today.

My limbs were already a rumor, a ghost story the world had started to forget. I gripped his hand so hard I thought I might drag him through the veil with me, if only I could anchor myself on his bones, his blood, his stubborn regret.

Cheshire stroked my shoulder, strangely tender. "Don't fret, love. You always belonged to yourself, anyway. It's the rest of us who must learn to do the same."

Theo scrabbled for my disappearing fingers, desperate.

"Alicia, please—I don't know how to do any of this without you. I don't even want to."

Tears streamed down my face as I felt myself fading further. "Will I ever see you again?"

Theo pulled me close, pressing a fierce kiss to my lips.

"I promise," he whispered. "Somehow, someway, I'll find my way back to you." The world tugged at me with the undertow of waking. I tried to fight it, wrenching myself back toward Theo with all the force of my wanting, but I was so light now, so gossamer—like the memory of a song after the last note dies.

For a moment—just a moment—our hands held, knuckles

white with refusal. And then the grip went through. Lost to another reality.

I fell up, not down, coughing flower petals and grief.

It was 2 A.M., and I was sprawled on my own bedroom carpet, surrounded by dirty laundry and the soft hiss of a jasmine candle I'd forgotten to blow out. The glow-in-the-dark stars on my ceiling were aligned all wrong. I blinked, and for a second, I was sure I could see the outline of Wonder-logic, the seams of a deeper place, but it faded as quick as rage.

I gasped for breath, lungs rebooting. My skin was damp but unmarked—except for a thin, crimson line beneath my jaw. A ghost of betrayal. Or maybe a souvenir of victory.

For a moment, I couldn't move. The air felt too thin here, too quiet. No whispering hearts, no living chessboards, no maddening cat grins hovering behind my ear.

But I could still feel Wonderland.

In the pulse beneath my fingers.

In the ache behind my eyes.

In the absence of Theo beside me.

I stood, unsteady, every limb heavy with something more than exhaustion—like gravity itself was mourning. I looked at my reflection in the mirror: same pajamas, same tangled hair, but there was something sharper behind my eyes. A new edge. A door once opened that wouldn't shut again. My eyes knew things now. I wasn't just a girl who stumbled into someone else's story.

I'd rewritten it.

On my nightstand. A single chess piece. The black queen. Burnt at the base. I picked it up with trembling fingers. It was warm.

I didn't remember bringing anything back. I didn't think I could.

But it was here. Just like the scar. Just like the memory.

And nestled beside the chess piece—though I *knew* it hadn't been there a second ago—was a note. Scrawled in ink so dark it shimmered when the candlelight hit it.

"The game isn't over, Key. Just paused. —W."

My breath caught.

Because the final line had already begun to fade, as if the ink itself were vanishing into sleep. Or waking.

And as I stared at the chess piece—at the burn that matched my scar—I knew two things for sure.

One: I'll do anything to get back to Theo.

And two: Who sent the note?

40

Lost in the Real World

Alicia

For the first three days, I assumed I'd lost my mind. Not in the way my therapist meant when she told me to try journaling the "intangible emotional disturbances" of my senior year. No, I mean lost: abandoned at a cosmic bus terminal, waiting for a ride that might never come. Every hour, I checked the chess piece to see if it would vanish, or sprout legs and run away, or whisper some new, uncrackable riddle.

Nothing.

On the fourth night, insomnia pressed me flat and awake until dawn. I lay in bed, palm cupped around the black queen—like maybe I could incubate it—and whispered every name I could remember. The names hurt my throat to speak: March. Caterpillar. Cheshire. And Theo, of course. Above all, Theo.

No answer.

It was only after months of crushing, ordinary days that the hallucinations came back. I was re-shelving a stack of YA dystopian romances at the shop, slouched and hungover on seven ounces of gas station coffee, I decided to open some of today's deliveries when I pulled out the book - a worn copy of *Alice's Adventures in Wonderland*.

A sad smile tugged at my lips as I flipped through the pages. The illustrations seemed pale and flat compared to the vivid reality I'd experienced. But as I neared the end of the book, something caught my eye. There, tucked between the last pages, was a small slip of paper that hadn't been there before. My heart racing, I unfolded it to find a message written in an elegant, familiar hand:

"My dearest Alicia,

Know that I am working tirelessly to find a way back to you. Wonderland misses its Key, and I... well, I simply miss you. Keep faith, my love. Our story is far from over.

Yours always,

Theo"

Tears blurred my vision as I read and reread the note. Somehow, impossibly, Theo had found a way to reach across worlds to send me this message.

In the days that followed, I threw myself into researching portals, dimensional travel, and anything that might help bridge the gap between worlds. I scoured every book on magic and fantasy in my shop, looking for clues.

At night, I dreamed of Wonderland - its vibrant colors, whimsical creatures, and most of all, Theo. I woke each morning with renewed determination to find a way back.

Weeks passed; I began to lose hope, wondering if I'd ever see Wonderland or Theo again. But I refused to give up completely.

By the time a month had come and gone, I felt defeated. I questioned if my journey to Wonderland ever really happened, or if it was a psychotic break on my part?

One night as the end of the workday approached, I was preparing to head up stairs for the night when the bell chimed one last time. "We're about to close," I called out automatically, not bothering to look up.

No answer. But footsteps. Measured, deliberate. And then, a voice—a voice I knew from the marrow out, low and gravelly and tired at the edges. "That's a shame. I was hoping to browse." I froze. There were a thousand rational choices: call 911, run, lock myself in the office, pretend I hadn't heard and pray the stranger would go away. Instead, I turned. Slowly, like the world would rip open if I did it too fast. He stood in the doorway, haloed by city dusk, hands in the pockets of a regal navy coat. He looked nothing like fairy-tale royalty; he looked exactly like himself. "Theo?" The sound slipped out of me, faint and wounded, like it had been hibernating in my chest all this time. He gave that signature, arrogant smile of the Mad Hatter. "Miss me?" His hair was longer than when I'd seen him last. He was no longer dressed as the dreaded Knave. He was more regal, less murdery.

He stepped forward, hands in his pockets, a chess piece glinting ever so slightly at his throat. Like a bruise, or a warning, or both. I didn't breathe, didn't dare. It was as if the world had become too thin for both of us, and in the pressure difference, nothing could move unless one of us broke first.

He reached the counter and hovered. "You look exactly the

same," he said, but the words meant more than they should have. I wondered what I looked like to him: paler, sharper, a little more brittle around the edges. He wasn't wrong.

I groped for the chess piece in my pocket, thumbed the burnt base like some kind of talisman. "You're here," I said, because it was the only thing I trusted to be true. "How?"

He shrugged, like traversing dimensions was no more difficult than jaywalking. "Cheshire's handiwork," he said. "Or maybe Wonderland's. Depends on whether you believe in metaphors or miracles."

I took a step around the counter, every nerve ending electrified.

He looked exhausted, older and younger at once, as if the entire mass of his lifetime had been shaken up and poured into a new vessel. He wore the city's dust on his boots and the rawness of old dreams in his eyes.

"I thought—" I started.

"So did I," he cut in, voice breaking, and then let the silence hang, trembling.

There was too much to say, and none of it belonged in the aisle between cookbooks and self-help. I stopped only when I could see the callouses on his knuckles. My hand hovered—then landed on his lapel, as if to anchor both of us to the here and now. "I lost my mind for a while after," I said. "Thought maybe you were just a fever dream." He grinned—not Mad Hatter wide, but soft, human. "I'd have made a terrible hallucination." He reached up and covered my hand with his. "Are you real?" I managed, because the question still mattered more than anything. He pressed his forehead to mine, our breath mingling. "We're both real, Alicia." He hesitated, the words trembling in the air. "And

I meant what I wrote." I didn't let him finish. I yanked him closer, his arms locking around me so tight the world could have collapsed and I'd never have noticed. For a second, we were both bracing, half-expecting the universe to correct for so much want. But it didn't. We were still standing. And then I was kissing him, and he was kissing back, and it was ugly and beautiful and nearly broke me in half. When we finally pulled away, the store was quieter than snowfall. He looked at me, new-minted awe in his eyes. "Wonderland's not the same," he said. "Not without its Key."

I snorted, wiping at my eyes with the heel of my hand. "I didn't do anything, you are the one who saved it."

He laughed—an unpolished, relieved sound that reminded me of midnight in the old cottage, the taste of stolen tea. "You changed everything. You changed the course of Wonderland by showing there was more to life than cowering to a power-hungry monarch. Cheshire, Caterpillar, March, even me. None of us would have stood up to her if it wasn't for you."

He laughed—an unpolished, relieved sound that reminded me of midnight in the old cottage, the taste of stolen tea. "You changed everything. Even Cheshire said so. Said you unraveled the whole tapestry—he meant it as a compliment, I think."

We stood there, holding on like gravity might reverse any second. The city outside pressed close, but in the warm cocoon of the shop, I could almost believe in parallel realities and happy endings.

He took my hand, his thumb tracing the edge of my scar with something like reverence. "They miss you, too." His voice was quieter now, and I knew he meant more than Wonderland. "March is running the tea house. Caterpillar finally got his garden. Even White Knight is learning how to lose, sometimes."

"And you?" I ask, worried about him most of all. "How are you doing as King of Wonderland?"

He snorted, looking away. "I'm very good at keeping Wonderland from eating itself, less good at pretending to belong there. I mostly haunt the gardens and yell at the croquet courts for not following the rules." There was a flash of mischief, but it faded fast. "It misses you, the place, even if it won't admit it. The magic's gone slippery, and half the river turned to gin last month."

I laughed, too sharply, and wiped my nose. "Sounds like poor management."

He grinned, bruised but happy. "We're trying."

He leaned against a shelf, gaze drinking me in as if cataloging changes. When the silence stretched, I filled it: "How long do you have here, before—" I couldn't decide what ending made sense. Before Wonderland pulled you back? Before you disappear again?

He shrugged, turning over his watchless wrist. "I'm not sure. It's like a tether, or maybe a veil. We can only cross it when it's at its thinnest as it is currently. He searched my face. "I came to ask you—"

"—Yes?" I ask, equal parts anxious and curious.

"Would you please do me the honor of accompanying me back to Wonderland? I cannot remain in this world for long as I am king, but I need you with me; and Wonderland needs its Queen."

He said it with a half-smile, like a man who'd practiced the line for a thousand daydreams and only just now allowed himself to say it aloud. It didn't sound corny, or desperate. It sounded necessary.

"Queen?" I managed, when I could trust my mouth to move. "I can barely run a used bookstore. You want me to run a reality-warping sovereign state full of sentient shrubs and anarchist rabbits?"

He met my gaze, steady and unblinking. "You already do. You just haven't signed the paperwork."

There was a madness to his certainty, but it was the good kind—the kind that made you say yes to things you'd always believed you weren't enough for. He pulled the chess queen from my pocket. Set it in my hand, his fingers curling around mine. "Wonderland needs you. I need you."

For a long minute we stood like that, the shop's old clock wheezing in the background, the world beyond the windows waiting to see if we'd jump, or stall. I said yes with a kiss, that held hope and promise.

Moving between worlds turned out to be a lot easier the second time. Or maybe the first trip had simply recalibrated what I understood about doors: the thin spots between shelves, the places where memory rubbed up against hope. The border is never a straight line; sometimes it's just the shape of a leap.

We locked the shop behind us and walked two blocks south, into the dead heart of the city. Theo paced every step like he was measuring it for later, like each crack and manhole would be mapped into some private geography. He stopped in front of an ATM vestibule where the lights had all blown out except for one: a flickering, pulsing red, an obvious invitation if you knew to look. He pressed his thumb against the greasy glass and smirked at me, conspiratorial. "A Wonderland thing," he explained. "Portals hate symmetry."

In the next blink, the alley dropped away. Reality performed a sleight of hand, and we were back—only not in the Queen's castle, which was now a tangle of wild roses and bright blue sky. We stood on the banks of a familiar creek, where glass-winged insects danced above a mess of impossible flowers, and I could see, in the near distance, the old cottage, battered but standing. My heart broke open with a joy I'd barely remembered how to choreograph.

The first to greet us was March, bounding from the reeds in checkered trousers and a sweatshirt that read "WORLD'S OKAYEST MARCH." He stopped short, blinking at the both of us. "Oh, it's you!" he said, as if we'd run into him at a hardware store. "I thought you'd died. Or gotten really, really into book retail."

Caterpillar, lounging on a rock nearby, lifted an eyebrow and blew a smoke ring so perfect it sat for a moment like a halo over March's head before shivering into nothing. "You took your time," he said, toneless but not unkind. "I started a pool, you know, on which century you'd return." He nodded at Theo, then at me, as if to say that the math had always pointed toward us coming back together, no matter how many universes intervened.

Cheshire phased in at my elbow, grin first, eyes wide with unspent mischief. "Welcome home, your Majesties," he purred, making an elaborate show of bowing so deep his face almost brushed Theo's shoes. Then, in an aside pitched only to me: "If you thought the last monarchy was unstable, wait 'til you meet your constituency."

The reunion, for a second, was just a chorus of bizarre affection. March insisted on a group hug, shouting "Huddle!" while wrestling both me and Theo into a nearly suffocating embrace. Caterpillar observed from his perch, dangling his cigarette like it was the scepter of some chill, lesser god.

I took it all in—the color, the collision of scents—and felt, acutely, how loss can be a kind of sharpening, a way of remembering what you can't bear to lose again.

We made our way to the new palace, close to the footings of the old one, though no longer ominous with the fear of execution now that the Queen was gone. No, now the feeling was lighter, happier with Theo on the throne.

March bounced up and down, unable to restrain himself. "Are we having a party? There's always a party. I brought muffins!" He produced a squashed brown bag and thrust it at me. "They're mostly edible."

The kitchen table was already set with mismatched cups and enough cake to sedate a small village. Even the river had put on its best shimmer, and the wild sunflowers leaned in from the windows as if they'd all RSVP'd to the impromptu party. I laughed, teary and unguarded, as the old rituals resumed— Cheshire twisting riddles into the frosting, Caterpillar announcing my arrival with the gravitas of a ringmaster, March accidentally setting the napkins on fire and blaming the wind.

Theo sat at the head, watching it all through half-lidded eyes, his hand never quite leaving mine. In the gentle chaos, he was different—not lighter, exactly, but loosened at the seams, less afraid to take up space in his own kingdom. Every time he glanced at me, something doubled and halved in my chest at once.

The crowd was nothing like a fairy tale; it was every edge and oddity I'd fallen for the first time around, dialed up to eleven. Every misfit and monster who'd helped us, or tried to kill us and failed, showed up with a bottle or a pie or a weirdly touching card. We were toasted with river gin, and the toasts veered between savage and surreal; no one got through a speech sober or unscathed.

When the sun rolled low and the shadows ran long, Theo raised his glass over the teetering pile of dessert crumbs. "To the Key," he said, voice ringing unsteady but clear. "To the reason any of us survived this mess. To Alicia, Wonderland's future Queen." He looked down at me then, love in his eyes.

I flushed, heat rising to the surface of my skin as every eye at the table landed on me. March Hare whooped, slapping his paw on the wood so hard cake shuddered and forks clattered. Caterpillar raised his teacup with a regal indifference and said, "A Key is nothing without the lock it opens." Cheshire raised two glasses—one for me, one for the world's ongoing absurdity.

I tried to reply, but the words stuck in the ruins of my self-doubt. "I mean," I began, the old defenses stumbling out on habit, "Are you sure I am qualified to be a Queen?"

Theo leaned in, lowering his voice just for me. "You opened Wonderland, Alicia. Doesn't matter if you use it for parties or for policy. You're already what it needs."

The others nodded. Some brought out confetti. It was not human confetti; it smelled faintly of mushrooms and laughter, and it stuck to my collarbone like the memory of a happy bruise.

By the time the party ran down and the last guest tumbled out under the indigo sky, Theo and I found ourselves alone on the terrace, the moon crooked above us like a knowing grin. The air smelled of grass and river and possibility.

We watched the castle's windows blink out, one by one, until only the light from the kitchen remained, where March snored into a plate and Caterpillar had arranged a tiny domino rally from cups and saucers all the way out the back door.

"So, what happens next?" I ask Theo.

"Next," He takes a deep sigh like a man walking to the gallows. "I ask for your hand in marriage. You, hopefully, agree. We marry, then you take your oath to serve Wonderland by my side as the queen."

I slap his arm playfully. "Why do you sound so monotone about that?"

He grinned, and I recognized the old, reckless joy—the Mad Hatter's signature, bubbling through the cracks of the king. "Because I'm mortally terrified of your answer. Because I'm not sure I deserve you. Because if you say yes, I'm out of excuses to be unhappy, and that's a deeply foreign sensation."

I bit my lip, considering him: the dimple somewhere under the stubble, the mismatched buttons, the haunted hope. "You didn't actually ask, you know," I said. "Not properly."

He straightened, then dropped to one knee—no ceremony, just momentum and nerves and the hush of a world trying to eavesdrop. The chess queen was palmed, trembling, in his hand. "Alicia," he said, "I've spent most of my life running from the idea of belonging to anyone or anywhere. I've been the villain and the hero. You stormed in and made Wonderland make sense for the first time." He caught my eyes and didn't let go. "Will you marry me? Will you be my queen?"

The air bristled, time stalling as if even the moon was holding its breath.

I reached for him, steadying the piece between us. "Yes," I said, "but only if you bring me coffee in bed and make this place weird and wonderful forever."

He laughed, relief and delight rolling off of him in waves.

"It's a deal. Although, I should warn you: the coffee occasionally bites back." He slid the chess queen onto my finger. It didn't fit, not really, but the symbolism was so perfect I thought I might cry. I pulled him up and kissed him, the two of us tangled under the moon as if we'd never known anything but this strange, second-chance happiness. From somewhere inside, March whooped and Caterpillar muttered a curse about "youth and indecency." Cheshire's purr was the low, secret thunder of a world remade.

Epilogue

Three Months Later

Weddings and coronations in Wonderland are much the same: excessive in every sense, destabilizing for bystanders, and ultimately not about the named principal at all, but about the theater of the world rearranging itself around a new rule. The invitations had gone out in every direction, finding their way up rivers and down roots, through libraries and under the doors of ancient, feuding houses. Some guests arrived in formalwear, others in carapace or rags, and more than a few materialized for the open bar alone.

It started with a parade—March's idea, obviously—forty-three bands, some of them literal, some just groups of people with opinions on what rhythm is. There were floats shaped like moons, cakes, and at one point a conscripted wolf pack in velvet footmen's livery. The air was so thick with confetti it choked out the clouds and the sun, and for two days, nobody in the city got any sleep.

I had taken the past three months to learn more about Wonderland, its people— and other beings— and still have not gotten any closer to understanding this crazy world. But, once you aren't fearing for your life at every turn, the place really grows on you. Sort of. I left my bookshop in the hands of a new employee, periodically checking in when the veil is thin and I need a break from the madness of Wonderland.

I reflect on everything that has brought me to this moment. The adventure, the heartbreak, the redemption. It's the kind of story written for the ages.

The White Knight volunteered to escort me down the aisle where my future husband awaits. Theo had insisted on a small ceremony—just friends, he'd said, knowing full well that in Wonderland, every guest list explodes on contact. He'd even adjusted his coat to an honest shade of blue, trimmed with the barest gold braid, and threatened March within an inch of his life to let the bride set the proceedings' tone. Unfortunately, even though he was king and I was set to become queen, he was overruled.

March, resplendent in a top hat covered in blinking LED lights and what could only be described as a ruffled shirt made out of leftover invitations, had declared himself "Master of Ceremonies, Cake, and Unmanageable Mischief." So, the wedding was held in the largest field on palace grounds, under a tent made from spider silk and improbable physics, with a guest list that sprawled across the countryside. So many people wept or howled or cackled at the vows that I lost count of which was which.

The White Knight— was decorated in ceremonial whites and a sash made of live doves (donated, I hoped, willingly)—led me down the aisle. My dress was a compromise: silk and georgette in the blue that Theo wore best, but laced up the back with red velvet, a secret rebellion I never intended to keep. My bouquet was less a collection of flowers and more a wild riot of broken teacups, ribbons, and the last surviving bloom from the Queen's old garden, shot through with streaks of gold.

As I walked, I saw the faces of monsters and men, misfits and friends: Caterpillar greeted me with a nod as I walked by, wearing a suit so powdery blue it could cause blindness; he was flanked by twin hookah pipes and what appeared to be a literal council of butterflies, wings all aflutter with the latest intrigue.

Hare, weeping openly, clutching two flower girls like emotional support animals; Cheshire, drifting above the crowd like a lazy smoke ring, mouth grinning at a private joke I hoped wasn't about me. Just this morning, Cheshire gave me a running commentary on the fashion decisions of every arriving dignitary. "I wouldn't trust the Duchess," he whispered into my ear, breath electric. "You know those aren't real— her *'improvements.'*"

And then there was Theo. At the far end of the aisle, blue suit, large top hat, and a grin that promised mischief. He stood beneath the arbor, hands folded, the wildness of his hair tamed by the hat and exactly one curl escaping above his brow. His eyes—crystal blue today—tracked my every step, calm and wild at once.

I felt the heat of his gaze with every stride, stripping away my anxieties, remaking me into something bold, almost regal. He had that effect, even—or especially—here, where every eye thirsted for spectacle and every secret was common knowledge by midnight.

He said later that the second he saw me, his heart dropped all the way to his shoes and stayed there, thumping like a trapped bird. I believed him, mostly because I felt the same— and because, just before I reached him, he exhaled so sharply I saw his shoulders drop, as if he'd been holding up the sky with his bare hands until now.

When we reached the altar, there was a heartbeat of silence, the crowd settling like a field of cats waiting for the precise moment to pounce and unravel the ceremony. The old chessboard aisle glimmered underfoot, each tile shifting color or shape with every step—at first black and white, then bleeding into wild mosaics, then briefly the exact tartan of March's scarf. I wondered, as always, whether the effect was intentional or if Wonderland simply couldn't help itself.

The White Knight bowed and relinquished me to Theo with a dignity so sincere it almost destabilized the moment. Theo looked at me, and—God help me—he looked a little scared, like it might actually be possible for him to lose this, to lose me. I squeezed his hand and felt him steady, the pulse of his thumb a reassuring drumming in the crook of my finger.

March, impossibly solemn for 0.7 seconds, cleared his throat and began with a eulogy for singlehood, followed by an epic poem about love's many deaths and rebirths. He was immediately heckled by Caterpillar, who suggested better rhymes, then by Cheshire, who offered to "Officiate by popular acclaim." The audience hissed and applauded. Theo grinned, and the tension broke, replaced by something like collective relief.

Nobody expected the vows to be beautiful, but they were. Theo had written his in the margins of a half-burnt deck of cards, and he read them with a steady, even voice that rang over everyone. "I promise you," he said, "the madness and the mercy; the moons that don't rise on time, and the certainty that on the other side of every disaster, I will be there—usually the cause, sometimes the cure, but always yours." The crowd erupted, some in tears, some in song, and at least two duels broke out in the back row over the emotional sincerity of it all.

When it was my turn, I wanted to be clever, devastating, unassailable—and instead, what came out was the truth. "You saved me," I said, and my voice was both too loud and too small. "Not from the Queen, or from Wonderland, or even from my ancient, evolutionary need to fix things that don't want fixing. You saved me from lonely. From never being enough. From thinking stories have to end in order to matter." I squeezed his palm, remembering all the nights I'd spent certain we'd ruined every chance. "I love you, even when you make me insane. Especially then." March Hare tried to sob quietly but failed and made it into a honk. I could hear Caterpillar exhale a cloud of blue that drifted in the air between us. Even the butterflies blinked, wings open and shut, caught for a moment out of their engineered indifference.

Theo bowed his head, just a little, so the brim of his hat hid the sudden rawness in his eyes. He recovered quickly—he always did—then slipped the ring on my finger and pulled me in, voice low enough for only me to hear, "You're my home, Alicia. Even when you burn it down."

"Ladies, gentleman, creatures of Wonderland," March yelled over the crowd. "May I present to you husband and wife, King Theo and Queen Alicia."

The crowd roared in approval—Wonderland's idea of reverence was total disregard for solemnity. March Hare threw both arms in the air, nearly concussing a passing hawk in his enthusiasm. And just like that, we were wed. The air lifted, as if the very physics of the place had awaited this ridiculous, beautiful collision.

As we made our way back down the aisle, the guests surged

after, the whole cortege dissolving into a parade of wild dancing, errant toasts, and amateur pyrotechnics courtesy of March. I don't remember every detail, but I remember the way Theo's hand never left mine. He grinned at everyone, but he kept his eyes on me, as if reminding himself that, yes, improbable as it was, we'd actually survived ourselves long enough to get here.

Later, there was revelry—three separate tented ballrooms sprung up, each themed to a different fever dream. At one, March presided over an endless croquet tournament that nobody understood the rules to, least of all March. In another, the musicians had conspired to play only palindromic songs, which set the dancers in orbits that made me dizzy just to watch. The final tent was pure hedonism: midnight pools, towers of uncut cakes, fountains that ran with something not quite wine and not quite truth.

Cheshire found me near one of the fountains, swirling a glass of iridescent liquid and smiling like a magician at the reveal. He offered a toast, slurred and sly: "To the couple who dared to knock Wonderland off its axis. May all your paradoxes be productive." He clinked my glass, winked, and vanished, leaving me with the sense I'd just been complimented and mocked in the same breath.

Theo tracked me through the party with a predator's accuracy, intercepting me just as the first real moon of the evening crested the sky. He pulled me into a makeshift alcove, the noise of the world dulled by velvet hangings and the thick presence of anticipation.

"If we run now," he said, mouth at my ear, "they'll rewrite the entire evening and no one will ever know we left."

"Let's go." I replied, eager, although my voice was already a whisper, already lost in the gravity well of what came next.

He kissed me, the way people do after a long siege: desperate, relieved, certain only of the present moment and the hope that it can be made to last. He tasted like river gin and the smoke of old regrets, but also like home. Always like home.

We slipped away through the candle-lit labyrinth of tents and tables, through groves where the flowers hummed old love songs and the night air pressed soft on our bare skin.

The castle, in moonlight, was barely there—a shifting patchwork of shadows and mirrors. He led me up the back stairs, laughter and fireworks echoing in the distance, and kicked open the door to the royal library, which now doubled as our secret rendezvous. For all the trappings, the place was a mess of teetering books and day-old teacups, the only true comfort either of us ever wanted.

We didn't bother with the lights. The hush of it let our nerves catch up to our bodies, and for a long, suspended second, we just looked at each other, hanging in that delicate space where anticipation is all that matters.

I smiled first, because someone had to break the spell. "So, what now?" I asked, as my hands found the lapels of his jacket, already starting to thread him closer.

Theo shrugged, a dazzling echo of his former, faintly infamous self. "Well, my love, tradition dictates we consummate, celebrate, and possibly instigate the next civil war. Depends how good I am." He bent his mouth to mine before I could mock him for it, but I felt the joke bloom anyway.

The world could have ended in that room, and I don't think I would have noticed. When we finally lay still, chests heaving, sticky with sweat and cake crumbs, he propped his head up on an elbow and brushed my hair from my face. "Can I confess something?" he asked, softer now.

I nodded, waiting for the punchline.

"My whole life, I thought love was a kind of hunger, a thing you could lose or win or defend. But you—" He broke off, searching for the words. "You're more like the answer to an impossible riddle, and all I want is to keep asking it. Over and over. Promise me, you won't disappear again."

I leaned in, kissing him hungrily once more. "I'm not going anywhere," I promised, reading his mind the way you do after surviving enough together. "Not unless you're with me."

Coming Soon

Coming Soon...

Hooked on Midnight

Once Upon Another Time, Book Two

Emberly Dawson doesn't believe in fairy tales. Which is awkward—because she's about to land in one. After a rough week and one too many reality-checks, Emberly stumbles into Alicia Hightower's quaint little bookshop looking for escapism and caffeine. What she finds instead is a strange copy of *Peter Pan* that refuses to be ignored...and an accidental one-way ticket to Neverland.

Only this isn't the story she remembers.

Peter's lost his charm. The Lost Boys bite. And the real danger? Wears a crimson waistcoat, commands a ship of cursed misfits, and introduces himself as Jace.

Tall. Dangerous. Entirely too composed.

And, of course, the infamous Captain Hook.

But Jace isn't what she expected. He's clever. Sharp. Aggravatingly attractive. And possibly the only one who can help Emberly survive this twisted version of Neverland.

The shadows are closing in. The magic is unraveling. And if Emberly wants to make it home—she'll have to decide which villain's story she's really a part of.

Because in Neverland, nothing is ever as it seems.

Especially the truth.

HOOKED ON MIDNIGHT

A darkly romantic Peter Pan retelling full of stormy seas, sharp banter, and a pirate who might just be the real hero of the story.

About the Author

While for her fictional tales she goes by her pen name, Eliza Nevius, you may know her by her real name, Erin Egnatz. When she isn't chasing ghosts, wrangling college students, or decoding ancient ruins, she's spinning tales that blend romance, fiction, and sometimes a touch of the paranormal. A published author, seasoned ghost hunter, and professor of history, archaeology, and English, she is also the creator of Hauntings Around America—a platform dedicated to all things eerie and unexplained. Armed with a BA from Central State University and an MEd from the American College of Education, she has been featured in Newsweek, Fox Chicago, WAVE TV, Fox Cincinnati, NBC Seattle, and beyond. She lives somewhere between chaos and caffeine with her husband, three kids, two dogs, four cats, and one incredibly judgmental bearded dragon.

You can connect with me on:

🌐 https://www.phantompublishing.com

🐦 https://x.com/PhantomPubllc

📘 https://www.facebook.com/alexa.phillips.16503

🔗 https://www.instagram.com/hauntingsaroundamerica

🔗 https://www.elizanevius.com

Subscribe to my newsletter:

✉ https://phantompublishing.com/newsletter

Also by Eliza Nevius

Hooked on Midnight Book 2 in the Once Upon Another Time Series
Emberly Dawson doesn't believe in fairy-tales. Which is awkward—because she's about to land in one.

After a rough week and one too many reality-checks, Emberly stumbles into Alicia Hightower's quaint little bookshop looking for escapism and caffeine. What she finds instead is a strange copy of *Peter Pan* that refuses to be ignored…and an accidental one-way ticket to Neverland. Only this isn't the story she remembers. Peter's lost his charm. The Lost Boys bite. And the real danger? Wears a crimson waistcoat, commands a ship of cursed misfits, and introduces himself as Jace.

Tall. Dangerous. Entirely too composed.

And, of course, the infamous Captain Hook.

But Jace isn't what she expected. He's clever. Sharp. Aggravatingly attractive. And possibly the only one who can help Emberly survive this twisted version of Neverland.

The shadows are closing in. The magic is unraveling. And if Emberly wants to make it home—she'll have to decide which villain's story she's really a part of.

Because in Neverland, nothing is ever as it seems.

Especially the truth.

HOOKED ON MIDNIGHT

A darkly romantic Peter Pan retelling full of stormy seas, sharp banter, and a pirate who might just be the real hero of the story.

The Jaded Knight Book 1 In The Lux Bellator Series
In a world where magic simmers just beneath the surface, one witch is about to shake the foundations of fate.

At just 21, Sadie never expected to be recruited into the **Lux Bellator**, an elite band of paranormal warriors sworn to defend the veil between worlds. With her rare blend of witchcraft and angel blood, she's a prodigy of power—telekinesis, clairvoyance, and more at her fingertips. But it's her sharp tongue and fearless spirit that really turn heads.

Thrust into a team of supernatural misfits—snarky shifters, brooding vampires, and icy fae—Sadie doesn't just survive; she thrives. Especially when it comes to Nathan, the devastatingly handsome team leader with a glare that could cut glass and eyes that see too much. Their chemistry is combustible. Their arguments? Legendary.

Magic. Mayhem. Slow-burn romance. If you love witty heroines, brooding heroes, found family vibes, and enemies-to-lovers heat with a supernatural twist—*this* is your next obsession.

The Burning Vow Book 2 in the Lux Bellator Series

Heart-pounding, magical, and laced with a slow-burn romance that scorches, The Burning Vow is a fierce continuation of the Lux Bellator series—where loyalty is tested, love is forged in fire, and the only way out… is through the flames.

Professionally Unprofessional (The Strategically Chaotic Series Book 1)

A Romantic Comedy

Lexie Phillips has a bestselling novel, a thriving start-up publishing house, and a closet full of sarcastic T-shirts—but not a clue how to share office space with the six-foot-tall finance bro next door who looks like he was raised by spreadsheets and arrogance.

After years of working out of coffee shops and converted garages, Lexie and her best friend Maci finally land their dream office in a sleek downtown Chicago high-rise. Bound Books Publishing is on the rise, the paint is barely dry, and success finally seems within reach.

Enter Ben Maddox: brooding, brilliant, and built like every bad decision Lexie's ever made. His financial firm occupies the space across the hall, and from the moment they meet, it's clear they're oil and water—with a side of combustible chemistry. He's precision and pressed collars. She's coffee stains and chaos. He thinks her "business" is cute. She thinks his face would look better with a book thrown at it.

Ben is precision in motion—until his firm needs him to impress a new client who values family men and flashy lifestyles. That's where Lexie comes in, his smart-mouthed neighbor and brand-new fake fiancé. Their fake engagement is supposed to be strictly business. No feelings. No drama. Definitely no flirting.

But when late-night strategy sessions turn into stolen glances and tequila-fueled confessions lead to lakeside kisses, things start feeling a little too real. Add one rockstar memoir, a random escape to Vegas, and a confession that rocks them to their core and all of a sudden being "professionally unprofessional" might be the smartest move either of them has ever made.

Fake dating was never meant to feel this good… or get this complicated.

Full of laugh-out-loud moments, sharp banter, and slow-burn heat, Professionally Unprofessional is a love letter to ambition, found family, and the kind of romance that shows up when you least expect it... usually wearing a tie.

If you loved The Hating Game and Beach Read, get ready to fall for the sarcastic slow burn of Professionally Unprofessional.

Professionally Unraveled (Book 1.5 in the Strategically Chaotic Series)

The other side of the chaos, control, and completely unplanned love story.

Benjamin Maddox has everything under control—his firm, his future, and his finely tailored life. As the youngest partner at one of Chicago's most prestigious financial firms, Ben lives by one rule: feelings complicate the bottom line. But all that control unravels the moment Lexie Phillips stumbles into his office building with a chaotic energy and a mouth that doesn't know when to quit.

Their fake engagement was supposed to be strategic. A polished illusion to help land a multimillion-dollar client. But the longer Ben plays the role of Lexie's fiancé, the more the lines blur—and the harder it becomes to remember where the performance ends and the truth begins.

From awkward elevator run-ins to tequila-fueled confessions, Ben is forced to confront the emotions he's spent a lifetime avoiding. Lexie challenges his every instinct—and makes him want more than just professional success. She makes him want her.

But when secrets, exes, and Lexie's fear of vulnerability collide with Ben's own emotional blind spots, their carefully built façade comes crashing down. To win her back, Ben will have to risk the one thing he's never risked before—his heart.

Told entirely from Ben's perspective as it dives into the mind of the man behind the suit, exposing the insecurities, passion, and quiet longing beneath his polished surface. Get ready to fall in love with Ben Maddox all over again.

Note: This is a companion novella to Professionally Unprofessional from Ben's Point of View.

Strategically Inappropriate (Book 2 in the Strategically Chaotic Series)

Maci has a plan for everything—except maybe her own love life. As the co-founder of Bound Books Publishing, she's used to controlling chaos, not starring in it. But after an alcohol fueled one-night stand with her friend Eli occurs, that chaos she has been trying to avoid hits her head on. Now, everything is messy. Crossing that line has made things awkward. Add to that the emotional crisis that is her best friend, Lexie, and Maci's life has turned into one big ball of drama.

Eli doesn't do relationships, emotions, or spontaneous anything, but Maci seems to be the exception to his rules. He thought they could keep things casual—until his ex resurfaces, his family starts pushing for a reconciliation, and Maci starts dodging him like he's contagious. Suddenly, he's not so sure detachment is working out.

When Lexie and Ben rope them into helping plan their wedding, the romantic tension between Maci and Eli goes from simmer to full-on inferno. Between rogue glitter explosions, cake disasters, and tipsy grandmas, the line between friends and lovers is not just blurred—it's basically a smoldering crater.

Now Maci has to decide: is she brave enough to break her own rules for a chance at something real? And can Eli finally open his carefully guarded heart—before he loses the one person who makes him want to?

Because love? It's never part of the plan... but sometimes it's exactly what you need.

www.ingramcontent.com/pod-product-compliance
Lightning Source LLC
Chambersburg PA
CBHW071156100726
47908CB00002B/396